**He needed a mother for the child
even if that meant taking a wife...**

"What I wondered...that is, I wanted to know..." He shifted uncomfortably in his chair. "If the opportunity to have a child were presented to you, would you take it? Would it interest you?"

Sarah stared at Reno. Now, she was really confused. What did this have to do with work?

She blinked. "Excuse me?"

Reno reached across the table and placed his hand on her arm. "I'm doing this badly. Just hear me out, okay?"

She nodded but withdrew her arm, the heat of his hand searing her skin through the silk fabric of her blouse.

"You know I have a six-month-old infant," he began. "I haven't done very well with her since Maggie's death. The circumstances are somewhat difficult."

"Difficult?" What could be so difficult about raising a child? Not to mention she had a hard time imagining this sexy as sin man with a child to begin with.

"My fault, nobody else's," he continued. "I can't seem to find a housekeeper, and my situation's desperate."

Sarah frowned. "Did you want me to check out some agencies? You didn't have to take me to dinner to ask me that. I'd be happy to help."

Reno shook his head. "No, that's not it at all. I don't really trust strangers, and I'm not comfortable having one live in my house. It hasn't worked so far."

"Reno, please. Just get to the point here."

"I'm sorry. I don't usually botch things this badly. Okay, here's the deal." He took a deep breath and exhaled. "Sarah, I'm asking you to marry me."

Killing Lies

by

Desiree Holt

Guardian Security Book 3

Killing Lies

COPYRIGHT © 2017 by Desiree Holt

Contact Information: info@thewildrosepress.com

Cover Art by *Diana Carlile*

The Wild Rose Press, Inc.
PO Box 708
Adams Basin, NY 14410-0708

Visit us at www.thewilderroses.com

Publishing History
First Scarlet Rose Edition, 2017
Print ISBN 978-1-5092-1648-2
Digital ISBN 978-1-5092-1649-9

Published in the United States of America

Dedication

As always, to what I now call Team Desiree: Margie ager, Janet Rodman, and Joseph Patrick Trainor, and to my daughter, Amy, who talked me through it when the idea of the story first took root in my brain.

Chapter One

"I can't believe you're actually doing this." Nick Vanetta stared at his partner, Reno Sullivan, a look of disbelief stamped on his face. They were in Reno's executive offices at Guardian Security, the corporate giant they'd built together.

"Doing what?" Tony Sullivan, Reno's younger brother, walked into the office and closed the door behind him. "What am I missing?"

"Your brother's screwy idea, that's what." Nick frowned, turning back to Reno. "Being your partner gives me certain privileges, so let me tell you I think you're out of what passes for your mind. She'll never go for it."

"Go for what?" Tony dropped into one of the soft client chairs. "Will someone please tell me what's going on around here?"

"Your brother has decided to resolve his situation with Molly by asking Sarah to marry him."

Tony gawked. "The incomparable Sarah? Marry you?"

Reno sat upright in his chair. "What, am I so repulsive? Will she run away from me?"

"If she's smart she will."

"I thought you said you were off marriage," Nick reminded him. "Your first try at it didn't win any prizes."

Reno recoiled as if from a blow. The guilt he carried around with him would have buried lesser men. Maggie, the child, their marriage, her death—all the fallout from his one lousy vacation, when he'd totally taken leave of his senses.

Regret flashed at once across Nick's face. "Sorry about that. I didn't mean it quite the way it sounded. It was a stupid remark and I apologize."

"I know how bad you think I handled everything," he said stiffly. "And yes, you're right. A lot of men would have handled things differently. But I created a situation, I was responsible for it, and I had to do what I thought was right."

He still cursed himself for getting into the mess in the first place, but honor was honor no matter what distasteful form it came in.

"I didn't realize you and Sarah were, um, you know…" Tony searched for the right word.

"Dating?" Reno shook his head. "We're not."

His brother scratched behind his ear. "Okay. I feel like I came in at the middle of a movie here. Did I skip over the beginning?"

"It's not really a marriage."

"Say that again?" His eyebrows rose nearly to his hairline.

"What he means," Nick explained slowly, "is that he wants to hire a mother for Molly, so she'll have at least one parent to care for her. Marrying someone, he says, is the best way to do this."

"Marrying Sarah," Reno protested. "Not just anyone."

"Jesus, Reno, you come up with a lot of crazy schemes, but this one takes the cake. What makes you think Sarah will even do this? She's liable to have you committed instead."

"Let me spell this out," he said through gritted teeth. "There's a child with my name, living in my house. She has that name because of lies and deception. But the betrayal was not hers and I still have a responsibility to her. If Mrs. Murray was still here, no sweat, but the housekeepers from hell don't quite solve the problem." He spread his hands. "I'm trying here, okay? Give me a break."

Reno Sullivan was a man who took charge of situations. His commanding presence automatically made people accept his air of control. The entire corporate community respected him for his razor sharp mind and keen business skills. How surprised these two men would be to know that underneath his air of self-confidence, he was panic-stricken, scared that Sarah would turn him down, and frightened she wouldn't.

"I think we've crossed this bridge one too many times already," Tony pointed out. "Anyway, I say she'll never do it. And you're liable to lose the best executive assistant anyone's ever had."

Reno shook his head in disgust. "Y'all tell me to get my life together. Move forward. Make sure the child is taken care of." He forced back the familiar anguish that always engulfed him at the mention of the little girl. God, would the pain of this never go away? "Did you not say that?"

"This isn't quite what we had in mind."

"People usually get married for different reasons," Nick argued. "Like falling in love?"

"I think I've figured out love isn't on my agenda. Most people aren't lucky enough to find someone like

Lindsey." Nick and his wife had one of the most solid marriages Reno had ever seen. "Anyway, this is totally different."

"No kidding."

"At least, with Sarah, I know her. I'm comfortable with her. If I have to bring another woman into that house, I want it to be someone I can handle being around." He raked his fingers through his hair. "I know that makes me sound like a jerk, but you both know the history."

"You're taking a big risk here," Tony pointed out. "Sarah could walk away from both the proposition and her job."

"But it's the only solution that makes any kind of sense to me. Financial security in exchange for a commitment to the child. It seems pretty straightforward to me."

Tony twisted his lips. "Do you know how cold that sounds? Like one of your business deals."

"It *is* a business deal." Reno glared at Tony. His partner and his brother weren't helping the cause at all. "That's what I do best, you know. And at this point in my life, it's about all I'm capable of. Do you think I'd even consider this if I thought there was a better answer? Damn Maggie anyway."

Maggie. Just her name conjured up such bitterness he could taste it. How had he ever gotten himself into such a mess? No one could possibly think worse of him than he did of himself.

At eighteen he'd had a different future planned for himself. Then his parents died and life became a constant battle, drastically altering his existence. One minute he was a college student with nothing on his mind except girls and classes, the next he was a man left with unexpected responsibilities. He'd had to grow up in a big hurry, fighting everyone for everything.

First the system, so he could hang onto Tony. Then fighting everyone else as he struggled to put both of them through college and keep a roof over their heads. And finally, with Nick, as two hot shot punks trying to break into the tight little world of high-end corporate security. No one had given an inch for him so he'd made his own rules. As a result, outside of Nick and Tony, he trusted no one but himself.

In the end that success cost him something. By the time he reached a point in life where he could think about a serious relationship, that part of him was buried so deep he didn't know how to find it. He never lacked for social or sexual partners, but after three or four dates he was always ready to move on. At the most basic level, he couldn't seem to connect.

He was scrupulous about not making promises to his women. He wasn't looking for anything permanent, maybe never would be. He'd have to expose his vulnerability to do that and he'd worked too long to bury it, to protect himself. Always up front and honest about this, somehow he managed to stay friends with all of them. As if his honesty created a bond between them.

He built walls around himself because, that way, he was protected. Any chinks in his armor were hidden from view. And he became a social creature who knew how to behave in public, but no matter how many people surrounded him, he was always alone.

It was a lonely way to live, but safer. He'd learned the pitfalls of making himself vulnerable to anyone. His marriage was a catastrophe from day one. But when

Molly was born, for the first time, he gave his heart to someone willingly and without reservation. At the first sight of that little girl his heart opened like a flower and scooped her in. Life was brighter, warmer, more joyful.

He raced home from the office every day to spend time with her. When he held her in his arms, inhaled her special baby scent, touched his lips to the skin as soft as peaches, he could convince himself Maggie was a small price to pay for this kind of happiness.

Until the night Maggie destroyed it all, hurling her vicious words at him, words of betrayal and deceit. With a few simple phrases, she'd managed to shatter him completely.

"She's not even yours, you arrogant jerk. Joke's on you. Ha ha ha." Slugging back the rest of her drink, she'd finished off her little speech. "I wanted a rich husband, there you were ready to be plucked, and the baby was just the bait I needed. You were my ticket to the big time, sucker."

"Do you even know who the father is?"

Her answer was more devastating than he could have imagined.

Maggie shrugged. "Don't know, don't care." Her mouth twisted in a sneer. "I don't even remember who all I slept with. No telling whose genes are running around in your precious baby girl's body." She shrieked with hysterical laughter.

"Stop it. Stop it right now." Anger welled up in him so violently he was shaking.

When she ran from the room, he didn't try to stop her. Hours later, she was dead, drunk enough to crash her car into an overpass, the gas tank bursting into flames.

Nothing he did wiped those words from his mind. For a year, he'd struggled with her bitter legacy, the truth about Molly. But his heart was damaged with a wound that wouldn't heal.

He shook off his depressing thought and looked up from his desk, realizing the two men in his office were watching him carefully.

"It isn't the baby's fault," Tony said softly.

"I know." Reno's voice was ragged with suffering. "You have no idea how I despise myself. For getting into this situation and for handling it—or mishandling it—the way I have. Honest to God. It's killing me, but I can't do what you want. I just can't." If Maggie were standing in front of him now, he didn't think he could be responsible for his actions.

"When do you plan to make your big pitch?" Nick asked.

Reno shook himself out of his reverie. "I'm taking her out to dinner tonight."

"Tonight?" Nick goggled at his partner. "Could you have cut things a little closer?"

"I'd say your social skills leave a lot of room for improvement." Tony shook his head.

"I'm not sure he has any social skills," Nick commented. "At least not anymore."

"I'll just present it to her in a reasonable manner," Reno went on, as if neither of them had spoken. "Sarah's very level-headed."

"Present it to her?" Tony raised his eyebrows. "Level-headed?"

"What a guy." Nick narrowed his eyes. "Giving her a whole meal to put her in the mood."

"At least you didn't plan on just stopping at her

desk and dropping it on her," Tony pointed out.

Reno Sullivan was a proud man, and the entire situation had devastated him. Always driven by his demons, he often felt like he was on the outside of life looking in. Only Molly had opened that door, and Maggie had slammed it shut. Neither of these men knew how many nights he lay in bed wishing he could cry and wash the pain away with tears.

The fact that he was about to do what he planned went against every rule in his personal code of behavior. But he was so desperate he was forcing himself to go ahead with it.

"What made you decide on Sarah for this?" Nick asked. "Or even think she'd accept your offer?"

"She has all the qualities I'm looking for—warmth, compassion, and excellent organizational skills. We know each other fairly well after five years in this office. I don't think she has any, um, emotional attachments. I'm hoping she will see the advantages in this arrangement."

"Jesus, you sound like you're interviewing her for the job she already has."

"In a way, I am. Just at my house instead of my office." He slammed the pen down on the desk. "She's perfect. I've made up my mind. Leave it at that."

"Okay, but why would you think a gorgeous woman like Sarah would be available on such short notice, anyway?" Nick asked.

"Gorgeous?" Reno frowned, puzzled. "Yeah, she's okay, I guess. She always looks good in the office." When he thought of Sarah, it was to admire her efficiency, her skills with people, with organizing. From day one, he'd never actually looked at her as a female. Why would he? She was just…Sarah.

"I can't believe you. Don't tell me you've never noticed how she looks. You *are* in another world."

"Anyway, it's a week night," Reno said, his voice edgy with irritation. "I'm pretty sure she wouldn't have plans."

Tony blew out a breath. "I know she'd be flattered to learn you have such a low opinion of her social life." He shook his head. "I'm with Nick on this. I think it's a bad idea."

"Well, hell. Thanks for all the support." Reno pushed himself away from his desk and went to stand at the window, his hands shoved into his pockets. "I'll talk her into it," he insisted, as much to himself as to the two men. "I have to. I'm out of options. This is all I have left."

At that moment, the buzzer on his intercom sounded.

He depressed the button. "Yes, Sarah?"

"There's a gentleman on the phone named Kip Balenger. He insists on talking to you, but he won't tell me why. Shall I put him through or get rid of him?"

Every muscle in Reno's body tightened. There was a name he'd hoped never to hear again. "It's all right. Go ahead and put him through."

"Mr. Sullivan?" Balenger's voice was as gravelly as he remembered.

"I'm almost afraid to ask why you're calling." He looked at Tony and Nick, both frozen in the doorway, their faces wearing identical expressions of concern. They knew who this was as well as he did.

"Well, it's not with good news, I'm sorry to say."

"Something's happened," Reno guessed.

"Unfortunately. Luis Aguilar was being transferred to a new location with some other prisoners this morning. The prison van was in an accident—real or manufactured."

"Do not tell me he's on the loose." Reno spat out the words.

"I wish I didn't have to." Balenger heaved an audible sigh. "The Feds are doing a full court press to find him, but I wanted to give you a heads up. You know he never forgave you for busting up his little game."

"Little game?" Reno curled his lip in distaste. "Are you fucking kidding me? He and his cartel kidnapped the daughter of the head of a conglomerate and held her for ransom. I guess he wasn't making enough with drugs."

Reno counted to ten, telling himself it wasn't Balenger's fault. But a combination of fear and rage raced through him. "Any idea where he is now?"

"No, but every state is on high alert. I just wanted to be sure you had a heads up on it. You know you were the one he said he'd be after."

"Let me know the minute you hear anything." He slammed the phone down.

"Please tell me it's not what I think it is," Nick bit off.

"I wish. That fucking asshole is on the loose." Reno gave them the story.

"I hope you aren't planning to bring Sarah into this mess." Nick scowled. "The situation's wonky enough as it is."

"As a matter of fact, it's an even better idea. I don't trust any of the damn housekeepers I've had."

"Then you'd better give her fair warning," Tony said. "She needs to know what she'll be stepping into."

"Yeah. No kidding. Nick, will you arrange for a new security system at the house? More cameras, more electronics. More outside sensors. The works."

"I'll get on it right away." He gave Reno a hard look. "And think carefully about how you're going to handle this whole thing. When are you planning to pop the dinner invitation? It's almost five o'clock."

"Right now, if you both will get out of my office and give me some privacy."

Nick held up his hands. "I'm going. I'm going. I'll go arrange for the system."

Tony grimaced. "Nothing like making her feel last minute."

"I've been working up my nerve for a week," Reno admitted sheepishly. "She intimidates me."

Reno frowned as Nick burst out laughing.

"What?"

"That's the most absurd statement I've heard. Sarah Madison is one of the warmest, most gracious individuals I have ever met. Well, you'd better get to it." He opened the door and threw one final word of warning over his shoulder. "You have to tell her the whole story. Including the kidnapping."

"I can't tell her what you want," he said. "She'd run in the other direction. And I wouldn't blame her."

Reno stood in the doorway, watching Sarah at her desk, busy with some last minute chores. From the first day he hired her, his office had run like a well-oiled machine. If there was ever a glitch, he never knew it. He had yet to see or hear of a disgruntled employee or client. Or have a piece of paper misplaced or miss an appointment. Sometimes he felt he just showed up at the office and Sarah took care of the rest.

He needed the same thing at his house, making order out of the chaos there, giving Molly the emotional security he wasn't able to. The idea of marriage to Sarah had risen from the fog of his miserable existence sharp and clear. She could just apply the skills she used at the office and everything would fall into place. Molly would have a parent to love her, and he would provide the best financial environment possible.

He reviewed again in his mind the little he'd been able to find out about her. Valerie in Human Resources had given him whatever information she had, which was meager at best. Five years ago, shortly before coming to work at Guardian, her husband had been killed in a carjacking and she'd had a difficult miscarriage.

"She never discusses her personal life," Valerie had told him, "but once a bunch of us were having coffee in the cafeteria, right after she started here. Everyone was talking about babies. She looked so sad and told us the loss of the child was devastating to her, especially since she didn't think she could have any more. Then she clammed up about it, but I always see that sadness in her eyes. Too bad. She has a lot of love to give some lucky child."

More than anything else, this was what had made him think his idea would work. And now it was even more imperative.

Sarah was well aware of the kind of work Guardian did. It wasn't all corporate security. She knew about the hostage they'd rescued from Luis Aguilar as well as some other dicey situations. She'd even insisted on learning to shoot. He'd taken her to the range himself, pleased at how well she did. Then he'd signed her up for classes to get a Concealed Carry license. She'd also taken some self-defense courses, telling him she wanted to be able to defend herself if the need arose. Talk about a lucky thing.

She was closing down her computer and locking her desk when he finally walked up to her. She turned to him, smiling.

"Whatever it is, we're closed for the day," she joked. "I understand the boss refuses to pay overtime."

He shoved his hands in his pockets and blurted out, "Sarah, would you have dinner with me tonight?"

As soon as he'd said it, he mentally kicked himself for his abrupt approach. So much for his well-rehearsed little speech. What was the matter with him? He felt like a teenager asking a girl out for his first date.

"I beg your pardon?" Her eyes widened and her jaw dropped.

His mouth went dry, and he tried to swallow. What if she turned him down? "Let's try this again. I was wondering if you were free for dinner tonight." There. That was a little smoother.

"You want me to have dinner with you?" She was still gaping at him.

Surprised at her unexpected loss for words, afraid she'd turn him down out of hand, he tried to dredge up what Tony called his famous Sullivan charm. "I can promise you a good steak and fine wine." He smiled and named one of San Antonio's top restaurants, located on the famous Riverwalk, the city's hot tourist spot.

"Well, I am a Texas girl born and bred," she

reminded him, the shock fading from her face, "so, yes, steak is my weakness." Curiosity was still reflected in her eyes. "But I'd like to know what this is all about. Why the sudden invitation? Something special come up?"

He raked his fingers through his hair. Had something come up? Oh, yes, more than she knew.

She watched him carefully, questions in her eyes. "Reno?" she prompted, still waiting for an answer.

"Yes, you might say that. I do have a project I'd like to discuss with you." Okay. Not far from the truth. "It's dinner time. We both have to eat. I thought it might be nice for a change to do it together, and we can discuss what I have in mind. Are you free? Do you have plans?" He wanted to sound casual, but he was afraid anxiety was creeping into his voice.

"Well…" She chuckled. "I guess it beats a frozen dinner. Right?"

Reno felt his shoulders sag in relief. "Good, good. I'll call the restaurant."

"I'd like to go home and change, though, if that's okay. It won't take me long. Or are you in a hurry?"

"No, of course not. How about if I pick you up at seven? Will that give you enough time?"

"Seven it is."

Chapter Two

Please let me get through this.

Sarah had been in an agony of indecision while getting dressed, discarding items, then pulling them back out again.

This is just a business dinner. That's all. Don't think it's anything else.

But she couldn't get rid of the flutter in her stomach. Just looking at Reno Sullivan made her nipples harden, her pussy dampen, and the muscles in her entire body tighten. It had taken a lot of discipline to put out of her mind the erotic dreams that left her shaking and go to work each day as if her boss were just a cardboard figure.

Yeah, right.

It wasn't as if she was looking for a relationship, for heaven's sake. Been there, done that. She and Mike had been on the verge of divorce when he'd been killed, and she'd sworn off men after that dismal experience. But that didn't mean she couldn't indulge in fantasies about one fantastic, erotic night with Reno Sullivan.

If she didn't get over this, she'd have to look for another job. Maybe her mistake was taking the job even though her body went into sensual overload the first time she'd seen him. But the pay Reno Sullivan offered was extraordinary and the work really interesting.

When he got married, it put him safely out of her reach. But now he was a widower with an infant daughter. So of course the dreams had come back with stunning force.

Cut it out and get dressed or you won't have a chance to find out what he wants.

Something was definitely up, and she tried to think what it could be. She enjoyed her job at Guardian, far more than she'd ever expected to. After five years they had settled into an easy give and take relationship. With her entire life devoted to her job, she was glad that they worked so well together and were so comfortable with each other.

Since the death of his wife he'd been driving himself even harder than before, working long hours, omitting any mention of either his late wife or his motherless daughter. His social calendar, beyond business obligations he couldn't avoid, was woefully bleak and bare. So why the sudden interest in dinner with her? What was up with this invitation?

Finally settling on a silk blouse and skirt she knew matched the blue of her eyes, she was fastening her earrings when the doorbell rang promptly at seven. She picked up her purse, automatically checking for the little gun she carried, although she didn't think she'd need a firearm for dinner with the boss. It had just become habit.

When she opened the front door, she swallowed a gasp at the sight of Reno in a dark gray slacks, white on white shirt, and paler gray tie. They complemented eyes framed by thick lashes, eyes so black you could fall into them. A square, masculine jaw set off his sensuous lips. The six-foot-four lean, muscular body was topped by a head of thick black hair.

She looked at him and saw the man as he appeared to the rest of the world—dangerous, dark, and edgy. He had a powerful presence that dominated every room he entered. His graceful movements belied the coiled energy that lay just below the surface. He was like a panther, always poised to leap. Even when dressed in his usual outfit of jeans and work shirt, he lost none of the power of his presence.

God, the man was too sexy for his own good. For *her* good.

"Ready?" His smile was a little strained.

All her original nervousness surged forward again. She swallowed and forced a smile. "Absolutely."

At the restaurant the maître d' showed them to a corner table, bowed them into their seats, shook open their napkins, and quietly handed them menus.

Sarah's palms sweated and her pulse raced, as much from nervousness as from sexual attraction, as she looked at the man across from her. She tried to ignore the tight look on Reno's face and let the quiet, elegant air of the restaurant work its magic on her. The polite tinkle of crystal sounded faintly in the air, punctuated by the genteel clink of silverware. Underneath it, muted conversation hummed at tables where carved tapers flickered in Waterford candlesticks, bathing the diners in a warm, amber glow.

"I've always loved this place," she said, thinking she should attempt conversation. "I don't get to come here as often as I used to, though. Thank you for choosing it." She rearranged her napkin in her lap and wet her lips. "And you're right about them serving the best steak in town."

"Score two points for the good guys." Reno grinned back at her, but the expression seemed forced.

The knot in Sarah's stomach grew to enormous proportions. This must be something terrible for him to be so uptight. Was he going to fire her? Surely, he wouldn't take her out to a fancy dinner to do it.

"Too bad none of the men you date are smart enough to bring you here," he added.

She looked at him, then down at the table, her mouth suddenly dry. "I don't date, Reno."

"I'm sure that disappoints a large part of the male population."

Sarah smiled politely, avoided commenting, and focused on the menu. She gave the waiter a weak smile as he took her order. An uneasy silence stretched between them as they worked their way through the meal, Sarah taking tiny bites of food, Reno merely pushing his around on his plate.

Reno stared at his dinner companion. She was such an obvious choice for his plan, the most together woman he had ever met. Very little rattled her. She was equally at home with corporate clients as she was with the construction crew. He saw her as the perfect combination of silk and steel. And he was sure she wouldn't demand any kind of personal relationship with him. Yes, she was exactly what he needed to stop his life from unraveling further. Except he'd avoided the subject all through the meal, unsure of how to begin.

Now, the meal was over, and he was still stalling.

"Coffee?" He raised his eyebrows.

"Yes, thank you." She looked at the waiter. "Some of your fabulous Spanish coffee, please."

Her choice surprised Reno. He wouldn't have

expected her to order something quite so exotic. He tucked this little fact away among all the other little things he didn't know about her, things he would have to learn. He hoped none of them held a trap for him to fall into.

"Just the French roast for me," he said.

He leaned back in his chair, studying Sarah, and Tony's words popped into his mind. His brother was right—the woman was stunning. She was maybe five foot four, but the heels she wore tonight added another three inches to her height. And her figure... Why hadn't he ever noticed it before? All he'd seen when he'd looked at her was a female in jeans and a shirt who efficiently handled everything he and Nick threw at her.

But the work clothes apparently had disguised a body with lush, feminine curves and a graceful line of neck and chin. The light from the candles on their table reflected the tawny highlights in her abundant, coffee-colored hair, its thickness she ruthlessly tamed into a French braid every day. It warmed her almost translucent skin, accenting her high cheekbones and delicate lips. Her eyes were warm brown pools of liquid chocolate with tiny flecks of gold in the irises, the most expressive part of her face. The light jasmine scent she wore drifted across to him and teased at his nose. An image of her graceful legs as she'd walked out of her house zapped his mind, but he suppressed it with great determination.

Shit. She's beautiful. I should have insisted we go someplace casual so she couldn't change out of her office clothes. She'd still be an anonymous female with excellent skills.

Maggie had been a carbon copy of all the other

women in his life—exotic women who were striking and out of the ordinary. In contrast, Sarah's beauty was understated but incandescent. It should have made her less attractive to him, but unfortunately for his plans, she stirred something long buried in him. He had an unexpected urge to release her coffee-colored hair from its braid, let it tumble about her shoulders, and run his fingers through it.

Damn! An unexpected stirring of desire, a heaviness in his groin that hadn't been there for a long time, shocked him.

What the hell?

"Have I spilled something?" Sarah asked, checking her blouse and brushing at an invisible spot.

He frowned. "No. Why?"

"You're staring at me with the most peculiar expression."

"Sorry." He twirled his wine glass, the liquid nearly sloshing out. "Just lost in my own thoughts."

"They must be pretty heavy." She grinned. "You look as if the world is weighing on you."

"I'm sorry." He sat up straighter in his chair, his mind working furiously. He was nervous as hell, a condition he wasn't used to. He couldn't afford to make a mistake with this. Or let his unexpectedly awakened libido lead him astray. He wiped his perspiring palms on his pant legs.

Sarah hadn't realized how difficult it would be to come out of her self-imposed shell and use her rusty social skills. Her catastrophic marriage had made her withdraw into herself. At work, she could look at all the men—Reno, Nick, Tony, and the others as sexless individuals. She did her job, and they were part of it.

Period.

But Reno's overpowering presence crowded her, and all she could think of was how she could go back to pretending he didn't make her panties wet or invade her dreams hot and naked. And how she would do her job after this. Maybe it would be better after all if he fired her.

Something was making him uneasy tonight, though, and it piqued her interest. It was so unusual for him. Whatever it was, she wished he'd get to it. And quickly.

"Sarah."

"Yes?" Okay. Was this finally it?

He cleared his throat. "You'd say we're a good team in the office, wouldn't you? We've developed a good working rhythm? We almost have a better relationship than some marriages."

What? Where was this going?

"You do such a great job," he continued. "I don't know how I ever got things accomplished before you came along. Guardian owes you a great deal."

"Thank you." She pushed away the remains of her coffee, suddenly losing her taste for the sweet drink, and took a deep breath. "This is very nice, your compliments are wonderful, the dinner was great, and I'm enjoying the evening. But I have no idea what's on your mind. What's going on here, Reno? What's so important you had to ask me to dinner?"

Reno swallowed the last of his coffee and set his cup down with careful precision. "You're right. It's time I got to it."

Sarah waited, forcing herself to sit quietly, even while her pulse began to accelerate. Something was definitely up, and something about Reno's attitude unnerved her.

He cleared his throat again. "I know that you lost a child when your husband was killed, and I can't tell you how sorry I am."

How the hell did he know that? It was carefully guarded information. *I wanted a child, but not Mike's. Not something I can tell a stranger.*

"What I wondered…that is, I wanted to know…" He shifted uncomfortably in his chair. "If the opportunity to have a child were presented to you, would you take it? Would it interest you?"

Sarah stared at him. Now, she was *really* confused. What did this have to do with work?

She blinked. "Excuse me?"

The air between them was suddenly so thick a saw couldn't have cut it.

Sarah dropped her napkin on the table and pushed back her chair back. "I think I'd like to go home now."

"Wait, please." Reno reached across the table and placed his hand on her arm. "I'm doing this badly. Just hear me out, okay?"

She nodded but withdrew her arm, the heat of his hand searing her skin through the silk fabric of her blouse.

"You know I have a six-month-old infant," he began. "I haven't done very well with her since Maggie's death. The circumstances are somewhat difficult."

"Difficult?"

What could be so difficult about raising a child? Not to mention the fact she had a hard time imagining this sexy as sin man with a child to begin with.

"My fault, nobody else's," he continued. "I can't seem to find a housekeeper, and my situation's desperate."

Sarah frowned. "Did you want me to check out some agencies? Really, Reno, you didn't have to take me to dinner to ask me that. I'd be happy to help."

Reno shook his head. "No, that's not it at all. I know people who've had really serious problems hiring through an agency. I don't really trust strangers, and I'm not comfortable having one live in my house. It hasn't worked so far."

"Reno, please. Enough. Just get to the point here."

"I'm sorry. I don't usually botch things this badly. Okay, here's the deal." He took a deep breath and exhaled. "Sarah, I'm asking you to marry me."

Sarah stared at Reno, speechless. If he'd asked her to take off her clothes, she couldn't have been more shocked. Of all the things she might have expected, this wasn't even on the radar. Cold liquid dripping on her skirt startled her, and she realized she'd knocked over her water glass.

"I'm sorry." Her face flamed, heat suffusing her skin.

Reno jumped up from his seat, agitation lining his face. "Here. Let me help you."

She brushed away his hand, blotting at her skirt with her napkin. "Thank you. I can handle it. I'm sorry for being so clumsy."

He stood so close to her his arm touched hers. The spicy scent of his aftershave, the heat radiating from his body, his overpowering masculinity threatened to suffocate her, and for a moment, she couldn't catch her breath. This was not the time for arousal to take over her senses. She needed a clear head to understand this totally unexpected situation. Then he moved, and she breathed again.

"Please don't apologize." His voice was tight. "I know this has to be a shock to you."

"Now there's an understatement for you." She waved her hand at him. "Please sit down. I'm fine."

No, I'm not, but it won't help if you hover over me.

She took a deep breath, steadying herself. "Reno, is this some kind of joke? If so, it's not very funny."

"I assure you there's nothing humorous about it." His voice was earnest, pleading. "And right now, it's especially important for me to have the right person there." He paused. "Luis Aguilar was being transferred today, the vehicle was in an accident, and he's escaped."

She felt the blood drain from her face. "He threatened to get his revenge on you."

"I remember. I already have Nick arranging for a more sophisticated security system. But I need someone with Molly who knows how to protect her. And you fit the bill."

Sarah didn't know what to say. She loved her job as it was, but the chance to care for a child, as well as use her skills to protect her…for the first time in a long time she really felt necessary. Valued.

Sarah, you don't get married to be a bodyguard.

She swallowed a laugh, but she couldn't ignore how appealing the idea was.

"How exactly would this work? I mean, I have a job now as you well know, and I like financial independence."

Reno nodded. "Understood. I hope it wouldn't

offend you if I said I'd continue your salary, the only thing that would change are your job responsibilities."

She sat back in her chair. "A salary. To be your wife. And bodyguard and mother to your child."

He nodded. "I have a child who needs permanence in her life. I can't give it to her. I can't tell you why, so you'll just have to accept that. I know you've been worried about your father and his health problems. And I'm sure he's concerned about taking care of your mother, since he can no longer work. Besides your salary, I propose to take care of your parents financially in exchange for you serving as the child's mother. And my hostess when I need one."

Sarah's pulse accelerated. Hostess. His hostess. What else would he expect?

"Again, this would be strictly a business arrangement," Reno went on to assure her. "You could hire someone to do the cleaning and laundry. I certainly wouldn't expect that of you. It would be nice if we could have dinner together, maybe share some time on the weekend. We do seem compatible, and we've known each other for five years. But that's strictly up to you."

"Dinner." She tried to follow everything he said. "Weekends."

"Yes. Sometimes, I go out to visit Nick and Lindsey at their ranch. Nick and I have known each other since our college days at UT, and we've been a good fit as partners in the business. You've probably been able to see that."

"Yes. That's true." Lindsey Vanetta was a sweet-faced blonde, and she and Nick were so obviously in love the air around them nearly crackled with flames when they were in the same room.

"She's really domesticated Nick. I think you'd enjoy spending time with them if you wanted to come along." He shifted in his chair, nervously crossing and uncrossing his legs. "There might even be other things we find we'd enjoy doing together."

"We'd be the same as housemates." She couldn't believe she was sitting here so outwardly calm, discussing this outrageous proposition. She grinned. "Except I'd also be a bodyguard."

"Yes." He actually smiled. "Housemates. A good description. You'd have your own room. Your entire focus would be on the child. Caregiver and bodyguard." He shifted his gaze away. "Of course, there'd be no expectation of intimacy."

Intimacy. The word brought her up short. If she said yes to this, they'd be living together. No going home at five o'clock. How on earth would she share a house with a man she lusted after without ever letting it show?

And what did he plan to do about sex? He wasn't the kind to cheat on his wife, real or otherwise, with a series of discreet affairs. But he also was a man known for his strong sexuality. How would that factor into things?

"I'll take care of the bills," she heard him say, "but you'll be in charge of everything else—the running of the house, normal chores and activities—those kinds of things. And the child. Especially the child. She'd be your primary focus."

"I see."

"We'd have an agreement so that, if it happened not to work out, you'd suffer no financial hardship." He looked down at his hands. "I had my attorney draw up a contract just in case you agreed."

Unexpectedly, she burst out laughing. "I can't believe I'm actually considering this. Just out of curiosity, how many others have you interviewed?"

"No one else." His voice was stiff. "Sarah, I didn't mean to offend you in any way. I…"

"It's all right. I'm just…stunned and not quite sure what to say." She took a sip of water, trying to collect her thoughts. "Reno, I'm curious. If you're so concerned about your daughter, why do you refer to her as 'the child'? Why don't you ever use her name? And why don't you want to play any role in her care?"

Lines of misery etched his face. "Please believe me when I say I can't tell you that. Sarah, you've known me for five years, and we've developed a comfortable relationship. I think we can take measure of each other. Can I just ask you to trust me on this and not ask any questions when I say there's a real need here?"

The amount of pain in his words shocked her. What kind of tragedy had he faced that he couldn't deal with a tiny child?

"But how can I make such a life-changing decision without all the facts in place? And why me?" That was the real question. "Surely there must be others you'd consider. I'd think you could have your pick of a dozen women. A hundred."

"You overestimate my present market value." A tight smile twisted his lips. "Especially these days. In any event, they would demand a commitment from me that I'm unwilling to make."

"Ah." Understanding dawned. "The intimacy issue."

"Among other things. Considering the trouble my libido has gotten me into, I'm pretty sure I could live without sex for the rest of my life."

She burst out laughing but immediately swallowed her laughter. This was not a time for it.

"I just find it strange," she said, "that you're willing to live in a celibate relationship."

"Believe me." Now his voice was bitter. "Celibacy has its virtues. I want a situation that won't be complicated by sex."

Sarah's eyes widened and her hands tightened on her napkin. "I beg your pardon?"

"Sarah, please don't take this the wrong way, but that's one of the reason's you're the ideal candidate. Sex is something we won't have to deal with."

She didn't know whether to be angry or laugh at him. "Have I just been insulted?"

"No." He shook his head. "Not at all. In fact, you might consider it a compliment."

"If you say so." How ironic.

"I have to have someone I trust to do this. And I trust you, Sarah. Implicitly. I'm convinced you're the person who could make this work. And of course, you have skills that others would lack."

"Ah, yes. The bodyguard side of the job."

He nodded. "Of course, if this does not work out, your job will always be ready for you."

Oh, really? If this blew up in their faces, did he really think she could go back to work for him?

Little fingers of warning danced on her neck, but she swallowed hard and banished them. Whatever the problem was, she'd find a way around it. Who could turn away from a child? Especially when she wanted one so badly and one who might be in danger.

"I admit you've caught me off guard." She wet her lips. "I don't know what to say."

"I'm sorry if this has upset you. I never meant—"

"No, please, it's all right. I think I'm just feeling a bit hysterical at the moment." She sipped at her water again, buying time to think. "You said I'd have full control in all matters where your child is concerned, right?" That was the key here. The heart of the matter. Whatever his problem with his daughter, she wanted to have no misunderstanding about her role. The child was the main attraction for her here.

"Totally." He was emphatic.

"And how much time do I have to think about this?"

"I wish I could give you as much time as possible to make your decision," he said, shifting in his chair, "but I have…let's say…a certain sense of urgency here. Especially with Aguilar on the loose, although I could always assign one of our agents to guard her in the interim."

"I'm, surprised you don't do that anyway."

He shook his head. "I think what we're doing will work. At least for now." He took a deep breath. "I hate to push you this way, but do you think you could give me an answer by tomorrow?"

Sarah thought she would faint. Tomorrow! She didn't know if she'd be able to answer him by next month or even next year. Her mind reeled. "Tomorrow. Well. I'll do my best to manage that. Could we leave now, please?"

"Of course. I understand." He signaled for the check. "I'm sure you have a lot of sorting out to do."

She was silent on the drive from the restaurant, very aware of Reno's presence next to her, his scent that filled the air in the car, his strong, lean fingers on the steering wheel. She kept stealing sideways glances at him, trying not to stare at this man whose entire meaning in her life had changed in seconds. What would it be like sitting across the table from him every day, watching the flex of muscles in his jaw and throat as he ate? Trying not to fall into the black pools of his eyes. Feeling the lingering traces of his presence when he left a room.

She was so preoccupied she barely noticed when the motion of the car stopped.

"We're here." His voice held a trace of amusement under the tension.

She blinked. They were parked in the driveway of her small house in northwest San Antonio. A two-story adobe structure with lots of wide windows, it was set back from the sidewalk on a tiny manicured lawn. A swing hung invitingly on the porch. She loved her tiny refuge, a little gem that she'd bought with Mike's insurance money. It gave her a sense of permanence. Would she have to give it up, too?

"Sorry." She shook herself. "What would I do about my house? I really don't want to let go of it." Her safety valve if this whole absurd situation blew up in their faces.

"Your decision. You can rent it out or just leave it empty. I'll pay the mortgage and the taxes on it, and we'll hire help to maintain it for you on a regular basis."

"I'll factor it in with everything else," she said, a touch of irony in her voice. "I understand this is a big responsibility you'd be handing me, and in fact, I'm flattered you think of me as the ideal candidate. But I have a lot to consider right now."

"I understand."

She stopped him as he unfastened his seat belt and started to open his door. "Please don't walk me to the door. I'll see you in the morning. I will try to have an answer for you then."

"Thank you."

Sarah unlocked her door and stepped inside, turning to wave to Reno before closing it again. She waited until she heard Reno pull out of the driveway. Then she locked the door and leaned against it, heart racing, head throbbing. How could Reno put her in this position? What was he thinking? That she could give him an answer by tomorrow?

But she closed her eyes and thought, not only of Reno, but of the unknown child that no one seemed to want.

****

Driving away from Sarah's house, Reno cursed himself steadily. Nick and Tony were right. He was an ignorant fool. Whatever had possessed him to bumble ahead with this stupid idea? He'd thought it so sensible until he looked at it through Sarah's eyes. She was right. He was hiring a wife.

But worse than that was his unexpected physical reaction to her, that unfamiliar tightening in his groin when he'd suddenly looked at her for the first time. He hadn't had sex in so long he'd almost forgotten how it felt, but he certainly hadn't thought of it in the same breath with Sarah. He shouldn't do it now, or he'd be in worse trouble than he already was. And she would certainly run as fast as she could in the opposite direction.

Sweat ran down his spine in rivulets and covered his face with a fine sheen, the aftereffects of nervous tension, and he suddenly felt as if he were choking. Yanking his tie loose and opening his collar, he drew in a deep breath and let it out slowly.

Did Sarah think he was a damned idiot? What if she turned him down? He hadn't even allowed for that possibility.

Come on, Sarah. Say yes. You're my only hope.

Chapter Three

The ringing of her phone brought Sarah back to reality. She pushed herself away from the door and rushed to catch it, her "Hello" coming out slightly breathless.

"Sarah?"

Oh, God, her mother. Just what she needed right now.

"Honey, are you all right?" Ellen Madison's voice had a touch of concern.

Sarah looked at the clock. Twelve-thirty. "Mother, what are you doing up this late? You never make it past the news." A terrible thought struck her. "Is it Daddy? Is he okay?"

"Yes, he's fine. I'm sorry. I didn't mean to scare you."

"Then what *are* you doing up so late?"

"I was worried about you. I tried you earlier several times but didn't get any answer."

Of course. I'm so predictable that the one night I'm out late, my parents push the panic button. You'd think I was eighteen years old. She hoped her father wasn't worrying himself into another heart attack. His condition was bad enough as it was.

"I'm fine. I was just out for the evening."

"Oh?" She could hear the curiosity in her mother's

voice. "Anything special?"

"Not really. Just dinner with my boss."

Please let her leave it at that.

"You had dinner with Reno? How nice. A real night out. I'm sure you had a great time."

Yes, Sarah the bore actually went out on a date. And Mother, you wouldn't believe what happened.

"Yes, I did. We had a lot of…business to discuss." *That's the understatement of the year.* "How's Dad?"

"He's doing okay, honey." Was that hesitation in her mother's voice? "Everything's fine."

But the underlying worry about health insurance and further treatments was always there. Sarah could sense it. And she had it in her power now to put that worry to sleep.

"That's good, Mom. But I'm very tired. How about if I call you back tomorrow? Okay?" Without waiting for an answer, she said, "Night, Mom," and disconnected the call. Tomorrow would be soon enough to open this particular Pandora's Box.

She popped two aspirins to ward off a threatening headache and crawled into bed, but sleep eluded her. No matter what she tried, she couldn't make her mind a blank. The evening repeated itself over and over in her head, like a television rerun she couldn't turn off.

The proposal tonight had rocked her, the offer coming from so far out in left field she had trouble coming to terms with it. And the terms of the marriage. A hired wife and mother. How trite! If the idea weren't so unsettling, she'd be laughing out loud.

If only she knew what secrets he hid. There had been a problem with his sudden marriage to Maggie, but neither Nick nor Tony had ever discussed it. The only time Reno had smiled in more than a year was when Molly was born. Then Maggie had died, and Reno hadn't mentioned either her or the child since. It was more than the grieving process. A hardness and bitterness had settled over him that hadn't been there before.

Too often, she caught a glimpse of such pain it made her want to weep. Tonight was the most outgoing she'd seen him since his marriage and the death of his wife. But of course, he had a reason for it. A plan he was following to hire her as his wife. He had obviously put his best foot forward.

She had an insane desire to giggle when she thought of yesterday's conversation with her mother.

"I do wish you'd get out once in a while," Ellen had said. "Solitude is only good for so long."

"I'm fine," Sarah had assured her. "I don't need anyone. I don't want anyone."

"Well, it's just not natural. It makes me sad to see what's happened to you. You're still young and beautiful, and you're wasting your life."

Okay, Mother. Wait until I tell you about tonight's dinner.

I must be insane even to consider his proposal. After the tragedy of her first marriage… Could she enter into another marriage, even one of convenience, when she hadn't yet put to rest the last one?

Again she wondered what it would be like living with Reno Sullivan. What did he eat? Watch on television? Read? Did he stay up late or go to bed early? Did he roam the house, and would she run into him if she made any nocturnal forays? Her mind drifted as she fell into a half-sleep.

****

He was standing beside the bed, wet from a shower, wearing only the towel wrapped around his lean hips…

The bedside lamp was on low, casting a golden glow on his toned body but shadowing his face. The glow in his eyes had nothing to do with artificial light, however.

"I want you." His voice was rough with desire. "I've wanted you from the first time I set eyes on you. You don't know how many times you came into my office and I couldn't get up from my desk because my cock was so hard."

"I want you, too," she whispered. "You don't know how many times I dreamed about you, just like this."

"I had my own dreams. But now we have the reality."

He tossed the towel aside, revealing an impressive erection and the sac with his balls resting heavy against his thighs. The muscles of her pussy quivered and moisture slid out onto her inner thighs. The ache inside her grew until she felt it in every throb of her pulse.

Reno pulled back the sheet covering her, lifted her to a sitting position, and deftly slid the thin nightgown over her head. His gaze raked over her, the heat in his eyes flaring brighter.

"Gorgeous," he breathed. "Absolutely gorgeous, just as I knew you'd be."

He lay down beside her, propping his head with one hand as he ran the other lightly over her body. His fingers traced a pattern along her cheek, down her neck and between the valley of her breasts. They glided across her puckered nipples, pausing to pinch each one lightly. *Shards of heat streaked directly to her cunt and spread throughout her body.*

As he explored her, his mouth found hers, taking her in a predatory kiss that roused her senses. He tasted every inch of her mouth, her own tongue dueling with his for possession. When he gently bit the tip of her tongue, she reached up to clutch at his head, trying to pull him even closer. When he broke the kiss, she was gasping for breath.

His palm rested a moment on her tummy, then his fingers trailed into the nests of curls covering her mound, finally probing the wetness of her slit. Her legs parted, giving him greater access to her, and the tip of one finger circled the entrance to her cunt. He inserted it barely past the first knuckle, and her inner muscles clenched in response. He shifted slightly beside her, and the full length of his cock pressed against her thigh.

She tried to urge him farther inside her with her hips, but he was intent on teasing. As his finger moved slowly in and out, never pushing all the way in, he bent his head and captured one tight nipple into his mouth and sucked. Hard.

Sarah moaned harder, the coil of need inside her winding tighter and tighter.

"Please," she murmured. "Oh, please."

"Please what?" he asked, lifting his mouth from her breast. "Please kiss you? Lick you? Fuck you?"

"Yes. Everything. All of it." She pressed one hand against the taut muscles of his back, feeling the play of sinews beneath the skin.

He pushed his finger all the way inside her, then added a second.

"You are so damn tight," he rasped, scissoring his

fingers. "*I can't wait to feel my dick inside you.*"

He moved his thumb to find the hot bud of her clitoris, rubbing it back and forth. Moisture flooded his fingers, and she clenched around them.

"That's it," he encouraged. "I want that wetness so I can slide into you."

She moved her hand from his back and tried to slide it between them, but he pulled it away.

"I want to touch you," she insisted.

"Not yet. If you do, I'm afraid we'll be finished before we barely get started. I've wanted to fuck you for so long I can barely control myself."

Those words, as much as what he was doing to her body, ratcheted up her pleasure even more. When he shifted again to move between her legs, she shivered in anticipation. But instead of positioning himself to enter her, he slid down, opened the lips of her pussy as if they were petals on a flower and licked the length of her with one long swipe of his tongue.

Sarah raised her knees, threaded her fingers through the black silk of his hair, and pulled his head tight against her.

"Yes," she moaned. "Oh, yes."

His tongue was like a flame heating her flesh. His hands slid beneath her buttocks, lifting her higher to his mouth as he licked and thrust and plundered. As an orgasm gathered deep inside her, muscles tightened, pulses throbbed. When it broke over her, she clutched at his head, lifting her hips to him and digging her heels into the bed. She shook with the spasms, her inner muscles trying to draw his tongue in deeper.

As she was still clenching, he withdrew his tongue, rose to his knees pressed the head of his cock against *her opening.*

"Now you can touch me," he whispered roughly. "Guide me home, Sarah."

Still in the throes of orgasm, she somehow managed to reach down for his shaft, widened her thighs and guided him into her body. He rolled his hip, and with one powerful thrust, he was inside her, stretching her, filling her until she couldn't breathe. One movement and she was plunged into another climax, this one even more powerful.

He held himself steady as she convulsed around him, bathing him with her liquid, wrapping her legs around him, and digging her heels into the base of his spine. When she was gasping, nails digging into his shoulders, he began to move, powerful strokes in and out in a steady rhythm.

"I can't," she told him in a breathless voice.

"Yes, you can. Ride with me."

He drove into her faster. Beneath the grip of her legs, his muscles tightened as his own climax gathered. His tempo increased as he pounded into her harder and harder. Finally he stopped, his entire body stiffening, and as he began to spurt inside her, another orgasm gripped her, this one the most intense yet.

Her pussy convulsed around his cock, her legs tightened around him, her entire body shuddered in the rhythm of the shared climax. She was spinning into space, rockets exploding in the black velvet that surrounded her. The spasms seemed to go on forever until she wondered how she would survive it.

And finally, finally, the intensity subsided, leaving her breathless and gasping for air. Her heart beat against her ribs so hard she was afraid it would shatter.

With great effort, she unwound her legs from him and lowered them to the bed.

Reno collapsed forward, catching himself on his forearms, his breath washing over her as he brushed her lips. His cock was still inside her, still filling her. He touched his forehead to hers and—

Sarah roused from her dream with a start. She was covered in perspiration, her covers tossed aside, nightgown rucked up, her hand between her legs, stroking her still-pulsing cunt.

Ohmigod!

She squeezed her thighs together and withdrew her hand guiltily. Another erotic dream about Reno. Her body was weak, nearly boneless, as if she'd actually had multiple orgasms. She was truly losing her mind.

On shaky legs, she stumbled into the bathroom where she dampened a washcloth with cold water and ran it over her face, her neck, and her arms. But it was going to take more than that to cool her feverish body. She drank two glasses of water, hoping that would help, but it barely took the edge off the arousal coursing through her. Filling the glass again, she wandered back into the bedroom.

She was standing by the bedroom window, rubbing the glass against her forehead, when the telephone rang, jerking her out of her thoughts.

She looked at the bedside clock. One-thirty a.m. Who could be calling at that hour? Nothing good came of calls after midnight. Again, her first thought was of her father. Her stomach knotted in fear as she picked up the receiver.

"Sarah?"

"Yes?" Her disoriented mind didn't recognize the

raspy voice at first.

"It's Reno." There was a slight pause. "I apologize for the late hour. I hope I didn't wake you."

Reno? Oh, God, now what? And why did his voice sound so strange? Maybe he'd decided he wanted his answer right away. That he couldn't wait until morning. Her stomach churned at the thought.

"No, I was awake." *After an unbelievable dream about you, so hot I'm still shaking.* "Is something wrong?"

"No. Yes. That is…"

"That is?" she prompted. She couldn't imagine this man ever fumbling for words.

"I was just thinking maybe I came across too strong tonight." His voice was slightly hoarse, and she caught the edge of anxiety. This had to be damn important to him. "I wanted to make sure I hadn't scared you away."

Too strong? She swallowed a hysterical laugh. A bulldozer would have been softer.

"I'm fine," she assured him. "Just turning a lot of things over in my mind."

"I'm sure you are." He cleared his throat. "Actually, I'm feeling kind of guilty. I don't think I realized I'd be asking you to turn your life upside down quite so much."

"Please don't worry. But I think we'd better hang up now. I'm still trying to sort through everything, and the night isn't getting any longer."

And I need to go to sleep and not dream about you.

"Of course. I'm sorry," he apologized. "I shouldn't have called this late in the first place."

"No, it's all right. Really."

Another pause. "To tell the truth, I think I was afraid you might decide I was totally crazy, pack up and leave."

"Not a chance." Though, after the dream, the idea had occurred to her. How could she agree to a sexless marriage with a man she wanted inside her every time she saw him? "I'm not going anywhere."

"Thank you for that. And Sarah? Whatever you decide, I want you to know it won't cost you your job."

Now she really did want to laugh. If she turned him down, how on earth could she go back to their everyday work arrangement—and keep dreaming at night—as if nothing had changed?

"We can discuss it if that turns out to be the case."

"Well, then." He seemed reluctant to break the connection. Again, silence stretched across the line. "See you in the morning."

"Good night."

More restless now than ever, Sarah went to the kitchen and made herself a cup of tea, sipping at it and staring out the window as if the answer waited for her out there somewhere.

She could only hope.

****

At six in the morning, Reno finally gave up trying to sleep, showered, and dressed. The child was still asleep, as was the dreadful housekeeper the last agency he'd called had sent him. If he didn't get her out of the house soon, he might have to shoot her.

At seven, he answered the door to let one of his agents in. He needed someone until Sarah moved in.

If she moved in.

He went over the layout with Gary Stern, the agent.

The housekeeper had been none too happy to have a strange man assigned to the house, especially since he hadn't given her any reason. Too bad. Hopefully, by afternoon he could boot her out.

The streets were just filling with morning traffic as he drove to work, and the parking garage was only partially filled. Most people wouldn't arrive until at least another hour. He was surprised when he walked into his office to find Nick already waiting for him.

He grinned at Reno. "Figure to dodge me by being an early bird? Not a chance."

"What about the security system?"

Nick looked at his watch. "They're on their way. As a matter of fact, they should be arriving any minute. I called Gary to let them in."

"Excellent."

"So. How did it go last night?"

"Please." Reno shook his head. "I've already had the speech from Tony. I woke him up in the middle of the night to tell him you're both right. I'm a fool."

And what a conversation that had been, prompting that incredibly stupid phone call to Sarah.

Nick frowned. "Does this mean she turned you down?"

"It means she said she'd give me an answer today." He sat down beside his desk and pretended to busy himself with a stack of change orders.

"You look as if you haven't slept in a year."

"That's how I feel."

Especially after the fantasies that popped into my head when I tried to sleep and now won't get out of my mind. Sarah naked in my bed. Sarah with her legs spread wide and her swollen, pink cunt—

"Reno?" Nick's voice cut into his mental wanderings. "Did you hear me? I asked how she reacted to the 'No Sex' clause?"

Reno frowned, remembering the mixture of relief and disappointment that crossed Sarah's face when he mentioned a sex-free marriage. "Actually, I think she was relieved."

"Well." Nick ambled toward the door. "I'd wish you good luck, but if Sarah says yes, she's the one who'll need it."

Reno said nothing. He was too edgy to argue and so uptight he was afraid he'd crack if he bent over. Although he tried, it was impossible to concentrate on the work orders in front of him. He brewed himself at least six cups of coffee from his handy one-cup coffeemaker. Within half an hour, his stomach had a sour feel and his head was buzzing from a caffeine high. His looked through the open doorway to Sarah's desk at least every two minutes, although she always got there on the dot of eight.

When she finally arrived, his entire body cramped. What if she said no? What were his choices? What if she said yes? Could he marry a woman his body suddenly craved with desperation and commit to a no-sex future?

She was dressed in her usual slacks and tailored blouse, clothes he had found decidedly unsexy where she was concerned. But today his mind imagined the satiny skin beneath it, and he wondered what her breasts would be like free of their restraining bra. If her nipples were large or small and how they would taste. How it would feel to be inside her. Was she tight? Would she be so wet for him it didn't matter?

Jesus! What the hell is wrong with me?

He watched her stow her purse in a bottom desk drawer, boot up her computer, and call the answering service for messages. Finally, she just sat there with her hands folded, not moving.

His head ached, and his stomach churned with anxiety. Was she trying to find a way to let him down easily? Had his stupid phone call in the middle of the night killed any possibility of the bargain he'd presented?

Frustrated, he tore off the sheet of paper he'd been writing on, crumpled it into a ball and threw it hard against the office wall.

"Is it safe to come in?"

He looked up. Sarah stood at the office door, a tentative smile on her face.

"Of course." He blew out a breath.

"You look as if you're chewing steel," she told him.

"I probably could right now." He motioned her forward. "Please. Come in."

She closed the door, probably to give them privacy in case anyone wandered in, then leaned back against it. Had she slept at all after he'd called? Or had she spent the night as he had, confounded by the whole situation? He gritted his teeth with the tension.

At last, she took a deep breath and let it out. "Before I give you my answer, it would help to go out to your house and see Molly. If I'm going to be her...mother, I don't think that's an unreasonable request."

Reno's body tightened. Of course she'd want to see what she was getting into. Maybe that would be the last nail in his coffin, but he nodded. "No problem. When do you want to go?"

"I think the sooner the better. Mornings are usually the quietest around here. I can forward calls to Nick's office and, of course, let him know we'll be leaving."

Reno could well imagine what those two would think. "All right. Let me know as soon as you're ready. FYI, the men are already on site installing the new security system. And I've got Gary Stern out there as a precaution until we, uh, see what's happening."

Well, didn't that just sound stupid?

"Good. I'm glad Molly will be protected."

Before nine o'clock, they were heading out I-10 in a tension-filled silence. Whatever sexual overtones might have popped up unexpectedly were certainly absent now.

Reno's house was located in Alamo Heights, a suburb of old money and executive wealth. He'd fallen in love with the architecture of the Georgian colonial and enjoyed living there until his life fell apart. Now, despite the oleanders and bougainvillea blooming in colorful profusion and two large crepe myrtles covered in soft lilac blossoms, everything looked cold and lifeless to him.

"It's beautiful," she commented, turning toward him.

If you only knew.

A black Guardian Security van was parked in the driveway. There was a man on the roof and two others crawling around on the ground. One of them stood up and waved at Reno.

"We'll be done by the end of the day, Mr. Sullivan."

"Great. Thanks."

Reno felt as if Armageddon was just beyond the doors. He had deliberately not called to give the housekeeper any warning, wanting Sarah to understand completely what she was walking into.

"Don't think the outside is an indication of the inside. I have an excellent lawn service." His voice was taut as a rubber band. "You may be in for more of a surprise than you thought. The housekeepers haven't done as good a job as the yardmen. This one can't seem to walk and chew gum at the same time."

"Where do you get them?" She raised one eyebrow in curiosity. "The housekeepers, I mean."

"An agency. And this isn't the first one I've tried. I've gone through six in as many weeks." Did that make him sound like an impossible perfectionist to work for? But surely she knew from the office how he was. And if anyone could make order out of chaos, it was Sarah.

He took a deep breath, feeling as if he were about to plunge off a cliff. "All right. Let's go on in."

Gary had seen them coming and opened the door from the garage to the house for them.

"Everything okay?" Reno asked.

The agent shrugged. "Yeah. Sort of."

Reno lifted an eyebrow. "What does that mean?"

"Not my place to say this boss, but it would be a hell of a lot better if you got rid of that harpy in there."

Embarrassment flushed through him. If he'd had any other choice, he'd never have let one of his men see what was going on.

Sarah frowned. What on earth? She'd been prepared for a sterile environment, with a little girl tended by robots on an orderly schedule. Robots who had no idea how to relate to a child. What greeted her was beyond anything she'd imagined.

A sharp voice drifted out from the kitchen. "Take this bottle. Open your mouth now, or I'll throw this away."

Sarah couldn't believe the animosity in the tone. But the room they stepped into was worse than any irritable voice. All around them was total disorder, the accumulation of neglect evident. The housekeeper sat in one of the kitchen chairs, a bottle in one hand, a screaming child in the other.

Sarah was stunned. Had Reno even noticed what was going on here? She looked at the distressed baby, and her heart lurched. At the center of the maelstrom was the most adorable baby girl she had ever seen, dressed in a onesie that was stained in the front. Blonde curls framed a pixie face with round cheeks, now more red than pink. Thick lashes fringed warm dark eyes, and dimples flashed at the corners of her mouth. There was very little resemblance to Reno so Sarah assumed she looked like her mother.

She spied Sarah and Reno and began to scream even louder.

The housekeeper turned, startled. "Oh, I'm sorry. I wasn't expecting you, Mr. Sullivan."

Sarah could believe that.

Reno cleared his throat. "Mrs. Randall, this is Sarah Madison."

"Hello." The woman got up from her chair, juggling the baby, and sighed. "I've been trying to get this bottle into her for ages without any success."

A jar of baby food sat on the counter, a spoon stuck

into it, obviously discarded. Reno made no acknowledgement of anything, simply stepped back as if removing himself from the scene.

Sarah's mind processed everything. So this was the reason for the urgent proposal. This woman obviously didn't like children, at least not this one. And her housekeeping skills wouldn't win any awards. Why on earth would she take a job caring for a house and child if she hated doing it? And why didn't Reno at least get a cleaning crew in here once in a while? Had he just washed his hands of everything to do with his personal life? This was a nightmare.

But the baby... Oh, that heartwarming child so badly needs someone to love her.

What on earth had happened in this house to bring it to the brink of such destruction? She looked at Reno, hoping for some kind of explanation, but he simply stood near the wall, his posture stiff and unyielding. Every line of his body shouted aversion to the whole thing. She would have thought him cold and unfeeling if not for the torment in his eyes. His gaze begged, *Please don't judge me so quickly.*

So many emotions bubbled up inside Sarah that, for a moment, she had trouble maintaining her composure. It included a pain that had never left her heart, a secret she hadn't felt the need to share with Reno. This was a disaster, and sooner or later, she had to get to the bottom of it. But not right now, when there were more urgent matters.

Suddenly, Molly hiccupped, stopped crying, and reached her chubby little arms out to Sarah. And Sarah's world turned upside down. Gone in an instant were her fears and misgivings at sharing a house with

Reno and her dismay at what faced her. With one gesture, Molly Sullivan became the focus of Sarah's world, and an unusual feeling of calm settled over her.

She was getting something she'd never thought to have, and that alone would help her do this. She could make it work. All she needed was to get past the emotional landmines she knew awaited her.

She stepped over to the chair. "May I?"

Without waiting for an answer, she dropped her purse on the counter and lifted the baby from the housekeeper's arms. As she nestled her cheek against the soft skin of the little girl's face, she felt a painful hitch in her heart. Tears pricked the inside of her eyelids, threatening to run down her cheeks, and she blinked hard to contain them.

"She needs cleaning up," Mrs. Randall said nervously.

No kidding!

"That's all right." Sarah smiled. "If you just show me where to go I'm happy to change her."

The housekeeper looked at Reno for answers.

He just nodded, looking like a caged eagle desperate to take flight. The message was clear to Sarah—do whatever needs to be done, but leave him out of it. If she'd had her car with her, she'd have told him to go on back to the office at once. She had never seen him this uptight.

"This way." He led her out of the kitchen, into the hall, then to the sweeping arc of the stairway.

Sarah stopped at the bottom step. "We have a lot to discuss, but I'll give you my answer now. Yes. I'll agree to this bizarre marriage arrangement. The sooner the better."

Reno visibly sagged with relief. "Sarah, I promise you I'll make sure you won't regret this. A bargain is a bargain, and I'll keep my end."

"Don't make promises you might not be able to keep," she said tautly. "Meanwhile, we have some immediate problems to resolve. Get rid of that dreadful woman. Pay her and send her on her way. This seems to be way beyond her capability, and I don't particularly care for her attitude toward Molly."

"Sarah, I—"

"It's all right. And call Nick. Ask him to look in my Rolodex for the number for the cleaning service we use for new construction." She stopped, suddenly worried. "I'm not presuming too much, am I? Overstepping my bounds?"

"You're kidding, right? This is more than I hoped for. But what about…"

She shook her head. "When I come back down."

Reno tried once again to say something, but Sarah hurried up the stairs with Molly in her arms. The upper floor had the same depressing air of neglect as the kitchen and a musty odor hung over everything.

What's wrong here? I can't understand why Reno would tolerate this kind of existence.

She located the nursery at the end of the hall. Not wanting to take the time for a tub bath, she stripped off the little girl's clothes, carried her into the adjoining bathroom, and ran a sink of warm water. While she bathed Molly gently with a washcloth, she talked to her and sang songs she dredged up from her childhood.

I have to be the dumbest person in the world to agree to this. But it's criminal what's happening with this adorable little girl. How could Reno ignore his child this way? He acts as if she's contagious. I would have expected a lot more from him.

But it was what it was, and without hesitation, she decided her next move.

Her mind raced, and her stomach did flip-flops at the thought of the very unSarah-like thing she was about to do. She worried that this really *was* pushing it, but the minute she'd seen Molly, everything else ceased to exist. This—a child to love who obviously needed her—was the only thing that mattered right now. And she would do whatever she had to where Molly's welfare was concerned. Protect her with her life if that animal Aguilar came anywhere near her.

Even if it meant suppressing those flames of desire that consumed her whenever she was in Reno's presence.

She opened a drawer and pulled out the first onesie she came to, thinking *inventory later*. In a few minutes, she carried a clean and freshly dressed Molly downstairs and went to find Reno. He stood in the kitchen, leaning against the wall, arms crossed, face set in granite.

"She's gone." He paused, his voice and posture indicating his discomfort. "Sarah, I know what you must be thinking…"

"One of these days you'll have to tell me what's going on here, but right now, this child needs attention."

"Shall I call the agency to send someone else?" he asked, his voice hesitant.

Sarah sat down with Molly in her lap, cuddling the infant against her. "No, I think not. You said I could make decisions, so I'm taking you at your word."

"Anything." His relief was evident. "Whatever you want, as long as you don't change your mind."

Okay, here goes.

"I think I should move into the house right away." She held her breath, waiting for him to say something, but he was silent. "Does that shock you? The situation with Molly is the most important thing right now. You said to do what's best for her. And we're going to be married quickly, right?"

Breath whooshed out of him in the biggest sigh of relief Sarah had ever heard. A smile, the first his mouth had formed in ages, tugged at his lips. "You really are full of surprises, aren't you? I was hoping that was what you'd do. Tackle it the way you do every project in the office."

For a moment, his reminder of the business-like nature of the situation chilled her, but she quickly brushed away the feeling. "I don't suppose that will cause any more gossip among your friends than the wedding itself."

"The hell with my friends. They were never there when I needed them anyway. I just want to be sensitive about appearances for your sake."

"I think appearances are the least of the problem here. The only people I'm concerned about are my parents, and I'll deal with that. Somehow." She hesitated. "But that presents another problem. This means I won't be coming back to the office. That will cause some problems for you." She nibbled at her lower lip, rocking the baby gently in her arms. "I'll call the temp agency we used when I took vacation. I'll tell them we're looking for a permanent replacement and to send us someone qualified who's looking for that."

"I can make the call if that would help," Reno ventured.

Sarah shook her head. "No. Not to step on your toes, but I know better what's needed in that job, so I'll take care of it. But I'll need to get my car, go by my house, put together a schedule to get everything done." Still feeding the hungry baby, she got up and looked in the pantry and the refrigerator. More disaster. "And grocery shop."

"I'll be getting you a new car, too." When she opened her mouth to object, he shook his head. "Not up for negotiation. I'd feel safer with her in an SUV. But the big thing is I'm sending it to Texas Armoring to make it completely bulletproof."

Sarah knew that many of their clients used TAC, as they were referred to. Vehicles that came out of that shop were safe from just about anything. Some of them even outfitted with gun ports and concealed weapons.

"Fine. I have to agree that's sensible, under the circumstances."

"I think we should take care of the license and the rings today. I'll call Judge Harrison about performing the ceremony, unless you have a preference of some kind. I'm leaving Gary here until we're settled back here at the end of the day. He can finish supervising the security system, too." The lines in his face deepened. "What about the child? Can you do something with her? I don't want to haul her around with us."

Sarah bit back the retort that jumped to her lips. "Do you think Lindsey might know of a babysitter we can trust?"

"I suppose. Nick has a big family, lots of nieces. Maybe one of them would do."

"Be sure to tell Lindsey about Gary. I'm sure Nick's already let her know about Aguilar."

He tore a sheet of paper from a pad on the counter. "Here's the number of the cleaning service."

"Fine. I'll talk to them while you call Lindsey. Then I think we should get going."

And just like that, Sarah's life turned upside down.

Chapter Four

While Sarah arranged for a cleaning crew, Reno called Nick to ask him about the baby sitter situation.

"He's put Lindsey on it," Reno told Sarah, disconnecting the call. "Everyone's in school until two o'clock but all the nieces have cell phones so she'll call and text. She'll have someone here by three. That will give us enough time to take care of business. We can do it right here in Alamo Heights."

"Good. The cleaning crew will be here at noon, so I'd better hustle. I asked for the biggest one they had and offered them double. I hope that's okay. We'll need it. They can bill Guardian." She shifted Molly in her arms. "Do you know where the carrier is?"

He tensed, then frowned as if searching for the answer. "I think Mrs. Randall put it in the garage."

Sarah stared at him. "You mean to tell me this baby has never been out of the house?"

His discomfort was obvious. "I'll go get it."

He brought it to her, holding it as if it would bite him, perplexed as to what to do with it. Sarah gritted her teeth and settled Molly into it. "Can you watch her for a minute? I need to run upstairs and get a light blanket to wrap her in and pack a diaper bag."

"Watch her?" Reno looked as if he'd bolt out the door.

Sarah fought back her impatience. "She won't get up and run away. Please. I'll be quick." Without giving him a chance to object, she raced up the stairs, dug in the chest of drawers in the nursery for some kind of light wrap, found the diaper bag in the closet, and pulled things from the changing table, stuffing them in as fast as she could. She literally ran back down the stairs.

Reno was standing exactly where she'd left him, staring at Molly who stared back at him, sucking on her tiny fist.

She picked up the carrier. "I think we're ready now. Do you want me to come in when we get to the office and get the temp settled?"

He shook his head. "We'll take care of it. We've done it before. Worst comes to worst, if she's a washout, I can get one of the payroll clerks to file and help with other things."

And those were the last words spoken until they reached the office parking lot. Sarah didn't even go inside, just shifted Molly, the diaper bag, and her purse to her own car.

"I'll pick you up at three," Reno said.

Was it her place to ask if he'd be home for dinner? She realized how much about him was still a mystery to her. "I don't know what time you usually prefer to eat."

"I don't expect you to cook tonight, with everything that's going on today. I'll just pick something up."

"No, please. I really want to fix dinner. I think I've overdosed on takeout and frozen dinners. Would eight be all right?"

"Whatever's convenient for you. I have some

things to take care of when we're through with the license and rings. I'll probably be home by seven."

"I'll see you this afternoon, then."

She slid into her car and backed out of her space. Glancing in the rearview mirror as she shifted into Drive, she saw Reno still standing where her car had been, watching her retreating taillights. Her heart pinched painfully when she thought about the look of torment he wore whenever he looked at his child.

Well, kiddo, fasten your seatbelt. You're probably in for a bumpy ride.

****

Reno sat in his office, staring at the folder in front of him. He'd gotten as far as opening it, but then his mind had shut down. He knew the decision he'd made was logical, a perfect solution to his dilemma. So why was he having such conflicting feelings about it?

It's the No Sex rule, dummy.

The last person he'd expected to make his cock sit up and take notice was Sarah Madison. But last night at dinner, he'd had to keep his napkin on his lap and direct his brain elsewhere, because every time he looked at her, every bit of blood rushed from his big head to his small one.

After the disaster with Maggie, sex hadn't even appealed to him—strange for a man with such a greedy appetite. Then he'd taken a really good look at Sarah. Suddenly, his cock swelled and his balls ached. He began to imagine her naked in his bed, rich sable-colored hair spread out on the pillow, rosy-tipped breasts pointing at him, begging for his mouth. He could almost feel his lips around a plump nipple or his tongue busy between her legs, lapping at her slit and tasting the juices in her cunt.

He shuddered inwardly as he thought of that idiotic phone call last night. It was a good thing he didn't drink, or he'd have blurted out the real reason. He wanted to change the No Sex rule. He could just imagine how she would have reacted to that. So he'd made up a lame excuse, hung up, and taken a cold shower, hoping that would help.

No such luck. When he'd gotten into bed, nude—a big mistake—and closed his eyes, his head had filled with images of Sarah under him, over him. In frustration, he'd grabbed his demanding cock, trying to squeeze it into submission, but instead, he'd imagined Sarah's slim fingers wrapped around it. Or that mouth that suddenly fascinated him so much. Or the tight muscles of her pussy clenching around him, pulsing with her climax, bathing him in liquid heat.

Before he realized it, his spine tingled, his balls drew up, and cum spilled over his fingers.

Great, just great.

He hadn't done that since he'd been sixteen years old. At least another cold shower had helped settle him for the night. He wished he had something to settle himself now.

A knock on the doorframe made him look up to see Nick and Tony standing there. He grimaced, then motioned to them. "Come in. You might as well hear all the gory details or you'll pester me to death."

****

Sarah's morning went by in a blur. She felt like a marathon runner, her mind still in turmoil and moving as fast as her feet. God only knew what Reno thought about her stepping into his life as if she'd always been there. Well, he'd told her to take charge, and that's exactly what she'd done.

First, she'd gone to her house for some clothes. She'd hurried since she was holding Molly in her carrier along with the diaper bag. But once there, she realized with a sinking feeling she hadn't bothered to get Molly's feeding schedule. She'd smiled down at the baby who sucked happily on her fists.

"Oh, well. We'll just wing it."

Packing two suitcases, she lugged them out to the car. Whatever else she needed she could come back for when she was better organized. Based on what time she'd arrived at Reno's and found the housekeeper struggling with breakfast—and a late one at that, for God's sake—she figured she had at least until noon before the baby was hungry again. That would give her time for grocery shopping and anything else she needed to do right away. Taking one last look around the house, she locked the door with a strange feeling. Tonight, she would be sleeping somewhere else.

Thanking her good luck that the grocery wasn't crowded, she filled the basket with staples and items for the meals she was planning. She had no idea what Reno's food preferences were except for steak, so tonight they'd have spaghetti and meatballs, a dish she figured was a safe choice. She stashed the groceries in the car and hurried back to Reno's, arriving just as the cleaning crew was pulling up in the driveway. Gary had been told about them, but she swallowed a smile when she saw him still giving them the fisheye.

"Top to bottom," she told the crew chief, a man she'd worked with many times. "Dump everything in the refrigerator and pantry and leave all the windows open. And let me know when I can get into the kitchen to put the groceries away."

He nodded. "Leave it to us."

Meanwhile, she stuck the perishables in a cooler she'd seen in the garage and luckily found some gel packs in the freezer so the stuff wouldn't spoil. She changed Molly, fed her, heated a bottle for her, and rocked her to sleep in the nursery. It felt good to hold the baby in her arms, to sing to her and watch her cherub face as she sucked on the nipple and watched Sarah with intense concentration. By the time she put Molly in her crib, the kitchen was ready for her. She unloaded groceries and put away things in the cheerful, yellow and white kitchen, now sparkling clean. Sun slanted in through the two huge windows that looked out on a wide backyard and patio.

She found vases for the flowers she'd bought on impulse and put the largest bunch in the center of the kitchen table. Already the air was sweetened with their gentle fragrance.

Finally, taking a deep breath, she called her mother.

"Well," Ellen Madison said, after Sarah had brought her up to date. "That must have been some dinner."

Sarah fielded questions, giving out minimal information. No, they hadn't been dating each other exactly, but the relationship had developed since she'd been working. Yes, his wife had died two months ago, but she understood the marriage was really over long before the baby was born.

"A baby!" her mother said. "No wonder he wants to move things along."

There was something in Ellen's voice that Sarah didn't want to think about. Time to end the conversation. "I've got to run, Mom, but I'll call you later tonight, and we'll have more time to talk. Okay. Bye."

Her last chore was to unpack her suitcases in the room adjoining the nursery and make up her bed with the sheets she'd found in the linen closet. There. At least, she had a place for herself, whatever that place turned out to be.

She glanced at her watch. Two-thirty. Reno would be there at three on the dot. Time to get ready. Too bad she wasn't looking forward to what should be the beginning of a happy chapter in her life.

****

Pulling into his garage, Reno felt every muscle in his body knot in tension. He had no idea what he'd find—Sarah gone in panicked flight, the babysitter watching the child? Or would he find Sarah inside, still dashing around in an attempt to make order out of the chaos?

He managed to stall by checking with the alarm crew who was just packing up. The crew chief gave him the code they'd used, but Reno would set his own. The diagrams and other information had been sent to his email so he'd open them up later on. Gary walked out to meet him, they shook hands, and Reno sent him on his way.

The moment he stepped inside, he stopped short, his senses jarred. He felt as if he'd walked into someone else's house. Everything was different. He heard James Taylor, a favorite of his, playing softly in the background, the soothing notes drifting through the air. A delicious aroma, drifting from the kitchen, tantalized his nose and blended with the delicate hint of something floral. His nose twitched at the pleasant but unfamiliar fragrance.

In the kitchen, he saw the verticals on the glass door and the window over the sink had been pulled wide, exposing the lawn and shrubs bathed in early evening diffused light. Funny, he'd never taken a good look at the well-manicured, well-tended area, even though he paid a fortune for its upkeep.

Sarah was just coming down the stairs with a young, ponytailed girl. "Reno, this is Nicki, Nick's niece. She's going to watch Molly for us."

"She's just so adorable," the teenager enthused.

Reno simply nodded. "Ready, Sarah?"

"Yes." She turned back to Nicki. "We should be back by five o'clock. Are you sure you're comfortable giving her the bottle and everything?"

Nicki grinned. "I've done it for two sisters and a brother when I was a lot younger. You can trust me. Besides, Uncle Nick wouldn't be too happy if I screwed up."

"Well, thank you for doing this on such short notice." She noticed Reno jingling his keys impatiently. "I'm coming."

****

As they pulled away from the house, he announced, "Judge Harrison can marry us next Friday at five. That's a week from tomorrow. Will that work for you?"

"Yes. Fine. That would be good."

"I've asked Tony to be my best man. You'll need to decide on who you want to stand up with you. I know it's short notice, but is there someone you're close to?" He suddenly realized how little he actually knew about her personal life.

"Oh."

He glanced sideways and noticed her discomfort. Didn't she have any close friends? What had she done with herself since her husband died, live like a hermit? And now he was consigning her to another kind of isolation. He needed to find a way to make this more comfortable for her. "Let me make a suggestion? You know Nick's wife, Lindsey. You've had lunch with her and talked to her when she's come into the office. If there's no one special you want to ask, I know she'd be happy to do this."

"Reno, she's your partner's wife, not really a personal friend." Sarah's voice was strained. "I'm sure she'd think it's a terrible imposition."

"I don't believe she'd see it that way." He softened his voice. "Call her. I'm sure she'd be honored."

"If you say so." She shrugged. "I'll call her when we get home. Thank you."

By four-thirty, they had applied for and received their license and stopped at a jewelry store to buy rings.

"Pick whatever appeals to you," Reno told her. "You don't need to worry about the price."

Red stained her cheeks, and she turned her head away. "I don't need anything expensive. It should be something that represents our…bargain."

Reno didn't know what to say after that, so he simply kept quiet while she chose a plain gold band. Her eyes held a shocked look when he purchased one for himself.

"Good protection," he said matter-of-factly.

He dropped her back at the house, his parting words brief. "See you about seven."

As he backed out of the driveway, he couldn't help but spare a glance for her slim figure climbing the steps to the front door, back straight, determination in every line of her body. Somehow, he had to find a way to make this pleasant for her. Make this work. But he'd be damned if he knew how.

He would have stayed at the office much later, finding busy work, if Nick hadn't chased him out at six-thirty.

"You're about to get married," he pointed out. "You got Sarah to agree to the bargain. At least behave with common courtesy."

Reluctantly, not knowing what kind of reception to expect when he got home, he put away the bid he was working on and went home. He held his breath as he walked into the house, hoping the earlier scene hadn't just been a dream. But the air was still fresh and a delicious aroma wafted from the kitchen.

Sarah was stirring something on the stove and humming along with the little under-the-counter stereo, her body moving to the music. She'd changed back into her jeans and pulled her hair back into a ponytail. The shiny mane swung in time to her movements. The soft denim of the jeans molded to her hips, and the T-shirt emphasized the fullness of her breasts. This was a Sarah he'd never seen before. She looked softer, more relaxed. Less businesslike. Certainly less tense than she'd been last night and earlier in the day.

He wanted to pinch himself because he still had trouble believing this warm, inviting atmosphere was his house. And this very sexy woman was about to become his wife.

Then he froze in place. What the hell was this? Shocked at the way his eyes roamed her body, at the hardening of his cock the minute he looked at her, he reminded himself this was an arrangement of convenience, nothing more. He couldn't let this assault on his mind and senses shove him off track. No good could come of that.

He moved, making a slight noise, and Sarah looked up, flushed from the heat of cooking. "Sorry. I guess I didn't hear you come in."

"Am I in the right place?" he asked. "This doesn't look or feel as if it's the same house."

"Thanks." Her smile was tentative. "Dinner will be in just a minute. It's really nothing special, just spaghetti and meatballs. I hope that's okay."

"It's fine. More than fine." He stood there stiffly, trying to figure out what to do with himself. "Well, I'll get rid of this jacket and tie and be right back. Sarah, I want to thank you again…"

"I told you. No thanks necessary." She turned her gaze back to the stove.

"You know," he said, "both times I came home today, I worried all day that you'd decided it was more than you wanted to handle. That you wanted to run back to your desk as fast as possible."

"Not when I see how much Molly needs me," she told him firmly.

"Speaking of the child, where is she?"

"Molly," she stressed the name, "has been fed and bathed and is sound asleep."

Reno just shook his head, completely amazed.

****

The atmosphere at the table was stilted, each of them trying to adjust to the idea that, from now on, they would be sitting down to meals together.

What should we talk about? How does he expect me to act? Lord, all the little things she hadn't thought about. Did Reno feel as out of place as she did?

By the time the meal was finished, they hadn't gotten much past the basics.

How did things go at the office?

Fine. The temp is very bright. I'll keep her a couple of weeks in the hope that she works out.

Would you like me to come by and go over anything with her?

No, I can handle it.

Fine. More iced tea?

When the dishes were cleared, Reno stood and filled his coffee mug from the freshly brewed pot. "I want to get out of these clothes. Can you meet me in my den in a few minutes? It's just past the stairs. I have some papers to go over with you."

Sarah tensed. "Is everything all right?"

"More than all right. I just want to make sure everything is in order before I ask you to sign anything."

Of course. The bargain.

She relaxed. "Okay."

"Then I want to show you about the alarm system."

But her nervousness returned as she waited for him. She wiped her sweating palms on her jeans and fiddled with her ponytail. The den was very much him. Wood paneling on the walls, thick carpeting, a heavy oak desk, with a credenza that held enough electronic equipment that Sarah was sure they could have launched a NASA expedition. The desk chair, the couch, and the large armchair were upholstered in the soft leather she knew he preferred. The only pieces of artwork in the room were a Russell painting he'd paid the earth for at a charity auction and a copy of the Remington bronze statue, *Broncobuster.* He'd tried and failed to get his hands on the original.

When Reno came in wearing sweat pants and a University of Texas T-shirt, her eyes widened. Oh, lord. How was she supposed to remain neutral and keep her mind on the reason she was there when he dressed this way. She couldn't help noticing the way the soft material clung to his narrow hips and emphasized the leanness of his body. Or the outline of a semi-erect cock pushing against the fabric. Dark, curling hair peeked over the neck of the shirt, the same masculine hair that dusted his corded arms and the backs of his strong-looking hands. His hair, wet from what was obviously a quick shower, looked even darker than usual and curled slightly at the nape of his neck. Delicious.

Get yourself under control before you make a mess of everything!

She swallowed, hard. This was not good.

"Sorry," he said stiffly, noticing her reaction. "I guess I dressed down a little too much. This is just what I'm used to throwing on when I get home."

"No, no, that's fine. This is your house. You should wear whatever you want. I'm…just not used to seeing you so…casual."

For a moment, his eyes darkened even more. "Same here." Then he sat down at his desk, indicating Sarah should take the armchair, and handed her a folder and an envelope in front of him.

In the next few minutes, she was alternately stunned and amazed. The amount of money stated in the agreement was completely absurd. More than she could need, even with the financial demands of her father's illness. She knew exactly how much money Guardian Security took in and that Reno could well afford this, but it still bothered her.

Her eyes widened when she opened the envelope to find a thick wad of cash with a rubber band around it and bank signature cards.

"This is ridiculous," she said when she could find her voice again. "I can't possibly sign this."

"Too little?" he asked, frowning.

"Too much," she insisted.

He picked up a pen from the desk and rolled it in his fingers. "You've agreed to turn your life upside down and enter into this crazy agreement with me. In addition, you'll be acting as a bodyguard to the child. There isn't enough money to express my gratitude. And you can't know at this point what financial assistance your parents will need. So please don't argue with me about the one thing I can provide in this arrangement, okay?"

Her pulse jumping at the enormity of what he was offering her, she finished the short document, reached for a pen, and signed it.

"The signature cards, too," he prompted. "I opened an account, but it will have your new—that is, your married name. The cash is to tide you over until then."

"It could probably tide me over until next year."

"Please, Sarah, just allow me this," he pleaded.

"I guess this will work out okay," she told him. "I

need to shop for Molly, anyway."

He frowned. "I also thought you might want to buy something new for the wedding." But he sounded as if the words were dredged up from six feet under.

She didn't know what to say so she just nodded.

"Well, then. Let's look at the alarm system."

He showed her the laptops set up, four in all—his den, the kitchen, his bedroom, and hers. Showed her how to scroll through all the camera angles and went over with her the diagram of where the concealed cameras and ground sensors were located. Then he took her back into the den where he gave her the code and explained how much time she'd have to enter it when she went in and out.

"Hopefully they'll find the asshole in record time, and this will just be overkill. But in the meantime, I feel better about having it."

She nodded. "So do I."

"And don't forget. If it's breeched, the alarm automatically sounds back at the office and the team is dispatched. It will also emit a screeching sound that hopefully will scare off whoever broke in."

Then silence dropped like a cement wall.

Sarah wet her lips. "I spoke to my mother today. Needless to say, this was a shock to her. I thought I'd take Molly by in the morning and see if I can talk my mother into going to the mall with us."

"Whatever you think best."

Whatever I think best? Don't you ever think about this?

"I grocery shopped today, but I really don't know the kinds of things you eat. If you'll give me a list I'll make sure we have them."

"I'm not fussy. Anything is fine."

"Fine."

Something simmered between them that neither of them wanted to acknowledge.

Reno cleared his throat. "I'm sure you must be exhausted and ready for bed."

"Yes. I guess I am." She rose on legs not quite steady and pushed back her chair.

When he handed her the folder with her copies of everything, their hands brushed, and she almost jumped at the spark that passed between them. He pulled his hand back, and she realized he'd felt it, too.

They stared at each other, the look a mixture of surprise, bewilderment, and panic.

Oh, this is so not good. This stupid agreement isn't twenty-four hours old, and already I can feel trouble.

"G—Goodnight," she stammered, backing out of the room. She literally ran for the stairs and up to her room, dropping onto her bed and throwing her arm over her eyes. Her heart raced, and her whole body felt flushed. Pulses she didn't even know she had throbbed as if they were some animated neon sign.

Was this what happened when you didn't have sex for years? Hadn't even wanted it? She'd better get control of herself, or her business arrangement would turn into a disaster. The fact that Reno had reacted, too, only made things worse. How had she gotten herself into this?

Forcing herself to sit up, she dug her cell phone out of her purse and called her parents to give them the details of the wedding ceremony. *That* ought to get her heated urges under control.

****

Reno sat at his desk with his head in his hands.

You stupid shit.

He was batting a thousand in his How To Fuck Up My Life program. Hadn't he learned a thing with Maggie? Of course, comparing her to Sarah was like comparing Hell's Kitchen to Park Avenue, but the end result was still the same. His dick kept getting him in trouble.

Sex had been the farthest thing from his mind when he'd concocted this crazy scheme. It was one good reason why Sarah had seemed the logical choice. Efficient well-groomed, sexless Sarah.

Sexless? Bull!

Damn Tony anyway. Ever since he'd rearranged Reno's thinking about the woman, Reno couldn't make his body behave. Definitely not his cock. Well, he'd better figure out how, or he'd be in deeper shit than he already was.

****

Sarah opened her laptop and surfed the Internet, looking for information on the care and feeding of six-month-olds, but it seemed no two babies were alike. She'd have to wing it, at least until she could throw herself on her mother's mercy and get some advice. She called Lindsey, who put Sarah at ease at once. And her mother agreed at once to go shopping, but Sarah knew she had an ulterior motive and prepared herself for what she knew would be a not-so-subtle interrogation. Finally, she showered and pulled on a robe over her nightgown. Molly was sure to wake soon for a bottle, and she didn't want to traipse around the house in a way that sent the wrong signals to Reno.

Actually, they're the right signals, but I'd better

shut them down. Fast.

At eleven, Molly woke, making little noises in her crib. Sarah managed to get down to the kitchen, heat a bottle, and get back in her room without running into Reno. She peeked down the hall and saw the den was dark, and when she passed his room, heading back to hers, the door was shut with a faint beam of light shining out beneath it. Was he in there reading? Thinking? Regretting the bargain? Pushing the thoughts from her mind, she fed Molly, rocking her to sleep before slipping back into her own bed.

Even as tired as she was, she had trouble falling asleep. The major changes in her life had her mind in turmoil. Applying for the license and buying the rings felt as if they'd happened to someone else. And of course, overriding everything was this unexpected and increasing sexual attraction to Reno. She closed her eyes, and immediately Reno's face swam before her.

"You're so beautiful." In her dream, he was lying beside her, his hand mapping her body with gentle strokes. *"I love your nipples, the way they feel when I put my lips around them."*

She felt the familiar flutters in her pussy, the surge of liquid inside the swollen, pink folds. His fingers danced through the curls surrounding her sex then dipped into her slit, finally probing at the entrance to her wet channel.

"Spread your legs for me." His voice was hoarse and thick with lust.

She complied but, at the same time, reached for his shaft, its thickness burning against her thigh. When she wrapped her fingers around its length, his breath hissed through his teeth.

"Do that too much, and we'll be over before we start."

She slowly slid her fingers from root to tip then raised her hand and moved it across his chest. She loved the soft feel of the fine hair covering his hard muscles as she twisted her fingers through it.

"You feel so good," she murmured, heat building inside her like a fire spiraling out of control.

"So do you. And you taste good, too."

He shifted his position and dipped his head between her thighs, his tongue lapping the trail his fingers had traced on her slit. When he reached her clit and rasped back and forth across the tip, her body began to shake with need. He teased her with his tongue, tormenting her, while one hand reached for a breast and fingers lightly pinched a nipple.

Her orgasm gathered deep inside her, and she pushed at his head.

"Inside me," she whispered. "I want you inside me."

He gave her cunt one last lick, then reached for the condom on the bedside table. Sheathing himself, he moved into position, lifted her with his hands, and plunged inside her with a swift stroke. The first flutters of orgasm clutched at her, drawing him deeper inside her. She wound her legs around him, locking them at the base of his spine and arching to ride his pulsing cock.

"I can't last." His breathing was harsh, uneven.

"I'm there." She moaned his name.

His eyes, dark with lust, bored into hers. "Now, Sarah. Now."

He thrust one last time, a powerful movement, and

they exploded together, shudders racking her as his body stiffened. She felt him spurt through the thin latex sheath and pressed his rigid body harder against her.

He rode her through the aftershocks, gasping for breath himself and...

Sarah sat up in bed, heart racing. Once again she'd fallen into an erotic dream. Her body was covered with perspiration, her hand between her legs. Panicked, she leaped out of bed and raced for the bathroom, turned the shower on, and stepped into it.

As she let the cool spray beat down on her body, she was thankful she'd closed her door. In her own home, she slept with it open, but here, she wanted the privacy. She could just imagine Reno's reaction if he'd stumbled on her little performance. The bargain would be ended before it even began.

Chapter Five

Reno was gone when Molly's cooing noises drifted in from the nursery to wake Sarah the next morning. Even though it was only six, she worried about running into him in the kitchen, but he must have been up at dawn and left the house. There was no sound of anyone in the house, his bedroom door was slightly ajar, and when she checked the garage, his car was gone.

Was he running away, escaping the confines of their situation? Did he have buyer's remorse? In any event, she felt relief, unsure if she could face him without the remnants of last night's dream showing on her face.

Back upstairs, she lifted the little girl from her crib.

"Oh, sweetheart, you are such a love." She nuzzled her cheek against the baby's soft skin. The pain she'd lived with for so long shifted, fading in the warmth of the tiny child she cradled.

Molly blinked at her and gave her a drooling smile.

Sarah hugged her tightly. Already she felt a sense of possession. After she'd changed and fed Molly, then put her back in her crib, she called her mother.

"I need help," she confessed. "I have absolutely no idea what Molly's schedule is, and I have to shop for her, too. There seems to have been some… miscommunication about what she needs."

And isn't that an interesting way to put it.

"I'm kind of winging it," she went on. "But she just had breakfast so she'll probably sleep for a couple of hours."

"You can figure she'll be up by ten," Ellen said. "I'm more than happy to help with the shopping."

"Thank you," Sarah breathed, relieved.

"Feed her, then come pick me up. Bring another bottle for backup, just in case. If you leave as soon as she's fed, we should be able to get enough done before she has to go down for her afternoon nap."

After she hung up, Sarah wandered through the house, exploring the place that was now her home. Although well designed and beautifully decorated, the atmosphere had a sterile quality with no personal objects of any kind anywhere, no hint of the child that lived within its walls or even a memory of Maggie. The house was wiped clean of her existence.

Sarah frowned, wondering if she could find a way to ask Reno about this. She had no idea yet what topic was forbidden and what wasn't.

Back upstairs, she peeked into Reno's room, noting the bed hadn't been made, and chastised herself for it. Of course, she should have checked this morning. Tomorrow, she would remember to take care of it.

While Molly napped, she made her own bed, showered, dressed in slacks and a short-sleeved sweater, and fixed herself a cup of coffee. Sitting at the kitchen table, sipping from the mug, she stared through one of the big windows at the peaceful scene outside and wondered for the thousandth time if she'd just made the biggest mistake of her life. A week from today, she'd be Mrs. Reno Sullivan. She would be able to ease some of the financial strain on her parents and, for once in her life, have no worries on that score herself.

And she'd have a child to love and care for, to watch grow into a young woman. Was it a fair enough trade? And could she fulfill her role for what seemed like an endless stretch of years? What about the growing attraction to Reno? Would she be able to hide her feelings indefinitely?

Her stomach cramping as tension rolled over her, she dumped the rest of her coffee and rinsed the mug. Time to put all that out of her mind. She could do this. She could. And she would.

****

They'd decided against the mall for a number of reasons, first and foremost being there didn't seem to be a stroller or carriage anywhere that she could use for Molly. In the end, they chose a huge baby store that had everything she needed. Dipping into the cash Reno had given her, and with her mother's guidance, she'd purchased everything she needed, including some adorable new clothes and what looked as if it were a year's supply of diapers.

Molly sat in her carrier on a chair between Sarah and Ellen, batting at a tiny mobile Sarah had fastened to the handle while the two women treated themselves at an exquisite French bakery and coffee shop.

"I have to say, Sarah, your father and I are completely stunned by this whole thing." Ellen Madison sipped at her hot tea, watching her over the rim of her cup.

"Yes, I'm sure you are." No more than she was. "But sometimes things happen that seem so right you can't say no."

Ellen sighed. "I just hope you know what you're doing." She looked over at Molly. "And this child. She's absolutely adorable, but what's the story here? Reno's wife has only been dead for a couple of months. Is he just looking for someone to raise his child?"

Sarah concentrated on pulling a tiny piece from her croissant. She didn't want to look directly at her mother, afraid her face would give too much away. "Of course, he wants someone who'd be good for Molly. But that's not the primary reason. We're good together. We know each other well. We fit."

She could feel her mother's eyes on her.

"I haven't heard you say yet that the two of you are in love with each other," Ellen pointed out.

"Of course, we are." Sarah concentrated harder on her pastry. "That goes without saying."

Ellen sighed. "It's your life, honey. I just don't want you to make another mistake."

"I'm fine, Mom. Honestly." Now, she looked up, then glanced at Molly and back at her mother. "And you get a grandchild without having to wait any longer."

At that moment, Molly gurgled, and the two women laughed.

"I guess I'll just have to trust you know what you're doing." Ellen squeezed Sarah's hand. "In any event, your father and I would like to have dinner with the two of you. We hardly know Reno."

She means, except as someone I work for. If I were in her place, I'd have the same reservations.

"Why don't you come to the house Saturday night, and I'll cook? That way you can see where I'm living, too."

"Yes, where you're living…"

Sarah leaned across the table. "Please don't judge me. I want to do this, and I need your support."

"Oh, honey." Ellen sighed. "You know you've got it."

****

She was in the kitchen putting the finishing touches on dinner when she heard Reno come in through the utility room. He punched in the alarm code before it began to screech, then stopped to survey the scene, much as he had done the night before.

"I guess I wanted to make sure I wasn't imagining things." He smiled. "Everything seems so…organized."

Sarah flushed with pleasure at his words. "Having a routine is nice," she agreed. "But you still haven't told me what you like to eat. I want to be sure to fix foods that appeal to you."

"I'll eat just about anything that I can chew," he told her. "Please, just fix whatever you want to."

"Why don't you go and change. Molly's down for the evening, and dinner is just about ready."

"All right."

She breathed an inward sigh of relief when he reappeared in a polo shirt and jeans rather than the too-revealing sweat pants. She filled their glasses with iced tea and served their food from the stove. When everything was in place, she sat down opposite Reno. The tension between them was almost visible, certainly obvious in their posture. Was she wrong, or was it more than just the climate of the situation? Was that heat she saw in his eyes as they swept over her or just wishful thinking on her part?

Sarah shook out her napkin and placed it in her lap, took a sip of iced tea, and set down her glass. Might as well get this over with now.

"I saw my mother today," she began.

Reno's features tightened. "How did that go?"

"Fine, fine." She sipped more tea. "She and my father have asked us to have dinner with them if that's all right with you."

He put his fork down. "Sarah, they're your parents. They know you're getting married. It's reasonable they would want to get to know me better."

A soft puff of breath whooshed from her in relief. One hurdle down. "I invited them here for dinner tomorrow night. Saturday. If we eat at eight," she continued in a hurry, "Molly will be down for the evening. If they want to see her, I'll take them up to the nursery. She won't be part of the…festivities."

A muscle jumped in Reno's jaw line. "Fine. If that's what you think would be best."

She'd hoped for a little more enthusiasm, but at least, he hadn't said no. "Thank you." She picked up her fork, then went on in a casual tone. "I was taking inventory for tomorrow night and noticed that your liquor cabinet is empty. Would you like me to restock it?"

"No." He bit off the word, his tone vicious. "No liquor in this house. Wine for dinner, but that's it."

Sarah was shocked. What was going on here? Did he have a problem with alcohol? She opened her mouth to ask him why, but at the look on his face, she changed her mind.

This is a minefield, and I'd better step very carefully.

"I apologize for not straightening your room today. I guess I was just too busy with everything else. I'll do it tomorrow, though."

Reno put his fork down carefully and squared his glass with his plate. "You don't need to do anything with my bedroom. There's no reason for you to go in there. You don't need to clean house, anyway. Set up a regular day with the service. They can change the sheets and towels when they're here."

What was wrong with her going into his room? Was there some secret she wasn't allowed to know? Sighing internally, she switched to a different topic, trying to diffuse the situation.

"All right. Thank you. I had a chance to really look at the house today. It's beautiful. Your wife had excellent taste." The moment the words were out, she could have bitten her tongue. Maggie was a closed subject—one of the rigid rules set down.

"My wife had nothing to do with it," he said, the edge of bitterness back in his voice. "It was done before we were married."

Things were getting more complicated by the minute. Sarah wondered if she would ever know the whole story or if she'd just keep falling into black holes. They finished dinner in silence, then he headed for his den. Sarah didn't know if he expected her to stay downstairs and talk to him or just make herself scarce. She was still struggling to adjust to a Reno completely unfamiliar to her.

In twenty-four hours, she'd discovered she was living with a man who was uncomfortable in his own house, who couldn't interact with his own daughter, and who hid painful secrets that laid traps she seemed to keep falling into.

But there was a need here so great there was no way she could turn away from it. She paused tentatively in the doorway to the den. "If there's nothing else, I'll go upstairs now."

He looked up, forcing a smile, then leaned back in his chair. "I'm sorry, Sarah. This is still very new for both of us. Don't worry. We'll figure it out as we go along."

"All right." What else could she say?

"I'll be leaving early in the morning again," he told her. "If you need anything just call me at the office or on my cell."

"Thank you." She backed away and headed upstairs.

****

Reno stayed in the den long after Sarah went to her room, disconnected thoughts bouncing around in his brain. In just two days, things here had improved beyond his wildest expectations. For the first time in months, he felt better about life, not so absorbed in his own misery.

When he finally felt tired enough to go upstairs, the nursery door stood open as well as the door to Sarah's room. Knowing he was making a big mistake, he walked silently down the hall to stand just beyond her door. She was turning back the covers on her bed. Backlit by the bedside lamp, the curves of her body were visible through the sheer fabric of her gown. At once, his rebellious cock hardened to almost painful rigidity.

Why couldn't he have married someone like her to begin with? But he knew the answer to that. He'd been down that road and had no one but himself to blame. The problem was what did he do with his body that refused to obey commands anymore?

She turned, startled at seeing him. "Oh!" She grabbed for the robe at the end of the bed. "I…didn't expect to see you."

Nor had he expected to be standing here. But he couldn't stop staring at her, at the body the robe couldn't hide very well or the cloud of dark sable hair floating to her shoulders. His hands itched to reach out and run his fingers through it, but thankfully, his feet were rooted to the floor.

"I'm sorry," he finally managed. "I was just checking to make sure you were all right."

"I'm fine. Thank you." Hugging her robe around herself, she walked to the door and put her hand on it to close it.

For a moment, she stood there. Her eyes met his, and the heat that flared between them was hotter than any fire he'd ever lit. Hell! This was a problem he didn't need. He was no doubt the world's biggest fool. One of them had to be sensible until the feeling went away. This whole situation was precarious enough without introducing sex into it.

"Goodnight," he finally managed.

"Goodnight." She closed the door firmly, clicking it shut with a definite finality.

Reno trudged back to his room, four walls that held some of the most unpleasant memories in the world. A prison of his own making. Would this torture never end?

At last, he got into bed, but he lay staring into the dark for a long time.

Chapter Six

"I'm in town, and I'm coming by for lunch, if that's okay." Lindsey Vanetta's voice was bubbling and just the tonic Sarah needed as she fretted over the coming evening.

"Great." Sarah smiled. Lindsey was obviously making an effort to smooth over an awkward situation. "I'll throw together a salad."

"I'll bring a fattening dessert."

Even though it was Saturday, Reno had been up early, just leaving for the office when she came downstairs to heat Molly's bottle. His way of avoiding things, Sarah was certain, so she was glad to have some company.

Lindsey arrived at twelve-thirty sharp, carrying a small bakery box and grinning broadly. "I never can resist Charlotte's goodies. They make the most wonderful French pastries."

"I've set us up in the kitchen." She had shut off the alarm to open the front door, but she quickly reset it.

"New addition," Lindsey noted approvingly. "Can't be too careful with that animal on the loose."

Sarah shuddered. "I remember when Reno and his team rescued that hostage and then he had to testify in court. Aguilar shouted the worst obscenities at him."

"I'm glad Reno is taking all these precautions."

Lindsey looked around as she walked down the hall to the big sunny room. "God, I can't believe the difference in this house in just two days. It even *smells* fresh."

"I raided a lilac bush I found in the back." Sarah pulled a big salad bowl from the fridge. "I haven't even had time to see what all is planted. I want to look at everything before the yard service comes next week."

"It's a real transformation, but I guess you know that."

Sarah busied herself pouring their iced tea.

"I know we don't know each other all that well, Sarah." Lindsey sipped the cold liquid. "So please tell me if I'm overstepping here. I just have to say, you have more guts than I think I would. This is quite an arrangement you've agreed to."

Sarah picked at her salad. "I figured Nick had told you all the details."

"Please don't be upset with him." Lindsey reached over and put a hand on Sarah's arm. "We have no secrets from each other, and Reno is a very close friend."

"I know, and it's all right." She sighed. "I guess I'm just glad he has someone to talk to."

"And you need someone, too." Lindsey fixed her with her clear blue eyes. "Like I said, we don't know each other that well yet, but I'm hoping that will change. I want to be your friend, Sarah. You've taken on an enormous job here, and I want to do what I can to make it easy for you."

Sarah had to swallow back sudden tears. "Molly is well worth it."

"This past year almost completely destroyed Reno, or I might have killed him for putting you in this position. It's just that, well, I know what he's been through so I can excuse a lot of things."

Sarah wanted to ask Lindsey what she was referring to and why things were so weird in the house, but she wasn't sure how to approach the subject. "Do you know the whole story of his marriage?"

Lindsey hesitated for a fraction of a second. "I think that has to be Reno's story to tell. And he will when he's ready."

"I hope so. Everyone at Guardian was so glad when he got married. He was always so controlled, so immersed in the business, we figured it would be good for him." She sighed. "But he never brought her to the office, never talked about her. One of the secretaries casually asked about her one time, and he just said she was fine and walked away. We all knew there was a problem, but no one knew what. He's such a private man."

"That he is" Lindsey chewed a bite of salad, her brow creased with thought. "All I can tell you is he's one of the finest men I've ever met. He was a rock for Nick and me when everything came down for us."

Sarah nodded. She knew that the Vanettas had run into some rocky times before they'd married, and Reno had been there for both of them. "I wouldn't have accepted this if I didn't admire and trust him a lot. Right now, everything is very fresh, though, and I think we're still feeling our way."

"'Each day in its own way,' my mother used to tell me, and I have to say I believe it. I just want you to know I'm here for you."

Sarah looked at the woman across from her, so calm and serene and warm. She was suddenly grateful to Reno for suggesting the phone call.

"Do you think Nicki could babysit for us next Friday? The wedding's at five, and it's a bad time to be juggling Molly's schedule. Not to mention the fact that Reno will freak if he has to be anywhere near her."

"I'm sure she'd love to. I'll call her tonight and give her a heads up."

The situation with the baby was another thing she wanted to ask about, but she was sure Lindsey would punt this back to Reno, also. Would he ever get around to telling her the whole story?

Reno still hadn't returned by late afternoon, and Sarah began to wonder if he was going to hide out until dinner was over. Dinner was in the oven, the dining room table set, and she was getting ready to go upstairs to feed and bathe Molly when Lindsey called to tell her she'd spoken to Nicki.

"She's happy to do it. And she only has a half-day of school next Friday, so she'll come early if you want. She can watch Molly while you and Reno dress for the wedding."

"That would be perfect. Thank you again." She hung up the phone.

"Who are you thanking for what?"

She'd been so engrossed in her conversation she hadn't even heard the garage door go up or Reno come into the house.

"That was Lindsey. Nicki's going to babysit Molly next Friday. She's going to come here a little early so we have time to dress."

"Good." Relief flashed across his face for a brief moment. "And I'm glad you and Lindsey connected. I think the two of you could become good friends."

"So do I." *And heaven knows I'll need one.*

Despite her misgivings, the evening with her parents went even better than she hoped. Of course, she shouldn't have been surprised. She'd seen Reno at work, talking, smiling, using the famous Sullivan charm. She knew how well he could play a part. In the role of the perfect host, he was on solid footing.

Her father kept squeezing her arm and whispering, "Smart move, Sarah. Very smart move."

"Thank you for tonight," she told Reno as they waved goodbye to her parents.

He frowned. "Sarah, you must have a very low opinion of me to think I wouldn't want your parents to feel comfortable with this situation."

"I'm sorry." She felt herself tense up. "I just didn't want to put you in an awkward situation."

He sighed. "I know, and I'm sorry you have to worry about it. I want to make things as easy for you as I can."

"They think Molly is adorable."

"Fine. That will make life a lot easier for you." His face was lined with now familiar pain, his eyes filled with such anguish, Sarah didn't know what to make of it.

"Don't you like children?" The words were out before she could stop herself, and she wished she'd bitten her tongue.

A muscle jumped in his cheek.

"More than you know," he said in a harsh whisper. There was no mistaking the heartbreak in his voice. He turned on his heel and headed toward his den.

Sarah blinked back her tears and slowly climbed the stairs to her room. Whatever was eating at his soul, she hoped they could fix it before it destroyed him. Or both of them.

****

The next week was a blur for Sarah. She moved her clothes and personal things from her house and shopped with her mother for a wedding outfit. She checked daily with Reno to make sure the temp was working out. And Friday moved closer and closer. She was glad for all the activity. It kept their problems at bay, and her hormones from getting out of hand.

Living in the same house with Reno was proving more of a challenge than she'd expected. If they accidentally touched, that same current sparked through them, like a miniature thunderbolt, startling them both. By unspoken agreement, they carefully avoided mentioning it, but it didn't seem to be going away. At least, she hadn't had any erotic dreams for a few nights.

She'd also gotten in the habit of keeping her gun in a small clutch that she took with her everywhere in the house. She was pretty sure it wouldn't be necessary. If Aguilar tried to break in, the alarm would sound. But she wasn't taking any chances.

Thursday night when Reno came home, he startled her with the news he'd made reservations for dinner after the ceremony.

"I thought we should do a little something to celebrate," he said.

"That's very nice of you." She hadn't expected a celebration of any kind.

"I want this to be a nice evening for you, Sarah. It may not be the most standard marriage in the world, but we should treat it as something special, don't you think?"

She was touched by his thoughtfulness and felt the tension begin to ease. She smiled her thanks at him.

Promptly at one-thirty on Friday, Nicki Vanetta rang the doorbell. Once Sarah had given her instructions, she hurried upstairs to get ready. She expected Reno home in a little while. He'd said they needed to leave at four.

Upstairs, Sarah organized everything she needed. Her treat for the day was going to be a long, relaxing soak before she dressed, something to soothe and relax her. She was determined to approach the ceremony and dinner with the right attitude, although she wasn't exactly sure what that would be. She closed the door from the bathroom to the nursery and locked it, giving herself complete privacy. Submerged in the hot water and bubbles, she closed her eyes and let her thoughts drift.

What would it be like once they were married? Could she find out what terrible secrets he couldn't share? Would they ever develop an intimacy? Could...

He stood at the door to the bathroom studying her in the tub, that same heat flaring in his eyes...

"That looks good. Is there room in there for me?"

Her body responded immediately. "It's a big tub. Come on in."

In seconds, his clothes were piled on the floor and he was lowering himself into the water behind her. His legs bracketed her on both sides, and the thick hardness of his cock pushed against her buttocks. His hands slid up the soapy slickness of her ribs and cupped her breasts, thumbs rasping against the already hardened nipples.

"I love to touch you everywhere." Reno's breath

was warm against her skin as he pressed his lips to the sensitive spot beneath her ear. "Your body is so responsive."

"Only with you," she murmured.

He pressed his thighs against her, gripping her, pushing more tightly against her. "You have no idea how much I love to fuck you. Your cunt is so tight it's all I can do not to come the minute I'm inside you." He nipped at her earlobe. "Is it the same for you?"

"Yes. Nothing's better than having you inside me."

"Nothing?" he teased. "What about this?" One hand slipped down to cover her mound and press against her folds. "And this?" His finger dipped into her flesh and rubbed up and down. "Or this?" He slid the finger inside her, curling it to scrape the sensitive nerves.

"Yes," she hissed, shifting to impale herself on the finger. "Oh, yes."

"And what about this?" The finger moved upward to touch her clit, lightly rubbing back and forth across the tip.

She felt the familiar flutters in her pussy, the clenching of her inner walls, and wriggled against him.

"I'd fuck you now, but I don't have a condom."

For a heart-stopping moment, she thought he'd leave her in this state of suspended arousal. Then he moved his hand back down to her opening, and this time, he thrust three fingers inside her. With the fingers of his other hand, he pinched her nipple, hard, then shifted it downward so his thumb and forefinger could grasp her clit. As his fingers moved in and out of her cunt, he stroked her clit with the same rhythm. His voice was almost harsh in her ear as he described to her over and over what he was doing to her and what he wanted to do.

Sarah had to clutch the edges of the tub to hold herself steady, leaning back against the solid wall of Reno's chest. The orgasm rose up and grabbed her so suddenly it took her breath away. She convulsed around his fingers over and over again, pushing down on them, needing to get them as deep into her as possible.

"That's it." His voice was heavy with lust. "Come like that for me, Sarah. More. Yes. Like that."

She was barely conscious of the water splashing over the side of the tub, rolling in little waves. For some strange reason, it was making a loud, banging sound. Like a knock.

"Sarah?" Reno's deep voice penetrated her fog. "Are you okay? I heard some strange noises and got worried about you."

Her eyes flew open.

Oh, shit.

That *was* a loud banging, Reno's knuckles on the door. She sat up, sloshing more water over the side, trying desperately to compose herself. She certainly didn't need him breaking in here because he thought she was in distress. Oh, it was distress, all right, but of a different kind.

"I-I'm fine," she called. "Doing great. Thanks."

There was a slight pause. "Okay. If you're sure. Remember, we need to leave at four."

"I'll be ready," she assured him.

The tub water soothed her body, but her face was steaming hot, not just from the dream but because she'd nearly been caught. What was she going to do? She couldn't keep doing this. Maybe she could take some kind of pill.

Yeah, right. She snickered at that. She'd need a lot more than a pill.

Sighing, she used her toes to release the plug, pulled herself out of the water, and stepped onto the bathmat. Every inch of her body still tingled, especially her sensitive nipples and the walls of her cunt. She definitely needed to pull herself together before facing Reno again. If he had the slightest inkling of what she felt, this could turn into a disaster of epic proportions.

****

What had she been doing in the bathroom that caused the noises he'd heard? Reno imagined her in the tub, and immediately, his cock hardened. That naked body under a froth of bubbles, maybe with her dark hair piled on top of her head, leaving her neck bare for him to…

Stop it. You'll ruin everything.

In his room, he stripped off his clothes, headed for the shower and turned it on full force. Maybe the water could beat whatever this was out of him.

Whatever this is? It's pure lust, damn it all to hell. Remember the trouble you got in last time? And this woman is going to be living in the house with you, so get over it.

But his body and his brain didn't seem to be in sync. He closed his eyes, and his stupid brain took off on its own again.

The spray from four showerheads danced on the satin skin of her naked body…

God, he didn't think he'd ever get tired of looking at it. High breasts with dusky rose, pointed nipples. Slender waist. Slightly rounded tummy, just enough to give it a sensuous curve. Hips curving down to her thighs, with the soft thatch of dark curls between them, covering her delicious cunt.

"Let me bathe you," he murmured, working the shower gel into a lather with his hands.

"All right," she whispered in a husky voice.

"Close your eyes."

When she did, he began sliding his hands down her body, from shoulder to hip, from neck to navel, pausing along the way to knead her breasts and tease her nipples until she was moaning softly. The moan turned into a hum when he smoothed the lather over her hips, her thighs, and down the length of her legs. He circled her ankles with his fingers, then trailed those same fingers up to the inside of her thighs.

She was trembling under his touch now. When he probed her slit, finding the entrance to her pussy, the humming sound grew louder and she flexed her hips at him. But before he could impale her on his fingers, she jerked away from him.

"What..."

She shook her head, smiling and reached for his iron-hard shaft. The feel of her fingers around him shattered every ounce of self-control. He had wanted this to be for her, but as always, she refused to take pleasure without giving. In his entire adult life, he had never had this kind of off-the-charts sex with a woman who gave as much as she took. It pierced him emotionally as well as physically.

"Lean back and enjoy," she murmured to him.

And so he did, propping himself against the tile wall of the shower, closing his eyes and giving himself over to the carnal enjoyment. One hand reached down to cup his balls while the other set up a steady rhythm, stroking his cock from root to tip, moving faster and faster.

Then he was there, hips rocking as he jerked in her hands, spilling over her fingers.

He opened his eyes, wanting to see the heat in her eyes as he came for her and...

Shit! Damn it all to hell.

The shower was empty except for him. It was his hands pumping his cock and squeezing his balls. He'd fucking done it again. He was angry, aroused, and panicked, all at the same time. Angry at his lack of control, aroused by the erotic images, and panicky because he had an underlying feeling that something was going on here that was more than just jerking himself off.

In disgust, he turned the shower to freezing cold and let it pound at him, hoping to beat the lust from his body and jumpstart his brain. If he didn't stop having these dreams, he was going to be so totally screwed.

For a fleeting moment, he wondered if, by some rare chance, the same thing was happening to Sarah. Was she having the same scorching fantasies about him? Ridiculous as it seemed, if she was and they ever actually did this for real, they would probably set the house on fire.

Meanwhile, he had to stuff himself back behind the walls he'd erected and get on with today's activities. And hope that what was going on in his mind didn't show on his face. Or worse, on his body.

****

Finished in the bathroom, Sarah took out the silk lingerie she'd bought and slipped it on. The feel of the smooth material against her skin was almost sensuous.

Why am I doing this? No one will ever see it.

It made her feel good, and she really needed that. Dressed in an ivory suit and matching heels, she took a look at herself in the mirror. It had been a long time since she'd dressed in anything but jeans and a blouse or T-shirt. That's what she wore to work, and that's what she wore at home. Her meager social life didn't demand anything else. She looked at the new dressed-up Sarah with a mixture of anxiety and pleasure. All she needed to add to her outfit was her jewelry and she'd be all set. She hoped. She was just tucking a pearl comb into the back of her hair when someone tapped on her bedroom door.

"It's Reno. May I come in?"

Reno? What now? "Yes, of course."

He came to stand behind her. Reflected in the mirror, he looked incredibly handsome in his dark suit and snow-white shirt. The cloth hung impeccably on his large body, the shirt setting off his dark, good looks. She knew his feet would be encased in his familiar trademark boots, polished to a high gloss.

He cleared his throat. "You're an extraordinary woman, Sarah. I appreciate the fact that you've agreed to do this. It appears to be working out well with the child. I want you to know I'm very grateful."

The stilted words weren't the romantic speech she'd hoped for in the unlikely event she ever remarried, but they certainly weren't words to take lightly. If gratitude was what she got, she'd take comfort from that. "I appreciate that."

With great care, he reached around in front of her and handed her a small box.

She frowned. "What's this?"

"Just a little wedding gift from the groom to the bride." There was a stiffness, both to his posture and his voice. "I believe it's appropriate."

She opened the box with fingers that shook a little then gasped. Nestled on blue velvet were a pair of exquisite pearl and diamond teardrop earrings. "Oh, Reno they're gorgeous. How did you know I love pearls?"

"Your mother is a great source of information." He smiled in relief at her reaction, obviously pleased with himself. "She was only too happy to make a suggestion. I see she was right. They're perfect."

He reached to take them out of the box, and their fingers touched for the briefest instant. They stared at each other in the mirror, wrapped in the heat they generated.

All Sarah could think was, *How I wish we were going to have a real wedding night?*

Her next thought was, *Will he ever get over the death of his wife and move forward with his life?*

Mentally shaking herself, she broke the spell. "This is very thoughtful of you. I'll treasure them."

His eyes never left her while she fastened the earrings in place. "You're a beautiful woman, Sarah. Today you're absolutely radiant. I'm proud that you'll be taking my name."

Sarah wanted to cry. It was the most personal thing he had said to her since that momentous dinner. "Thank you," was all she could manage.

He took a slim leather portfolio from his pocket, all business again. "Here's your checkbook, with money already in the account. I'll put money in every month for your personal everyday needs and for the child's. Spend it, save it, do whatever you wish with it."

Sarah looked at the checkbook and stifled a gasp. "This is so much," she protested. "And I still have a great deal of the cash you gave me."

"There are also two credit cards in your name. You don't need to worry about a spending limit. Use those whenever you can and save your cash for when you need it. Oh, and I'm adding your parents to the company health insurance policy. This"—he indicated what he'd just given her—"should help you take care of any other needs they have that might arise. I think that should take care of everything."

She didn't know what to say. It wasn't as if he were bankrupting himself to do this. No one knew better than she did that he didn't have to pinch pennies. Guardian Security was booming. Nick was even bidding on out of state projects. Well, Reno had done what he'd said he would, and now she would do her part.

"I think I'm ready," she finally managed. "Let me check on Nicki and the baby, and we can leave."

Molly had just awakened, and Nicki was in the process of changing her. Sarah bent over and planted a soft kiss on the tiny forehead. The baby gurgled at her.

"She's so sweet," Nicki said, deftly taping the diaper in place.

"Yes, she is." And Sarah's heart turned over. No matter that the baby's father didn't seem to want her. She would make sure Molly was loved and cherished.

The teenager hefted the baby to her shoulder and smiled. "Don't worry, we'll have a great time, won't we, cutie pie?"

Reno waited by the front door when Sarah came downstairs. "I left the car in the driveway. I didn't think the bride should exit through the garage."

She appreciated how hard he was trying to make the day as pleasant for her as possible. It had to be twice as difficult for him. "I guess we're set then."

Reno took an extra moment to instruct Nicki again about the alarm and to show her how to scroll through the shots on the kitchen laptop if she heard anything suspicious. He also made sure she had his number and Sarah's on speed dial.

"I'm good, Mr. Sullivan." She nodded solemnly. "Nothing's going to happen to this sweetheart while I'm watching her."

"All right, then."

Everyone else was waiting for them at Judge Hoffman's office when they arrived. The judge shook hands with Reno and kissed Sarah on the cheek when they were introduced.

"I always kiss the bride," he twinkled.

Sarah's mother hugged her, as did Lindsey, and her father kissed her forehead.

Even Tony gave her a brotherly peck. "You've got guts, girl," he whispered. "If he gives you a rough time, just give me a call. I'll straighten him out."

"We're always here for you, Sarah," Nick said in a quiet voice when it was his turn. "Don't forget that."

She was so grateful for their support she almost wept.

Then they were standing before Judge Hoffman, Lindsey to one side and Tony to the other, and the judge delivered the words that would bind them together. For better or worse. That covered a lot of territory for them. Tony handed them the rings to exchange, and they became man and wife.

Sarah was dazed. There was an awkward moment when it was time for the bride and groom to kiss, but Reno never faltered, touching his lips to hers. For a moment, that spark hovering around them threatened to explode, but they quickly broke apart. Everyone hugged and kissed again, and she felt Reno's firm hand at her elbow.

"We have reservations at the restaurant for six o'clock," he told everyone, "so we should get going. We'll meet you all there." He shook hands again with Judge Hoffman, then led Sarah from the chambers, his hand still firmly on her elbow.

Unexpectedly, the dinner turned into a festive occasion, and it was well after ten before everyone said their goodnights and headed for home.

At the house, Sarah paid Nicki and saw the young girl off to her car. Then she and Reno both headed upstairs. She had checked on Molly and was sitting on her bed in her robe and gown, her hair down and curling softly below her shoulders, when she looked up and saw Reno in the doorway.

"I just wanted to say goodnight." His eyes scanned the room. "I didn't think to ask. Are you comfortable in here? Is this room all right for you? Do you have everything you need?"

"Yes, I'm fine. Everything worked out very well." When he showed no sign of moving, she asked, "Did you need something else?"

Before she could react, he walked to the bed, pulled her gently to her feet and brought his lips down to hers. They were pressed together from shoulder to knee, her breasts against the heated wall of his chest, his erection outlined against the softness of her abdomen. Skyrockets went off in her body. Her nipples hardened into sharp points, and wetness flooded her pussy.

When Reno moved his tongue against the seam of her lips, she opened for him without protest. Oh so slowly, his tongue slipped into her mouth. She felt the texture of it as he danced through her warm, wet recess, the softness of his lips pressed against hers. The hands holding her were like burning fingers of flame, and his spicy cologne surrounded her. Her senses were on overload. She couldn't pull away, and the kiss seemed to last forever.

At last, Reno lifted his head, but his face was still only inches from hers. He cupped her cheeks in his large, gentle hands. "I've wanted to do that every day since our first dinner. God, Sarah, you taste like heaven."

She stared at him, heat rising in her face and her legs shaking. She didn't know which affected her more—the kiss or the fact that she'd responded. Reno looked as if he was about to say something else, then turned on his heel and strode from the room, leaving Sarah more confused than ever.

****

Shutting himself in his room, Reno fell across the bed still fully clothed, his cock still harder than steel, his balls aching. It was all he could do to keep himself from yanking Sarah's robe and gown from her body and throwing her down on the bed. Just the feel of her against him spiked his desire to an almost unmanageable level. This was way off the charts for him. What the hell had he been thinking?

The answer was simple. He hadn't been. His little head was leading his big head around in a chokehold. It wanted to be inside Sarah Madison so badly it was driving him crazy.

What a stupid thing he'd done, but he'd been drawn to Sarah like a magnet. She was beautiful, desirable, and not in the cheap way Maggie had been. Sarah was a woman who deserved to be possessed with dignity, and he'd attacked her as if he were a horny teenager. The feel of her body when he'd given into impulse and pulled her into that kiss was imprinted on him, and he could still taste her mouth. Another minute and he'd have had her naked on the bed, plunging himself into her.

God, wouldn't that have just taken the cake. But he'd felt her respond to him, heard her breathy little moans as his tongue plundered her mouth. She had to have been as turned on as he was.

So much for his emphasis on celibacy. She must think him either the most arrogant jerk or an insufferable ass. Had he ruined a perfectly good arrangement because he couldn't keep his hands to himself? Was she insulted because he wanted her or hurt because he thrust her away before he lost his head completely? Now what did he do? Could they wake up tomorrow and act as if nothing had changed? But it had and it would take superhuman effort from both of them to pretend otherwise.

His fingers curled as the memory of the feel of her breasts and the hard buds of her nipples shot through him. He'd been a nanosecond away from sliding his hand beneath her nightgown to feel just how wet her cunt was. To dip his finger into that delicious liquid… At least, he was sure it was delicious. He was dying for a chance to taste her, to slide his tongue through her swollen pink flesh and probe at the entrance to her pussy. To take her clit between his lips and draw on it until she was ready to explode.

Her hand closed around his shaft and he was sure she could feel the pulsing of his blood through the thick veins. The feeling was so sensual, like velvet stretched over a rod of steel.

He tossed her nightgown to the floor, exposing her flesh to him from head to toe. He lowered himself to the bed beside her, his hands going again to her breasts even as his mouth sought hers once more. Her hardened nipples pressed against his heated palms, and he bent to take them in his mouth, one then the other.

She was pliant in his arms as he sucked, caressed, and nibbled the pebbled tips gently with his teeth. But not unaffected, as he could tell by the rapid beat of her pulse at the hollow of her throat and the erotic little moans whispering from her mouth. He shifted to press the hard, thick shaft of his cock against her thigh, the moisture at the slit dropping onto her skin. When she rubbed herself against him, he had to exert every bit of effort not to go off like a teenager. He groaned, and his hands began a further exploration of her body, drifting down the softness of her stomach, brushing the soft curls covering her mound, until he found her labia, already damp from stimulation.

Slowly, slowly, he separated the lips, his thumb rasping back and forth against her engorged clitoris. With a gentle touch, he nudged her thighs farther apart, spreading her opening and inserting one finger. Sliding a second one in beside it, he began a slow, stroking motion that had her body nearly jackknifing. She reached for him, anchoring her hands in the hair on the plane of his chest. The heavy thud of his heartbeat reverberated through him...

Shit!

He was doing it again.

He pushed himself off the bed, stripped off his clothes, and went into the bathroom. He turned on the shower to icy cold. It helped but only marginally. Toweling himself off, he crawled into bed, wondering how he was going to face his brand new wife in the morning, knowing he had already violated one of the rules of this arrangement he'd set himself.

Chapter Seven

Needed to do some things with Tony. Be back in time for dinner. Don't cook. I'll bring home food. Call me on my cell if you need anything. Be sure alarm is set. R.

Sarah read the note propped up on the kitchen counter. Just before she and Reno had returned home from last night's dinner, Nicki had given Molly a bottle. Wonder of wonders, the baby actually slept until quarter to seven this morning. Sarah walked softly into the kitchen, wondering if Reno was wandering around at that hour, only to find the note he'd left. Apparently, he'd had the same thoughts she had.

She sighed. Saturday morning, the day after the wedding and her brand new husband had made himself scarce.

In a way, she was glad. She needed the space to deal with their encounter last night and get her raging hormones under control. Not to mention the fact that another erotic dream had consumed her last night and was still vivid in her mind. She shivered just remembering images of the hot coupling of their bodies. She couldn't seem to shut them away.

Somehow, by the time Reno came home, she had to put distance between them, find a place where they could get past this little bump in the road, be cool, reserved Sarah again and stay that way, without making him uncomfortable that they'd nearly violated their No Sex rule.

She looked around the house before going back upstairs to get the baby. The cleaning crew had been back twice, and the windows sparkled and the wood cabinets shone. Everything had a fresh, new garden smell to it. The blinds in all the rooms were open, and sunlight flooded everywhere, casting a golden angel's kiss glow.

She had yet to venture into Reno's room, mindful of his orders. But her room was filled with her personal knick-knacks, and she'd hung some prints on the walls. The nursery was now a zoo of stuffed animals in every conceivable color, the same animals marching across the wall in prints she'd found in the children's store. Instead of the depressing environment she'd seen that first day, the room was lively, cheerful, and smelled of the strawberry-scented lotion she used on Molly after every bath.

"Okay, sugar," she told the little girl, plucking her from her crib.

Molly sucked on her fist and stared at her with huge blue eyes.

Sarah smiled, hugged the child to her heart, and kissed her soft cheek. "Looks as if it's just you and me today, kiddo. How about if, after we eat, we get out the stroller and take a look around the neighborhood?"

For a brief moment, she wondered if it would be safe taking Molly for a walk. Was Aguilar anywhere in the area? No, she was pretty sure the FBI would let them know if he'd been spotted.

But what if they don't know?

Damn! But she couldn't hide in the house forever. That's what she had her gun and pepper spray for. They'd just take a walk around the block, that's all. Get a little fresh air.

Feeding Molly was accomplished with a minimum of fuss and a lot of giggles. Once she'd washed the chubby little face and hands, she pulled out the stroller and placed Molly in the seat. She checked her gun, placed it in a small shoulder bag that had a special slot for it, and added the pepper spray and her cell phone. She wanted to laugh at the absurdity of the whole thing, strolling in a gorgeous upscale neighborhood on such a beautiful day fully armed. But she knew too well what happened to people who weren't prepared.

"Let's see who's out and about today, shall we?"

Spring in Central Texas was always balmy, just on the verge of being sultry. This beautiful late spring morning was a perfect example, warm but not hot. The scent of fresh cut grass mingled with the perfume of freshly blooming flowers, swirled together on the fingers of a gentle breeze. The air had the heady feel of approaching summer.

"Guaranteed to put us in a good mood, right, sweetheart?" Sarah asked, fastening the safety straps.

They walked up one street and down another, letting the warmth of the day wash over them, the faint breeze kissing Molly's skin. If Sarah hadn't known better, she'd have thought the infant actually smiled. It was just after ten when they made it back to the house. She was barely inside when her cell phone rang.

"Where the hell are you?"

She was stunned at the anger in Reno's voice. "Reno? What's the matter?"

"Where are you?" he repeated.

"I just walked back in the house. Molly and I took a little stroll around the block."

Was he angry because she'd gone out? Did he think she'd taken the baby and run away? What was wrong with him?

"Lindsey just called me for your cell number. She said she'd been calling the house, and there was no answer."

Sarah looked at the answering machine on the counter and saw the light flashing.

"I'm sorry, but we weren't gone long. And yes, I had my gun and pepper spray with me. Please. I'm not stupid."

There was a moment of silence.

"I'm sorry I yelled," he said at last. "I was just worried."

"I understand, but you have to learn to trust me, okay? I can't hide in the house with Molly, but I will always make sure we're protected."

"You're right. Of course." His voice softened.

"Listen, let me call you back. There's a call coming in, and I'm sure it's Lindsey. Do you know what she wants?"

"She and Nick want us to come out to the ranch tomorrow for lunch." He paused for a moment. "And bring the child, I suppose."

Or what? Lock her in a closet for the day?

"That sounds terrific. Let me take this call."

"Go ahead. I'll be home about six. I'll pick up Chinese take-out."

He disconnected, and Sarah pressed the icon to accept Lindsey's call.

"I'm sorry if I created an uproar," Lindsey said. "When I told Reno there was no answer at the house, he went ballistic."

"It's all this business with Aguilar," Sarah explained. "And I should have given you my cell number the other day."

"Maybe he thought you'd had second thoughts, run off and left him." She laughed. "It would serve him right."

After last night, Sarah could believe it. "No such luck. I'm still here."

"Anyway, he may have already told you, but I wanted to invite you to the ranch tomorrow. Nick wants to barbecue ribs, and he's got enough to feed a regiment of Marines. What do you say, about one o'clock? We'll eat around four."

"That sounds great. Can I bring anything?"

"Just yourselves. See you tomorrow. We'll have fun."

****

Across town, in his brother's condo, Reno Sullivan stared at his cell phone, then shoved it into his pocket, feeling like a fool and an idiot.

Tony scowled at him, apparently having heard one side of the phone conversation. "Well, that went well," he commented. "I thought you were going to bite her head off. That should endear you to her. Don't you think you should go home? You've been pacing and fidgeting all morning."

This morning, climbing out of the bed he'd grown to hate, Reno had felt suffocated even as his body experienced an unfamiliar emptiness. Unnerved by his actions the night before and fighting a new assault of thoughts and emotions, he'd pounded on Tony's door when the sun was barely in the sky.

Now Tony pretended to read the paper, watching his brother but keeping his mouth shut while Reno alternately paced and threw himself into an easy chair.

"I had to get out of the house."

"You just got married, and you're spending the day with me?" Tony stared, incredulous. "Are you nuts?"

"This is going to be harder than I thought." He rested his elbows on his knees and dropped his head into his hands.

"Especially if you keep running away from home," Tony pointed out.

"Can it, will you? This morning I felt I'd choke if I didn't get away."

Tony quirked an eyebrow. "Is there something going on here I don't understand?"

"I don't know. I'm trying to make this work. Everything's just...weird. I can't explain it."

"So you're hiding here with me?" He shook his head, a grin teasing his mouth. "God, you do have a problem."

"People tell me that a lot lately." He leaned his head back in his chair and rubbed his eyes. "I didn't mean to yell at her. I just didn't know where she was. I thought...she'd left."

"With or without Molly?" Tony put the paper down. "Did you do something to piss her off?"

Reno was silent, staring out across the balcony.

Tony snapped his fingers. "You want to have sex with her, don't you? That's it. Ha! I knew that ball of ice where your dick is would melt sooner or later."

"Just shut up, okay?"

"Jesus, it's not a sin to fuck your wife. Maybe she'd even be willing."

Reno glared at him. "I said shut up."

"Fine. Tell me. Don't tell me. But whatever it is, you'll have to deal with it sooner or later."

After a while, Tony made sandwiches, and they ate them on the balcony, Reno still brooding and Tony watchful.

"You think I'm a real jerk, don't you?" Reno asked after a long time.

"Sometimes," Tony said with irritation. "Listen, nobody knows more than I do what you've been through. But you can't keep running away from your life."

He let out a whoosh of air. "It doesn't seem to do much good, does it?"

"Nope. And you married a woman most men would snap up in a hot minute. You need to go home and figure out what you're going to do. So why don't you see if you can make this a real marriage?"

That was exactly what he wanted to do. Run home and carry Sarah off to his bedroom. But he was sure he'd really screw himself over if he did that. He couldn't figure out where all this was coming from when he'd been prepared to live like a monk for the rest of his life. He was afraid to acknowledge the undercurrent of desire that swelled every time he looked at Sarah. Or the dreams that plagued him. What the hell was he going to do about it?

He sat out on the balcony long after Tony had gone inside. His mind was such a jumble he wondered if he'd ever get it straightened out.

Tony was watching a baseball game when Reno

went back into the living room.

"I guess I need to go home," he ventured.

"No kidding. Don't forget, you promised Sarah you'd bring dinner."

****

Sarah was upstairs bathing Molly when she heard the garage door open and close. In a few minutes, she heard Reno clear his throat. Looking over her shoulder she saw him standing in the door to the bathroom, watching her. He looked uncomfortable, as if he didn't know quite what to do with himself. After a moment, he walked to the other side of the bathroom where the baby would be out of his line of sight. She'd sympathize with him if she knew what the hell his problem was. Without information she had to tamp down her irritation.

He cleared his throat. "I owe you an apology."

"Yes, you do," she said, not turning to look at him, her voice very calm. "Which particular thing are you apologizing for—running off for the day or shouting at me on the telephone? I'll take either one." She carefully avoided mentioning the scene from the night before.

"Both, as a matter of fact." He leaned against the wall. "I was stupid and thoughtless today. I'm sorry. I'll try not to do it again."

"Fine." She ignored him while she diapered Molly and dressed her for the night. "I just fed her, and I need to give her a bottle. I'm hoping she'll sleep through the night again."

"I've got food downstairs," Reno said. "I'll get it ready to heat in the microwave."

Molly's eyelids were drooping by the time the bottle was finished. Laying the little girl down in the crib, Sarah switched on the mobile. Then, after turning out all the lights except the night-light, she forced herself to go downstairs.

In the kitchen, she poured herself a glass of water, leaned against the counter and eyed her husband. The air between them crackled.

"Everything's heated," he said, indicating the array of white cartons on the table. He'd also gotten out plates and silverware.

Good. Apparently, he wasn't going to mention last night either.

"Then why don't we eat? I don't know about you, but I'm starved."

They ate in a silence filled with electricity and tension. At last, Sarah put down her fork and looked at him. "I don't know what's going on here, Reno. There's a lot you haven't bothered to tell me. Of course, that's your choice. But there's so much tension in the air you could slice it."

He watched her through narrowed eyes, saying nothing.

She hoped he couldn't see the slight trembling in her hands. "Whatever it is, don't you think you should accept the fact that everything's got to come out sooner or later? The appropriate time will make itself known, but I wouldn't wait too long if I were you."

Panic flashed across his face. "Sarah, please, I—"

"Not now. I'm really tired. I think I'll go on upstairs."

She walked out of the room with dignity, leaving a frustrated Reno behind. But no more frustrated than she was. Secrets were going to kill them if she couldn't find a way to break down the wall he'd built. And she'd better do it before it collapsed on them, destroying everything.

****

Sunday morning heralded another bright and beautiful day. With Reno hiding in his den, Sarah took advantage of the early morning cool to push Molly around the block in her stroller again. It wasn't the relaxing walk it would have been under other circumstances, wondering if every car that passed or every stranger on the sidewalk was danger. She made sure she could access her gun in seconds if she needed to. She just hoped they caught the damn man soon.

She fixed sandwiches for lunch, but when Reno didn't emerge from his self-imposed exile, she left his food on the counter and went upstairs to dress herself and the baby for the afternoon.

They said very little to each other on the drive to the Vanetta ranch. Molly was wide awake, for which Sarah gave thanks. That meant the baby would nap during the afternoon. Sarah felt as if the trip was thirty hours long instead of thirty minutes and sighed with relief when they drove down the narrow road and pulled up before the ranch house.

"My God, Lindsey, this is gorgeous," Sarah said when the Vanettas came out to meet them. She sniffed the air, a heady mix of prairie grass, hay, horseflesh, and leather.

Lindsey grinned. "We love it here. Nick was a city boy all his life, but now he wouldn't live anywhere else."

The afternoon proved a respite for Sarah. She and Lindsey sat on the porch drinking lemonade and eating sugar cookies baked by Mary, the Vanettas' housekeeper. Jason, the Vanettas' one-year-old child, sat in the playpen burbling to himself and playing with his toys. Molly napped in the portable crib Lindsey had set up.

Nick and Reno headed out the back door. Sarah sat up in surprise when she saw Emilio, Mary's husband, lead two horses from the stable as the two men approached.

"I didn't know Reno could ride," she commented.

"He rides a lot when he comes out here. Says it works out the cobwebs."

Sarah eyed her husband carefully as he and Nick swung into their saddles. In his faded jeans, denim shirt, and scuffed boots, he looked every inch the cowboy, sitting on the horse as if he'd been doing it for years. Her breath caught in her throat, and she forced herself to swallow hard. No sex, they'd agreed, and after last night, she needed to make sure she didn't give him the wrong signals. Why had her body chosen this particular time to decide to come out of the deep freeze?

She tried to focus on conversation with Lindsey, but her mind kept drifting. She was glad when the men returned and Mary announced it was time to eat.

They had dinner at a picnic table under a huge oak tree, the heat of the day fading and the huge oaks providing a leafy canopy against the sun. Despite the fact they had Molly with them, Reno seemed more relaxed, more at ease, sprawled in a chair as he laughed and joked. His enjoyment was evident in his body language and his easy conversation. Sarah almost regretted when it was time to leave.

By the time she settled the baby in her crib at home, Reno had once again gone directly to his den.

Avoiding the issue, she told herself, but she was grateful not to have to deal with the awkwardness tonight. Sighing as she climbed into bed, she wondered what was going to happen to this relationship that seemed to be turning itself upside down.

He still hadn't taken down the invisible walls around his bedroom, seeming to be much more comfortable in her room. And bed...

By now, she was familiar with his body as he was with hers. Foreplay didn't require testing and experimentation anymore. Now they remembered which touches elicited the sounds of pleasure, which ones brought forth the most heated response.

Sarah loved when he took her nipples in his mouth as he was doing now, sucking on them and biting them gently until they were aching and swollen, each touch sending darts of pleasure through her body. His warm hands cradled each plump breast, kneading them while he drew on her tips, knowing the effect it had on her and chuckling softly against her flesh.

His mouth moved farther down her body, trailing wet kisses to her navel where he circled the indentation with the tip of his tongue. But when she tried to urge him lower, he moved his head completely and placed soft kisses at the crook of each elbow and the soft inner side of each wrists. Not until Reno had she realized how many erogenous zones lurked on her body.

"Reno." His name rolled from her lips on an urgent sigh.

"Tell me what you want," he commanded, his mouth just above the curls on her mound.

"You know," she whispered. "You always know."

"Tell me," he repeated.

Sarah licked her lips. He always liked to hear her say it aloud. "Suck my pussy. Lick me with your tongue. Please." This last a little more frantic.

His low chuckle had a hoarse sound to it. "Right now."

He opened her labia as if he were unwrapping a present and lapped at her flesh as if he were a man dying of thirst. Darting inside her quivering channel, then out, then in, then tracing the entire length of her slit. Her hands fisted in the sheet as pleasure raced through her in a rush of heat. Her hips automatically lifted to urge him on more and more. When he slid two, then three fingers into her waiting cunt and closed his lips around her clit, it took barely one or two movements before her orgasm crested and rippled through her like waves crashing on a shore.

Sarah bucked against his mouth and hands, barely recognizing the keening sound low in her throat as spasm after spasm rocked her. The more she convulsed, the more rapidly Reno moved his fingers in and out and the harder he sucked on her clit, until he'd wrung the last drop of liquid and the last spasm of response from her convulsing body.

"Did you like that?" he asked, his words uneven.
"Yes."

Before she could say more, he'd rolled on a condom and slid inside her. She loved the fullness of the feeling, the pleasure that shot through her body. And despite the fact that he'd just wrung an intense orgasm from her, she was riding the crest with him again and tumbling over the edge.

Afterward he caught his weight on his forearms and kissed her with infinite tenderness.

"Now you are truly mine." His voice was ragged as he labored to breathe, but his words were firm. *"Mine."*

"Yes. I am." She reached her arms up to him and...

The sensation of falling woke Sarah. When she could brush the cobwebs from her brain, she realized the dream had been so real she'd reached for Reno and nearly fallen out of bed. She rolled back onto the tangled bedclothes and pressed her hands to her hot cheeks.

Hell!

This was really getting out of hand, but what could she do? How was she supposed to stop it?

****

She woke in the morning more tired than when she went to bed. This time the erotic dream was even more graphic than previous ones. She swore she could feel the imprint of Reno's hands on her breasts and thighs, feel his semen on her skin, but when she looked at herself in the mirror, there were no visible marks. Nothing there. Only an insistent throbbing that demanded release.

She stared at herself in the bathroom mirror.

What's happening to me? I never had dreams like this about Mike.

Or this kind of sex with Mike, if she were honest. She shivered, hoping cold showers would work as well for her as she heard they did for men.

For the rest of the week, Reno made it a point to avoid her. He left early each morning before she was up, calling during the day to check on her in a very formal voice and telling her he would work late and eat dinner out. Well, he'd hired her to be a single mother, and it seemed that was exactly what she'd turned out to be.

Sarah longed to use Lindsey as a sounding board, but the situation was too intimate to discuss. She would have felt uncomfortable sharing the details, so she kept everything locked inside and wondered how she and Reno were ever going to find some kind of even footing.

****

Reno threw himself into the routine at the office. If he'd worked with a frenzy before, now he was in overdrive. No one had any idea the agony he was suffering, sitting in his office long after others had left, staring out the window into the darkened night, wondering what he was going to do.

At odd moments, in the office or in meetings, he found his thoughts drifting and images of Sarah would flit across his mind. She moved with such a graceful economy of movement, always in control, the light scent of her perfume an aura around her. He didn't trust himself to go home to her, to be alone with her.

Added to that was the constant worry about Luis Aguilar. He called Balenger twice, but the man had nothing to report. Aguilar seemed to have vanished off the face of the earth. Reno knew the cartel leader had people everywhere willing to hide him and help him. This waiting for the other shoe to drop was excruciating.

On the other hand, his original idea seemed to be working, because it was obvious Molly adored her. He heard baby sounds that, if she were older, could be construed as words until he wanted to scream. It just wasn't fair. He had what most men dreamed about—a gorgeous wife and an adorable child—and he couldn't bear to be around one or trust himself with the other. Now, in addition to the child, he had to stay away from his wife.

Sometimes, when he climbed the stairs late at night, he'd pause at the door of Sarah's room, the way he had that first time, and watch her sleeping. He gave thanks she couldn't see the enormous erection that sprang to life just by looking at her. How had he gotten himself into this mess?

When he couldn't stand there anymore, he would go to his room, lie in the bed he hated, and stay awake until dawn, anguishing over his stupidity and his mistakes and his raw hunger for what might have been.

****

Friday afternoon, while Molly was napping, Sarah poured herself a glass of iced tea and took a new book and the baby monitor out to the patio. It was another gorgeous Texas spring day, and she didn't want to be cooped up in the house. The sun was warm, the breeze like a soft caress on her face, and she slowly began to relax. She was so engrossed in reading, she didn't hear Reno come out of the house.

"Good book?" he asked.

She was startled. He never came home early in the day.

"Yes, it is. Thank you for asking." She frowned up at him. "Is something wrong? You're home early."

"Wrong? No, not at all. Can you call Nicki Vanetta and ask her to sit for a couple of hours?"

"I'll call her." Sarah tried to keep the surprise out of her voice. This was the first conversation they'd had all week, and she wasn't about to break the mood. "What did you have in mind?"

"We're going to pick up your new car."

She blinked. "Excuse me?"

"Don't you remember? I told you I was getting you an SUV and having it outfitted at Texas Armoring."

So he did. She wanted to say how nice it would have been if she'd had some choice in the matter, but it was a small thing to make an issue out of. He was struggling with the role he'd been thrust into as it was.

"What about the car I have? What should I do with it?"

"Take everything out of it you need before we leave and park it in the driveway. Gary Stern's going to pick it up and take it to the dealer we use. He'll sell it, and the money will go into your checking account."

She wanted to resent what she saw as high-handed, but again, he was so uptight, trying to do the right thing, that she didn't think it was enough to make an issue of. "Okay. Let me call Nicki and see if she can come over."

Reno leaned against the counter, hands in his pocket, watching her in frustration. He couldn't seem to do anything right, and he was afraid he was losing the battle in his desire for her. They'd go would pick up her car, maybe have a quiet dinner someplace, and he'd try to get his libido under control before Sarah washed her hands of him.

"She'll be here in thirty minutes," Sarah told him, hanging up the phone. "Molly's still asleep, and when she gets up, Nicki can feed her supper. How long will we be gone?"

"I thought maybe we'd road test the new car and

grab a quick bite while we're out. Does that sound okay?"

"Oh. Of course. Just let me put myself together."

He wanted to tell her she looked totally together, but he was afraid a compliment would give her the wrong message. God, he'd made such a mess of things he was afraid to even tell his wife she looked nice.

****

Sarah had to admit Reno made a good choice with the vehicle. The Chevy Equinox wasn't so large she felt overwhelmed by it, and the silver color made it look less threatening. He made her get behind the wheel and drive it herself as they left TAC.

"No time like the present to get used to it," he said.

"What about your car? Are you just going to leave it here?"

"I've got someone coming to pick it up. No sweat."

It didn't take her long to get used to the vehicle as they drove through the Hill Country, enjoying the scenery cast in bronze by the late day sun. They stopped for an early meal at a small, little-known Italian restaurant that Reno had discovered years ago. The place was jammed, but the owner greeted them as if they were long lost family and set up a corner table for them.

"I found this place by accident one night," he explained as they were seated. "The food is excellent, and the atmosphere's casual and relaxing."

And that it was. The aroma of garlic teased at their nostrils and stimulated their hunger. They shared an antipasto, savoring the sharp taste of their food and sipped on a bold, red wine. For the first time since the night of their wedding, the atmosphere between them eased. Over the main course, they chatted about common subjects—books they enjoyed, movies they'd seen, things they liked and things they didn't. It amazed them both that they agreed in so many areas.

By the time they finished the meal, they were both feeling loose, without the tension that had gripped them. Reno took the keys to drive home, and when they pulled out of the parking lot, he took a CD from his pocket and slipped it into the player.

"New music for a new car," he told her. "I heard you listening to Springsteen one night when you were cooking dinner. This is his latest."

She was touched that he'd remembered and that he would take the time to do something so thoughtful. Maybe there was hope for them after all.

****

Their social life, with the exception of one or two business dinners when Sarah acted as hostess, consisted for the most part of time spent with Lindsey and Nick, but Sarah was content with that. She felt comfortable with them. They knew the truth about the marriage so she didn't have to pretend, and she and Lindsey had become close friends.

And they spent more time with her parents than she had since Mike died. The Madisons adored Reno, and he seemed to genuinely like them. But it made it harder to hide the reality of their situation from her mother.

"You look, I don't know, contented but not completely, Sarah," Ellen said one day when she dropped by. "Sometimes you seem as if you're living in limbo. Is everything all right with you and Reno?"

"Yes, Mother. I'm doing fine. It's a good marriage, and he makes me happy."

"I hope so, darling. You deserve to be happy. Not that we don't like Reno. We're crazy about him. I'm just concerned about you."

"Please don't worry. Everything's great."

"You're sure?"

"Yes. Positive. I have a wonderful life." She made a mental note to act less distracted when they were together. "By the way, did someone call you about information on you and Dad? Reno's adding you to the company health insurance policy."

"Yes. I meant to ask you about that." Ellen's voice sounded puzzled. "Why on earth is he doing that?"

"It's very common in situations like this." Sarah had rehearsed her answer. "A lot of companies include extended families."

"Well, you be sure and thank him for us. It certainly makes things a lot easier."

And it means he's kept his part of the bargain.

She and Reno were finally at a point where they were more comfortable with each other, but only concentrated effort tamped down the sexual tension both felt bubbling beneath the surface. They dealt with it by avoiding physical contact and by going up to bed at different times.

The other problem wasn't going away, either. Weekends, Reno locked himself in his den so he wouldn't have to deal with Molly. Sarah wanted to weep with frustration. She had no idea how to break down the wall he'd built around himself, and every time she tried to bring up the subject, he shut her down at once.

"I don't know what to do," she told Lindsey. "If I could just find out what's behind it, maybe I could come up with a solution. I've just never seen a man reject his own child this way, especially one so affectionate and lovable."

"He's fighting a lot of demons," Lindsey told her. "I keep hoping he'll pull himself out of it before it destroys him."

"Can you at least give me a hint?"

Lindsey's sigh was so heavy Sarah heard it through the phone wires. "If it were my story to tell, I would. Reno has to realize he can't keep secrets forever and tell you himself."

Once again, he avoided both her and Molly on the weekend except for the stilted dinners when they averted their eyes and made stilted conversation. The following Monday, he came home and told her he had to go to Colorado to meet with a new client.

"I should be able to wrap this up in a day or two, but it may take a little longer," he told her, his voice uninflected. He might have been giving her a report. "There's a major corporation interested in having us set up their security. We'd be training their security personnel, also. Lots of money involved so the partners often travel with a protective agent."

"We'll be fine," Sarah assured him. "Just go and do what you have to."

"I hate to be gone with Aguilar still on the loose. I spoke with Balenger this morning, and he said they may have a lead on him. I fucking hope so because this is nuts."

"We'll be fine," she assured him.

"One other thing. I've put security on the house while I'm gone. And don't bother to argue," he told her when she opened her mouth to do just that. "I need it for my piece of mind. You'll never know they're here."

She found she was actually glad to have him gone for a few days. It gave her a little breathing space and, at least temporarily, took care of the problem of two strangers living in the same house. And despite what he said, she was acutely aware of the car parked in her driveway every night. She brought whichever agent was sitting in it fresh coffee before she went to bed, along with whatever she had recently baked.

"We have a guest room," she told the man on duty the second night. "I'm perfectly happy for you to use it."

"Not in our orders, Mrs. Sullivan." He smiled. "Thanks anyway, but we're used to this."

A larger problem was the erotic dreams that wouldn't go away. She awoke every morning feeling as if she'd spent the entire night in heated lovemaking. Her nipples would be hard, and she could feel fluid between her legs. She tried staying up late and reading, watching documentaries on television, exercising before bedtime—nothing worked. She was thankful Reno was gone for a few days. At least, she didn't always have to be on her guard.

He said little about the trip when he returned except that it was successful, and he'd tell her more about it when he had all the details together. He knew she was still interested in what went on at the office, and it was a safe area of conversation for them. The one night of easy camaraderie didn't seem about to repeat itself.

A week later, Reno came home to tell her two of the Colorado executives were coming to town with their wives. They were combining a short vacation with a meeting at the Guardian offices to meet everyone and formalize the contracts.

"I'll be taking them to dinner on the Riverwalk. Can you arrange for Nicki to sit so you can join us? I think having you there would make their wives more comfortable."

"Of course. I'll call her right away."

She made all the arrangements at the restaurant, and Reno came home from work to change and pick her up.

"Thank you for doing this," he told her.

"It's part of the bargain," she assured him and turned away. She didn't need his impersonal thanks. She'd rather have nothing. But she'd walked into this bargain with her eyes wide open so she certainly couldn't shut them now.

Sitting in the restaurant, she glanced at Reno seated at the opposite end of the table. He was looking at her with an unreadable expression in his eyes, almost as if he were seeing her for the first time. A sudden shiver ran through her body as she remembered that brief scene in her bedroom. She smiled at him, and he returned the smile, raising his glass to her in a silent toast.

God, she's beautiful, Reno thought to himself, not for the first time. He watched his clients falling under her charm, as did nearly everyone. She had taken to wearing her hair clipped back with a barrette or in a loose braid at home, but tonight she wore it loose around her shoulders, a look that reminded him of clouds of soft, brown silk. The earrings he'd given her on their wedding day glistened and shimmered in the muted light whenever she moved her head. He'd been doing well keeping his feelings under control, but he felt a sudden surge of possessiveness that came at him out of nowhere.

He was shocked to realize how much he wanted his stamp on her. He loved to see that coffee-colored hair with its warm golden highlights hanging loose, the way it was when she got ready for bed, and run his fingers through it. He wanted to touch that skin with its honeyed glow and make her eyes blaze with passion. He wanted the world to know this exquisite creature was his wife. That she belonged to him.

What could he say to her? *Sarah, I'm sorry I was so clumsy about this before, but I want you?* Yes, in a way he'd never wanted any of the other women in his life. *I love you?* He wasn't sure he even knew what love was anymore, except it led to vulnerability and pain. All he had to do was think of Molly to know how right he was.

Damn. He'd made a bargain and, if nothing else, he was a man of his word. Now, he was choking on it.

Chapter Eight

Reno and Sarah fell into a somewhat easier pattern to their existence. Dinners were not quite so uncomfortable, and she could tell Reno was making a real effort at conversation. He still avoided Molly except when it was totally unavoidable, but at least, he was making an effort to make Sarah feel more comfortable. The dreams came in intervals now, giving her some nights completely free of them. But she knew whatever she felt was still there.

She saw it in Reno's eyes, too, this unspoken sexual desire. But he'd made it plain from the very first night. No sex. She was so careful not to let whatever this was break free, but secretly she suspected it couldn't go on forever. And she was pretty sure he felt the same way.

Fall arrived and with it the football season. Often on Sundays, the three of them would troop out to the Vanetta ranch to barbecue and watch the games. The visits eased the weekend tension, allowing Reno to be part of the activities and still retain his remoteness from Molly.

The days passed in the routine they'd fallen into. Sometimes when he watched her, Reno had the urge to tell her how much she'd come to mean to him, but he was afraid to open that Pandora's Box. He had enough trouble dealing with the threads of desire lurking in his subconscious. No Sex. What a stupid rule he'd established. At the time, he'd been so sure no woman would ever tempt him again. Maggie had destroyed his normal sexual desires, perverting them and degrading them, and he wasn't about to make himself vulnerable again. Even if the situation was different.

Now, of course, he was hung by his own rules.

"I wonder what she was like before her husband was killed," he mused one day when Tony asked how things were going. "I only know how she's been since she came to work for us."

"I would guess a lot like she is now," Tony told him. "You don't get to be that self-possessed and composed overnight." He looked at Reno, searching his face for something. "Still fighting those feelings about your wife, huh?"

Reno shrugged. The last person he wanted to admit anything to was his brother. "Just curious, is all. She's stepped into this whole thing so naturally."

How could he tell anyone what was really in his mind? That he didn't think he could any longer avoid the fact he was falling in love with her? That he wanted to change the rules of this ridiculous marriage?

****

Months passed since Luis Aguilar had escaped from prison. She told Reno maybe he'd gone home to Mexico to the obscenely huge estancia he owned, surrounded by his own private army. He'd probably forgotten all about his thirst for revenge.

"If only," Reno said. "He's probably waiting until we drop our guard and he can swoop in. That's his style when he's got someone in his sights. I won't rest until that man is dead."

In late October, Molly celebrated her one-year birthday. Painfully aware Reno would not want to be reminded of the date, she drove out to the ranch where she, Lindsey, and Jason celebrated the event. Molly didn't seem to care that there weren't a lot of people. Mary made her a chocolate birthday cake, and Sarah and Lindsey had a great time shopping for toys.

She realized Reno was aware of the date when he called her to say he'd be out of town with a client for a couple of days. That way he could avoid any reminder of the event. He never paid attention to Molly's toys, anyway, so when he came home what she played with would be of no interest to him.

It broke Sarah's heart, but she knew, at least for now, there was nothing she could do about it.

In November, Sarah took a chance and told Reno she'd like to have a big Thanksgiving dinner at the house. Invite her parents, the Vanettas, and Tony.

"I need to do something," she pleaded when he frowned. "We've been to the ranch so many times I'm beginning to feel as if I'm a hospitality hog. I don't want to impose on my mother by adding extra people, and I'd like to have a good holiday for Tony, too."

"Fine," he bit off. "We'll have Thanksgiving. Just keep the child out of my way."

Oh, goody, what a swell holiday we'll have. Maybe, he can hang around and be the Grinch for Christmas, too.

Sarah shopped and cooked for three days, choosing the menu with care and refusing all offers of help. By the time the day arrived, she was in too good a humor even to be annoyed when Reno shut himself in his den for the morning. She knocked on his door when she went to get Molly from her nap.

"Everyone will be here in an hour," she hollered at him.

"I'll be ready," came the muffled answer.

Sarah shrugged and went on upstairs.

She bathed and fed Molly, then dressed herself in a long hostess skirt and silk blouse she'd bought just for the occasion. Molly was adorable in ruffled pink and white. She had grown so much in eight short months. As Sarah came down the stairs, her nose caught the tantalizing scents of the roasting turkey, sweet potatoes, pumpkin and apple pies, and the spicy aroma of her special hot punch—all the Thanksgiving smells filling the house. They always gave her such a good feeling.

She had very high hopes for this holiday. The heat between her and Reno had been increasing in its intensity, no matter how carefully they tiptoed their way around it. Many nights Reno hid in his den while she headed for her bedroom right after dinner, and she knew it was just to avoid their being alone together.

She had finally admitted to herself that the erotic dreams weren't going to go away, and she had feelings for this man with whom she'd entered into this strange marriage, feelings it might be time to explore—if she could find a way that didn't bring them a tipping. She'd expected nothing out of this arrangement in the beginning except a child to lavish her love on. Now, it seemed Fate had taken a hand and turned things upside down for her.

Maybe this would be the night to heal whatever was wrong between Reno and Molly. The holiday spirit could open a lot of doors. Tonight, after everyone was gone, she'd find a way to test the waters.

Her parents arrived first, bringing wine and fall flowers, then Tony with more wine.

Lindsey and Nick arrived a few minutes later, both of them wearing an air of barely controlled excitement and bringing a box of their housekeeper's special cookies. They insisted on seeing Molly and playing with her for a few minutes. Reno excused himself, announcing that he needed to carve the turkey and taking the sting out of what was turning into an awkward moment. When the little girl's eyes began to droop, Sarah carried her upstairs, followed by Lindsey and Ellen. They all talked nonsense to Molly while Sarah put on her sleeper and settled her in her crib.

When everyone was seated at the dining room table, Nick lifted his wine glass. "I want to make a toast. Here's to the newest Vanetta, who will be joining us sometime in June." His eyes sparkled, and he reached for his wife's hand.

"Do you mean what I think you do?" Sarah gasped.

"Yup. Lindsey's pregnant. We saw the doctor yesterday afternoon."

Sarah watched Reno, and his reaction to Nick's announcement stunned her. His eyes were filled with such despair and longing she didn't know what to do. She quickly jumped up from the table and hugged Nick and Lindsey in turn.

"I am so glad for you," she told them. "That's such great news. Does the doctor say everything's okay?"

"Yes," Lindsey told her. "I have to take it very easy again, and this is my last glass of wine for a while. But the doctor said he doesn't foresee any more problems than before. This one might even be a little easier."

"How wonderful for you. Isn't that great, Reno?" She turned to her husband, who was trying hard to rearrange the expression on his face.

"Yes, it is. That's terrific." He managed a stiff smile. "Congratulations to both of you." He shook Nick's hand and kissed Lindsey on the cheek. "It will be nice for Jason to have a little brother or sister."

The turkey was roasted to perfection, the sweet potato casserole fluffy and light, the yeast rolls hot and crusty. Compliments flew across the table. Everyone seemed immersed in the holiday spirit, and Sarah's sense of expectation rose.

She kept an eye on Reno, and as the meal progressed, he visibly relaxed, although the amount of wine he consumed might have had a lot to do with it. She didn't remember ever seeing him drink more than a glass or two except for the night of his strange proposal. She tried not to stare at him, wondering what he was thinking. But the flex of the muscles in his throat as he swallowed, the movement of his strong jaw as he talked, the deft way his long, lean fingers handled the wine goblet fascinated her.

Lindsey and Nick were the first to leave.

"Gotta get Mama home." Nick winked, ushering his wife out the door.

Tony and the Madisons were the next to go. Sarah stood in the doorway, waving and smiling until the last car had pulled away, then she turned back to Reno. "Well, I thought everything went well, didn't you?"

"Yes. You did a great job. Everyone enjoyed themselves." He cleared his throat. "It was a wonderful evening."

"Molly was good as gold when we had her

downstairs," Sarah pointed out. "Don't you just want to give her the warmest hug?"

As soon as she looked at Reno's face, she knew she'd made a mistake.

"Don't presume beyond your job description." His voice was harsh, his tone cutting.

Sarah's heart shifted painfully, but she reached out and touched his arm, not willing to give up. If anything were to happen between the two of them, Molly would have to be a part of it.

"Just try holding her." She made her voice soft rather than demanding. "Just once. Please. You'll see. You'll fall right in love with her. I just know it."

Reno froze, then slammed the front door so hard the walls echoed with it. He nearly knocked both of them down in his haste to move away.

"You run this house," he shouted, "you run the child, you run the basic structure of my existence, all with frightening efficiency, which I completely appreciate. That's what you're paid to do." His eyes blazed with fury. "Leave it at that. Do not attempt to run this one tiny corner of my life. Can you not learn to mind your own business?"

She turned away with more grace than he had any right to expect. "I think I'll go upstairs now. Good night."

Sarah made it to the rocking chair in the nursery before she collapsed, forcing back the tears that threatened. All she could do for a long time was sit in the chair, shaking like a leaf, staring at Molly sleeping so peacefully.

Well, now what?

All day, her growing feelings for Reno had kept

bubbling to the surface. Every time she sensed his eyes on her and raised her own, there was no mistaking the heat that flashed between them. Little shivers of anticipation had chased themselves along her spine as she'd thought of what tonight might bring. Would her erotic dreams finally come true?

The confrontation had destroyed all of that and wiped it away as if it had never happened. The harsh words lay there like unexploded bombs. She was as angry as Reno but wounded that he could say the things he did. Why had she forced the situation? She knew better. Clearly, after all these months, his head was still in the same place. He was a long way from dealing with whatever pain he carried. Trying to ease him into interacting with Molly hadn't been a raging success. Even today, he'd found a way to leave the room when the little girl was downstairs.

She had been so sure, with everyone wrapped in the holiday spirit, that this was the time to try moving forward. Instead, she feared she'd only made things worse. What dreadful thing had happened to turn him against his adorable daughter? What tragedy in his life had closed him off from a child who was so easy to love? The hidden hope that their feelings for each other might be something real was swallowed up by the bitterness of the words he'd flung at her like so many sharp knives.

I knew better. That was a stupid thing for me to do. Now he'll hate both of us, and any hope for the future is down the drain.

Whatever drove him might just end up destroying them all.

She kept listening for his car to start, wondering if

she should go out there and make sure he was all right to drive. But she couldn't face him at the moment. Her pain was too intense, too sharp. She was barely holding herself together as it was.

What was he waiting for out there? Was he planning to come back inside?

Then she realized, knowing Reno, he was waiting until he was sure it was safe for him to drive.

After a long time, she finally heard the growl of the engine turning over and the squeal of tires as he backed out of the garage. She managed to rouse herself and, assured that Molly was still sound asleep, went into her own room and took off her clothes. Throwing them on the chair, she pulled on the first nightgown she found in the drawer.

Tired to the bone, she crawled into bed, resisting the urge to pull the covers over her head. She closed her eyes, willing herself to sleep, praying that tonight the erotic dreams wouldn't plague her. But her restless subconscious sought the pleasures she was denied when she was awake.

****

Cursing himself for his stupidity, Reno had slammed out of the house, not even bothering with a jacket. He'd gone to the garage and stood for a moment, breathing in the unseasonably cold evening, letting it shock the effects of the wine from his system. Bracing himself against the car, he'd waited a moment to make sure he was competent to drive. The last thing he needed was to be arrested for drunk driving. Secretly, he'd hoped Sarah would come looking for him, but after a long time, it was painfully obvious that wasn't going to happen.

Finally, when his head had cleared and his hands were steady, he'd started the car and backed out into the street.

Reno felt sick to his stomach. Well, he'd done it now. What the hell was the matter with him? How could he say something like that to Sarah who deserved so much better?

As soon as the words had left his mouth, he'd wanted to take them back. Sarah looked as if he'd slapped her. Her face had gone paper-white, and her hands trembled. When he turned to say he was sorry, that he didn't mean it, she was already gone. An intense pain had captured his heart, worse than the night he'd found out about Molly's parentage. A pain that still stabbed at him.

Nice going, jerk.

That was the price he paid for drinking too much wine. Or anything. His mouth got ahead of his brain. Hadn't he learned his lesson yet?

Sarah, Sarah, Sarah. Oh, God, how I want you. I didn't even have the chance to tell you. I need you to let me put my arms around you, apologize, try to tell you how I feel. For a man who's such a raging success in business, I certainly manage to keep screwing up my private life big time.

Reno banged his fist against the steering wheel.

You finally figure out you're in love with the woman, so you show it by insulting her. Big time. Way to go, jerk-off.

He'd give anything if he could take back the words he'd flung at her. What Sarah had done was the most natural thing in the world, connecting father and child on a holiday. Her intentions came from the heart.

Unfortunately, she had no idea why he felt the way he did.

It was all that damn wine he'd drunk, way past his two-glass limit. Still, a drink seemed the only logical choice to blunt his pain. And he knew right where he could get one. Nick's office, where he kept liquor for celebratory drinks.

For everyone but me and rightfully so.

They had keys to each other's offices, so access there wasn't a problem, but the cabinet with the liquor was also locked.

Shit. Paranoid son of a bitch.

In his own office, he dug through a junk drawer, looking for anything to help, finally coming up with a screwdriver. Nick would kill him for sure, he thought, as he worked to pry open the lock, but this was an emergency. At last, the cabinet was open, the door hanging lopsided. Pulling out a bottle of bourbon, he poured a shot straight and raised the glass.

"To the world's greatest screw-up," he toasted himself and gulped down the liquid. Then he refilled the glass, took it and the bottle back to his office, and sprawled on the couch.

But one drink followed another and soon all he could think of was Sarah. He still remembered that clumsy scene in her bedroom the night of the wedding ceremony, felt the softness of her mouth when he'd touched it, the silkiness of her skin against his palms. The heady scent of her perfume still lingered in his nostrils. He knew he couldn't run from the truth any longer. All those nights he'd lain awake in his bedroom craving her, all those erotic dreams when he'd fucked her every way possible. His body had been sending him messages. So had his heart, but he was too bitter to recognize it

Desire had grown within him all day today. He'd been impatient for everyone to leave so they could be alone, and he could try to tell her how he felt. He was filled with an almost overpowering need to make love to her and tell her how she'd made a place for herself in his heart. Then in seconds, with a few thoughtless words, he'd killed that chance.

So Maggie had made a fool of him, played a cruel joke on him. He was the one who'd gotten into the mess to begin with, and he was the one who refused to deal with its aftermath. Everyone was right. He'd turned into a self-pitying wreck that no one even wanted to be around anymore, including himself.

He wanted what Nick and Lindsey had—a loving marriage, children—and he wanted it all with Sarah. He was gripped with a fierce desire to hold her naked in his arms, her breasts warmly covered by his hands, her body arched against him. He couldn't stand the thought he might lose her and he might not ever have that opportunity. Right then, he wanted her more than he'd ever thought it possible to want a woman. But what could he do about it now?

He had no idea how long he sat there, drinking steadily. The more he drank, the more depressed he became. *What if she leaves me?*

Panic coursed through him, chilling his blood. He didn't think he could stand it without her. He could not lose her. Somehow, he had to make her understand, let her know how he felt.

He'd blamed what happened on the alcohol. It was easier than blaming himself. If he hadn't gotten drunk, none of it would have happened. In his right mind, he'd have slept it off and waited for the sober light of day to plead his case. But the liquor had wiped away all sense of sanity, urging him to yet greater folly. He swallowed the last of the bourbon and headed for his car.

His alcohol-fogged brain had lost all ability to reason. He had no idea how he managed to get home without running the car off the road or into a tree. He hoped Sarah had not come back downstairs and set the alarm because he didn't think he could remember the code tonight.

Chapter Nine

Sarah stirred restlessly in her sleep, twisting her body. The dream had engulfed her again.

A naked Reno stood beside her bed, holding his pulsating erection in his hand, staring down at her...

"I can't wait." His voice was thick with desire.

He didn't bother stripping off her nightgown, just pulled it up to expose her body. He pressed her back against the pillows and pushed the gown up to her neck. She felt his heavy, naked presence as he lay down in her bed, caressing her, murmuring to her. Her hands, reaching up, touched hot, naked flesh covered with the now-familiar mat of chest hair.

She woke with a start, suddenly aware of the naked male body in bed next to her.

"Sarah," he moaned. "Sarah, Sarah, Sarah. I've wanted to do this every day."

Reno! Oh, god. She should push him away, out of her bed, but her body was primed for him, an erotic fog clouding her mind.

"Let me touch you like this." His voice was low and husky. "Let me taste you, feel you. I want you so badly."

At last. Oh, at last.

His big hands caressed her breasts, tugging at the sensitive nipples, laving them with a hot, wet tongue the way she had dreamed about. Nipping with little bites then soothing with the warm moisture of his mouth.

Bite them. She wanted to scream the words. Instead, she pressed against his body, sliding back and forth against the hair on his chest until her skin felt stretched to bursting.

He moved his lips to her mouth, and that's when it hit her. The smell of alcohol.

Oh, god! He's drunk! Does he even know what he's doing?

"Reno." She had to force the words out, his lips were pressed so hard to hers. She shoved at his shoulders and tried to squirm away from him. "Reno. Wake up."

"Sarah, Sarah, don't leave me. I need you, Sarah." His mouth slanted over hers again, his tongue probing insistently, giving her a taste of herself. "I want you, Sarah. Please. We'll be so good together."

I want you, too, Reno.

"I'm so sorry," he mumbled. "I never meant to hurt you. Don't leave me. Please. I need you."

Damn it! Her stomach knotted, and a dull ache began at the base of her skull. She wanted him to make love to her, but not like this. Never like this. All this would bring was disaster. She wanted to push him away, but he lay pressed heavily against her, making it impossible to move.

"Reno," she shouted the word in his ear and dug her fingernails into his skin. She gritted her teeth and pushed harder. She didn't want to raise her voice too loud and wake Molly. That's all this god-awful nightmare needed. Somehow something finally got through to him, because he lifted his head, his eyes glazed from the effects of the alcohol.

"Wha—" He blinked. "Sarah?"

"Get off me. Now, Reno. This minute."

He looked down at her, bewilderment etched on his face.

She knew the moment awareness struck him. His body recoiled as if struck by ice water. Just like that, the effects of the alcohol were banished as the truth struck him. Shaking, he climbed off the bed.

Shock replaced bewilderment on his face as his eyes raked over her, lying in a rumpled bed, nightgown pushed up, clutching the sheet like a shield. He took in his own nakedness, and all the color drained from his face. For a minute, he looked as if he would be ill.

"Oh, god. What have I done? Please tell me I'm imagining this. I didn't mean..." He sat up and shoved his fingers through his hair. "Sarah, I'm so sorry. So very sorry. Oh, god. I just wanted..." His voice cracked. His throat muscles worked with his effort to swallow. "This isn't the way I wanted it. Not the way at all. I don't even..."

Even what? Want me?

He turned and stumbled out of her room without finishing his sentence, head down. After a moment, the sound of the front door slamming reverberated through the house. Slightly hysterical, she hoped he'd remembered to put his clothes back on.

She fell back against the pillows, trying to gather the tattered remnants of her scattered mind. She struggled to find a shred of self-respect and a reason for the way she'd almost given in to him.

Nice, Sarah. Where's your self-respect?

Finally, the tears she'd been forcing back all night

flooded her eyes and cascaded down her cheeks. She made no effort to wipe them away, just let them keep flowing. They were tears of rage as much as disappointment, in both herself and Reno. She wanted to scream, to beat the walls at the stupidity of what had just happened.

At last, she pulled herself out of bed and went to the shower, standing under it for a long time, as if she could wash away the searing memory of the night. She dried herself off, pulled a fresh nightgown from the drawer, and crawled back into her bed. She had no idea how she would face the next day.

There was no sign of Reno in the morning and no note, but Sarah wasn't expecting any. In fact, his absence was a relief. She felt as if she'd been in a prolonged battle, her senses and pride battered and bruised. She had no idea how they were going to get past all this.

The memory of last night was burned into her mind—the brief but terrible argument, the deep, exhausted sleep she'd fallen into, and the dream that wasn't a dream after all. She could still feel the imprint of his body on hers, the slide of their skin together, and his touch that had drawn her up the spiral into explosive ecstasy. As much time as they'd spent dancing around it, last night should have been wonderful, not the unbelievable disaster it really was.

On the one hand, she wanted to lock herself in a closet until she could forget what happened. On the other, she wanted to flay him alive, to let out every bit of her anger at the way he treated her, and not just last night. She was getting sick of his self-serving control and his refusal to deal with the past. It wasn't just about the two of them. In the end, if he didn't face whatever truth he was hiding from, innocent Molly would be the one to suffer. And that made her angry all over again.

The worst part of it was she'd gone and fallen in love with him. What kind of idiocy was that?

"Oh, Reno," she whispered. "Why can't you tell me the awful secret that keeps that haunted look in your eyes? Why can't we love each other the way I know we both want?"

Well, it was all blown to hell now. Any chance they might have had was certainly wrecked by what had happened. If not for Molly needing her, she would have gone back to bed and hoped she didn't wake up until next year.

"Oh, sweetie," she whispered to Molly as she dressed her, "I think your mama has finally run into a problem she can't solve. Whatever's got your daddy hurting so bad is more than I can handle." She pressed her lips to Molly's baby-soft skin. "If it weren't for you, I'd be gone in a flash. But don't you worry. Mama will never, ever leave you. I just wish you were old enough to give me some answers."

Molly cooed and reached up a chubby little hand, patting Sarah's cheeks.

Tears pricked Sarah's eyelids. No, there was no way she'd leave this child. But how could she and Reno get past this nightmare? Could they even talk to each other? What would she say to him, for God's sake?

She made a pot of coffee, then burned her lip drinking it while it was too hot. But the strong, black liquid seemed to shock her brain into motion and allowed her to perform her necessary tasks. She had a child to care for. A self-indulgent collapse would have to wait.

The phone rang several times while she fed Molly breakfast. She ignored it, letting the machine pick up. There was no way she could talk to Reno right now, or anyone else, so she just listened numbly as the messages played.

"Sarah?" Her mother's voice. "Darling, are you there? Can you pick up? I just want to tell you what a great time we had yesterday. Well, all right. Call me when you get back from wherever you are."

I'm in hell, Mother. I don't know if I'll ever be back.

Four or five hang-up calls. Reno? What could he possibly say to her? Or she to him?

Then Nick. "Sarah? Can you please answer? I just want to talk to you for a minute."

Not on your life.

"Please? Sarah?"

Two more calls from Nick, the message the same. Then a call from the ranch.

"Sarah? It's Lindsey. I guess you must be busy with Molly. Please give me a call."

Lindsey was the one person she even thought about talking to, but what would she say?

My husband hurt me last night with words that still sting. Then he got drunk, climbed into my bed, and I welcomed him with open arms. Until I realized he was stinking drunk.

The only thing she was grateful for was the fact she had realized his drunken state in time and pushed him away.

Wouldn't that just make for great conversation?

She turned the volume down on the answering

machine, but the ringing still drove her nuts, so she unplugged the phones. For a long time, she sat in the nursery with Molly, rocking in the chair while the little girl lay in her playpen and played with her toys. She wondered if her heart could possibly ache more than it did. Finally, needing the closeness, she picked Molly up and snuggled her in her lap, laying her cheek against the warm skin.

"Mama's having a bad day, sweetheart. Maybe a bad year."

Maybe a bad life.

****

Reno sat on the couch in his office, his head in his hands, sure he'd have to die to get better. What the fuck had he been thinking, breaking into Nick's liquor cabinet and downing all that bourbon.

Don't you remember what happened the last time you went on a bender, asshole?

This time he'd really outdone himself. Every time he thought of the scene with Sarah, he wanted to hide in a dark hole.

He was trying to decide if he was functional enough to make some coffee when he heard the outer door to the office open. Who the hell would that be? They'd given everyone the day after Thanksgiving off.

"Well, this is another fine mess you've gotten yourself into, Ollie."

Reno looked up to see Nick standing in the entrance. "Go away," he growled. "Leave me the hell alone."

"Jesus Christ. Look at you. Your clothes are a wreck, your hair looks like it hasn't been combed in a year, and it's obvious you didn't shave." He sniffed the air. "Fuck. Is that bourbon I smell?"

Reno looked up at him and shook his head, then thought better of it as the hammers took up a rhythm in his head again. He just hoped to hell Nick didn't notice he'd been crying.

"Jesus, Reno." Nick crouched down in front of him. "What the hell happened? You didn't look this bad during the Maggie crisis. Why aren't you home with your wife and child?"

"It isn't my child." He spat the words. "And if my wife has any sense, she should pack up and leave me."

Nick rose and shoved his hands into his pockets. "You want to tell me what's going on?"

"Not really." Reno scrubbed at his face. "I'm a miserable bastard. That's what's going on."

"I'll agree to that if you want, but I still want to know what the hell put you in this shape. You haven't had anything but a glass or two of wine in two years." He took a step back. "Did you do something stupid again?"

"Stupid. Yeah, that's a good word." Reno leaned against the couch, his eyes closed. "First, I blew up at Sarah, insulted her, said things she'll never forgive. Then I got drunk, went home, and climbed into bed with her, naked. How's that for a happy holiday?"

Nick was silent for so long Reno forced his eyes open and grimaced at the look of shock on his partner's face.

"Is that why you broke into my cabinet and stole my liquor like some teenager? I'm sure there's a saner explanation than that."

"I wish I hadn't had so much bourbon. How's that for sane? I could probably use another drink to blot everything out. Maybe I wouldn't hate myself so much."

"Yeah, right. That's a wonderful remedy."

"The worst part?" He shook his head. "She realized I was drunk, finally got my attention, and pushed me away."

"It's a good thing one of you is smart. All right, enough with the self-pity. Go wash your face and pull yourself together while I make coffee."

Reno flipped on the light in the bathroom, took a look at himself in the mirror...and nearly threw up in disgust. His eyes were bloodshot with circles beneath them. His skin had the slightly ruddy cast of someone who'd had way too much to drink. His clothes were wrinkled, and a motherfucker of a headache was building behind his eyes.

What the hell was the matter with him? Alcohol didn't solve anything, especially for someone who didn't metabolize it properly.

He turned on the cold water, splashed handfuls of it on his face, and finally ducking his head beneath the faucet to see if he could shock his brain into functioning. What a mess he'd made out of things, as if they weren't already bad enough. How in the hell was he ever going to get past this?

He dried his face, raked his fingers through his damp hair, and returned to the office, feeling only marginally better.

Nick hung up from a call on his cell phone, slid it into his pocket, and handed him a fresh mug of coffee. "Don't spill it, please."

Reno wrapped his hands wrapped around the mug. "Thanks. But you better go home to your wife and child. It's a holiday, remember? What are you doing here, anyway?"

"I came in for a file I wanted to review. It's a damn good thing, or you might not have been found until Monday. I'm not leaving here until you tell me how this happened. Or do you want me to call Sarah?"

"God, no." Reno took another sip of coffee. "That's the last thing I want."

"Then start talking."

And so he did, laying out every sordid detail, from the day he approached Sarah about the deal, including the times he'd been miserable to her. He threw all his conflicted feelings on the table, figuring things couldn't be any worse. Maybe it was time to finally bring it all out into the open. He didn't know how long he talked, but he managed to get it all out. When he was finished, he was afraid to look at his friend. Afraid of what he'd see on his face. But the only thing there was compassion, and that made him feel even worse. If anyone deserved compassion it was Sarah.

The Reno Sullivan the world saw was missing this morning, replaced by a human being whose mistakes had all come back to haunt him in one big explosion. He'd finally managed to fall into the hole he'd been digging for himself.

"Jesus, Reno," Nick said at last. "What the hell got into you? And to get drunk the way you did? What did you think that would accomplish? Remember what happened the last time you got into the booze. You're supposed to be an adult. It's time to start acting like one again."

"I know, I know." Reno rubbed his face.

"Well, you can't stay here," Nick told him. "You

need to go home, throw yourself on the ground in front of your wife, and beg her forgiveness."

"Go back to that house? That's part of the problem, all the ghosts I live with. Sarah—"

"Is going to the ranch with Lindsey for the weekend. She needs to be away for the weekend to get some perspective on this. Ah, here are reinforcements."

Reno looked up as Tony walked in. "Did you broadcast it to the world?"

"I can't believe this is the same man who kicked my ass growing up and taught me self-control and respect for other people." Tony's voice held a mixture of both anger and disappointment. "This Molly and Maggie thing has left a festering sore on his soul. It needs to be lanced and drained before it becomes terminal."

"Well, if we can't help him patch this up with Sarah, it may not make a difference." Nick paused. "He needs space to get some perspective here. He and Sarah both need to be out of that house until they can face each other and move forward. Can I dump him on your doorstep for the weekend?"

Tony snorted. "Do I have a choice?"

"Not much." Nick laughed grimly. "Lindsey's taking Sarah and Molly out to the ranch, and I damn sure don't want to leave him to his own devices. And I do not want him alone in that house until he deals with the mess that screwed up his life. It's hiding there, waiting for him in every corner."

"Sure, I'll babysit him. When you get done beating on him, I can take my turn."

Reno looked from one man to the other. "What the hell got into me?"

"Be nice to know the answer to that." Nick shook his head. "I think you were looking for one more way to punish yourself and took Sarah along for the ride."

"You want to know something else?"

Nick narrowed his eyes. "You mean there's more?"

"Oh, yeah." Reno ran his fingers through his hair again. "I was jealous of you and Lindsey and the new baby coming. How's that for being a good friend? I wanted a baby of my own, a child with Sarah. But I didn't know how to change the rules."

Nick sighed. "Well, you sure picked the wrong way to do it."

"Do you think she'll ever talk to me again?"

"Let's hope so. But you've got to give her—and yourself—some time."

"I wanted her, Nick, but I sure hadn't meant for it to happen this way."

Nick scowled at him. "And we're done with the pity party."

"Let's go," Tony urged. "We'll swing by the house so you can pack a bag. I'll come in with you and supervise."

"And get him the hell out of there ASAP. He needs to shape up over the weekend so the staff doesn't get a sniff of this on Monday. I'll clean up the mess here in the office."

"Done and done."

Nick looked at Reno again. "Answer one question for me, and you damn well better tell me the truth. Are you honest to god in love with her? No bullshit. Say it out loud so we both hear it."

"I'm not sure I even know what love is." Reno rubbed his bristly jaw. "I just know whatever I feel is killing me. I couldn't... I didn't know how—"

"All right, all right," Nick cut him off. "Will you do whatever we tell you to get her back?"

"Anything. I'll do whatever it takes. I can't lose her, Nick." His voice was raw with need and hunger, the pain in his heart coloring his words.

"Okay. Then let's get this show on the road."

Following his brother from the office, Reno wondering how he, a man who had built a successful security business with nothing but grit and determination, had made such a fucked up mess of his life. And if, indeed, he could do what it took to salvage it.

Chapter Ten

Sarah had no idea what to do next. All she knew was she needed to get out of here, out of this house that held so many painful memories for her. Everywhere she looked, she saw Reno, the good and the bad. She had kept her own house as backup, and that seemed the most logical place to go. She had no idea where Reno was, and at the moment, she was torn between not giving a damn and worrying about what condition he was in.

I'm a sucker, plain and simple. Maybe I should tattoo it on my forehead.

She'd need a crib for Molly. Maybe she could pay extra and get one delivered and set up today. It was Black Friday when shoppers ruled. There must be some store that would accommodate her. Most of the other things she could take from here.

The doorbell rang as she finished feeding Molly her lunch. She tried ignoring it, even when it rang three more times. There wasn't a person in the world she wanted to see right now. The ringing stopped, but heavy pounding on the door replaced it.

Then she heard Lindsey's voice. "Sarah, if you don't open this door and let me in, I'm breaking a window and coming in that way. You don't want to do that to a pregnant woman, do you?"

Reluctantly, she opened the front door. Lindsey stood there, her eyes intent on Sarah's face. Emilio was just behind her.

"You look like hell," she said. "Come on." She grabbed Sarah's arm and marched her into the kitchen, Emilio on her heels.

Molly was banging noisily on her highchair tray. The little girl looked up at everyone and smiled, showing two new teeth. Lindsey sat Sarah down in a chair, found a teething cookie in the pantry, and handed it to the baby.

"All right." She dropped into a chair. "Don't open your mouth until I'm finished. I know what happened last night, and before you start feeling uncomfortable and trying to hide, Nick had to tell me because he was worried about you."

"Nick knows?" Sarah's face turned red then white. "Oh, my god. Everything?"

"And Tony," Lindsey added.

"Has Reno told the whole world?" Sarah's eyes filled with tears. She covered her face with her hands.

Lindsey tugged gently at her hands, forcing Sarah to look at her. "He didn't want to tell anyone, but when Nick found him holed up at the office this morning and got the whole story out of him."

"Oh, my god," she whispered. "Lindsey, there are other things you might as well know. Although I'm ashamed to even talk about them."

Very slowly, she spilled all the wretched details. Molly. What happened the night of the wedding? And what she'd hoped for with the Thanksgiving holiday.

"So you see, it's an impossible situation," she finished. "I want him, I love him, but we have so many problems lying between us now. I don't know if we can ever face each other again. I don't even know if I can trust him again."

Lindsey put her hand on Sarah's arm. "Just know this; Reno's a bigger mess than you are. Nick found him at the office looking like the trash someone forgot to pick up. He called to tell me he's sending him to Tony's for the weekend to get his head on straight."

Sarah frowned. "Tony's?"

"Yes. None of us think it's healthy for him to be in this house by himself, and I'm taking you and Molly to the ranch with me."

Sarah just stared at her. "To the ranch?"

"Yes. You need to get out of this wretched house for at least a couple of days." She cleared her throat. "Sarah, how you play this is up to you. But you've known Reno long enough to know he's a good person. He's just got his life twisted in a knot he can't undo. What happened last night—him blowing up at you, what happened afterward—is all part of that."

"Why won't he tell me what's wrong?" Sarah persisted.

"There are reasons, and he needs to tell you those himself. You need to let him explain everything to you."

"I guess you're right," Sarah said miserably. "Now more than ever I have to get out of this house. I was thinking of taking Molly to my place for a while."

"Good idea." Lindsey nodded. "But you shouldn't be alone right now, so you're coming to the ranch with me. And no argument. Everything's already set up. You and Molly will have my old room. Mary's wonderful about taking care of people with emotional wounds. I should know. She did it for me many times. And we'll all give you as much space as you want."

Sarah chewed on her bottom lip. It certainly sounded better than being in her old house with just Molly. And in *this* house, she'd see Reno and his ghosts in every corner. Call her weak and a coward, but that was more than she wanted to deal with right now.

"If I just knew what he was hiding…" She shook her head. "What is so awful that he can't tell me about it? Why does he hate Molly so much? Why did he get so drunk? Why couldn't he just come to me and…" Sarah drew in a calming breath.

I will not break down. There's been enough tears. I am going to be strong for me and Molly. And maybe eventually Reno, if he will ever open that door.

"Stop. Not another word. You need some space to think, and the ranch is just the place for that. So let's get going."

"But Nick will be there and…"

"Sarah." Lindsey took Sarah's hands and pulled them away from her face. "Nick is one of the gentlest, most sensitive people in the world. He has his own history. I guarantee you he will go out of his way to respect your privacy and make you feel comfortable." She chuckled. "On the other hand, if I don't have any success with you, he's going to come here, throw you over his shoulder and drag you out to the ranch himself."

Sarah smiled weakly at the thought.

"All right." Lindsey wiped Molly's face and hands and lifted the little girl out of the highchair, handing her to Sarah. "Tell Emilio where the luggage is so he can bring it upstairs. We're going to pack whatever you need for a few days for you and Molly. What we forget we can buy. And don't argue with me. Stress isn't good for a pregnant woman."

Sarah had to admit getting away from the house would be a relief. She needed to sort out her feelings. The ranch was such a soothing place to be, and it would be great for Molly.

"You're right," she said, giving in. "The luggage is in the garage. If you can keep Molly busy, I'll get us packed." She handed Molly back and hugged her friend. "Thanks. I don't… I just…"

"It's all right. You don't need to say anything else."

Mary was waiting for them when Emilio brought the suitcases into the ranch house. She reached at once for Molly, who smiled and gurgled at her. The woman gave the little girl a warm smile.

"She hasn't had her nap today," Sarah told her.

"We'll take care of that right now. We'll just get her into bed, and she'll go off like a rock. If you want to come up with us, Mrs. Sullivan, I'll show you how the room is fixed, and you can let me know if you need any changes."

"Sarah. Please call me Sarah." Formality certainly wouldn't work in this situation. She hugged Mary. "And thank you so much."

She was touched at the trouble they'd gone to, trying to make her comfortable. Lindsey's old bedroom was huge, with a king-sized bed and a large dresser. The crib was set up close to the bed and even had a mobile attached to it. Jason's old changing table was set up in a corner and Mary had stocked it with everything she'd need. Fresh flowers stood in a vase on the dresser and a stack of mysteries sat on the bedside table. There was even a rocking chair. Sun poured in through the oversized windows, giving everything a warm glow.

Sarah was overwhelmed. She could feel the tears starting again. "I don't know what to say except thank you."

Lindsey took Sarah's arm and steered her to the door. "Why don't you let Mary put Molly down, and we'll go dig into the pot of hot chocolate that's waiting."

Lindsey carried the tray with the mugs and a plate of Mexican wedding cookies into the living room, where Emilio had built a fire that now roared and crackled in the fireplace. Sitting on the big couch, she patted the cushions for Sarah to sit next to her. "Just kick back and relax, okay?"

****

Time passed in a blur for Sarah. Her mind was as battered as her body. She was so cold on the inside she didn't think she'd ever get warm again, yet she sat outside, rocking on the porch in the chilly weather.

"Something hot for you."

She hadn't even heard Mary come out.

The woman pressed a cup of hot chocolate into her hands. "You should come inside, though."

Sarah shook her head. "I'm fine. Really." But she wasn't, and they all knew it.

Nick tiptoed around her when he came home later. Sarah saw him whispering to Lindsey, sure they were discussing Reno, but she couldn't find it in her at the moment to ask about him. She needed to get her brain and her emotions straightened out before she could move forward.

"Is she okay?" Sarah overheard him ask Lindsey in a low voice. "She hardly says a word."

"She needs to work this out herself," Lindsey whispered back. "She'll talk when she's ready. I'll make sure of it."

They all left her pretty much alone, watching her wrestle with her feelings. And she said little as she kept to herself. She responded politely when spoken to, but other than that, she said nothing.

After dinner the next night, Sarah pulled on her jacket and went out on the porch again. She'd finally reached a point at which she could go no further. Her mind was paralyzed with the necessity to make some decisions, but she couldn't focus on what they should be.

In a minute, Emilio came out and sat down in the other rocker. He rocked silently with her for a minute before he started to speak. "You know, Sarah, life is full of challenges. Every day, we make decisions that affect us and the people around us. We just hope for the best. My parents lived in a little town in Mexico I'm sure you've never heard of. We were dirt poor, scrabbling out a living. There were seven of us kids to support. We all worked from the minute we were old enough, but our parents still insisted we all go to school and to church every Sunday.

"They loved each other very much. They just weren't very good at saying the words. But we saw it in the way they treated each other and the love they passed along to us." He stopped for a minute, as if gathering his thoughts. "One time, something happened between them. None of us knew what it was, but we heard angry words, long into the night. Then my father stomped out of the house, slamming doors on the way.

"In the morning, when he came back, they acted as if nothing had happened, but we all knew. We never found out what caused the argument, only that it was so bad my mother stopped speaking to him. All those good years together down the drain.

"After that they might as well have been two strangers under the same roof. No matter what he did, she turned him away. You could look into her eyes and see that, whatever it was, it had bruised her soul.

"Then one day, my father came down with the flu, and, bang, just like that he was gone. My mother mourned every minute, not just for his death but also for what she'd wasted by never healing the breach between them. She died a year later. We always believed it was because her heart was broken. Don't let your heart break, Sarah. Reno is a good man. I don't know the whole story here, and I don't want to. But if you don't deal with it, you'll never get past it, your life will be gone and maybe you'll have missed something very important."

He stood up, went to her rocker, and patted her shoulder.

His touch unlocked the floodgates. She began to cry in huge, rasping sobs, her body shuddering and her cries those of a wounded animal. Emilio just kept his arm on her shoulder and let her weep. She heard Nick come to the door and speak to Emilio, who waved him away.

Finally, when she was totally exhausted, when there were no more tears to cry, she wiped her eyes on her sleeve and sat back. "Emilio, I…"

"That's okay, Sarah." He was a solid presence next

to her. "I know."

"Would you please ask Lindsey to come out here?" She sniffled and blinked her eyes. "I think I'm ready to talk now."

"Why don't you come inside, and I'll chase Nick upstairs. Mary and I are going to our own place next door, and he can keep an ear out for the kids. I don't want either of you girls freezing to death in this chill."

They sat in front of the fire, with fresh mugs of hot chocolate.

"I'm ready to go back now," Sarah told her friend. "I can't call that place home, but I need to go back with Molly and find a way for Reno and I to face this. No more avoiding and running away. Once it's all out in the open, I can make a rational decision. I hope."

"Well, then." Lindsey let out a breath. "Let me just add one more thing to the mix. You may not realize, but Reno is desperately in love with you."

"What?" Sarah's head jerked up. "What did you say?"

"I said he's desperately in love with you. We've all seen it coming for months, and he admitted as much when Nick asked him. Nick thinks Reno's been in love with you since you came to work for them but was too stupid to recognize it, especially after the disaster with Maggie."

"Oh, Lindsey, I don't think so," Sarah disagreed. "He married me because he thought I was the best candidate to pick up the pieces of his life."

"Maybe he fooled himself in the beginning, but not now. That's why he's so busy beating himself up. He's convinced he's destroyed the one good thing in his life."

Sarah was stunned.

Lindsey was silent for a long moment. "This is a complicated situation. But I think he's ready to be honest with you now, whatever the consequences. Just listen to him. Then you can decide what you want to do."

"I guess I'm just nervous about facing him." Sarah twisted her fingers together. "I'm not sure I'll even know how to act."

"He's scared, too," Lindsey said. "Just talk to him and see what happens. Is that fair enough?"

Sarah nodded slowly. "I guess so. I can't hide from this forever. I think tomorrow I need to go home. I need to face that house and hopefully, Reno."

"Are you sure?"

"I can't run away from this forever," she told her friend. "It's time I took matters into my own hands. One way or another, I'm going to force the truth out of him."

"Okay. I'll have Emilio take you in the morning. And call me if you need reinforcement."

Sarah laughed. "I will."

Emilio dropped her off just after ten the next morning, carrying her suitcases into the house.

"It will be okay," he told her in his solemn way and squeezed her shoulder.

Ten minutes later, after viewing the discouraging sight in her refrigerator, she put Molly in her car for a run to the grocery store. She'd make a special meal tonight and call Tony to tell him his brother should get his ass home this minute. Tonight was Armageddon, whether Reno realized it or not.

Sarah was glad to be home, even if the house was

filled with painful memories that kept prodding at her. She felt, if not refreshed by her stay at the ranch, at least released from the grip of emotional disaster. Regardless of the circumstances, she and Reno had taken a leap into intimacy. Somewhere in all this mess were real feelings propelling both of them. If they could just negotiate the obstacle course, maybe they could examine how they really felt about each other.

She wasn't sure how she would ever sleep in her bed again without thinking about that night. She still had so many unresolved conflictions. Loving Reno was not enough if he didn't love her back. Despite what Lindsey said, she needed him to tell her that himself. She would listen to whatever he had to say, then decide what to do next.

"We'll just have to find a way to make your daddy talk to us," she told Molly, opening the passenger door. "He's really a good man. We have to make him believe it."

She was about to lift Molly from her car seat when an unfamiliar car pulled into the driveway. Had it followed her? Been waiting for her? Panic seized her as two Hispanic men climbed out and walked toward her. Aguilar! She went to pull her gun from her purse but realized she'd left it on the seat to get Molly.

"Your husband will learn he's fucked with the wrong man," the one closest to her said.

She tried to shield Molly with her body, but she heard a soft pop! And searing pain engulfed her side. She screamed as the other man grabbed Molly from her seat. The last thing she heard was the baby crying as blackness overtook her.

****

"You need to stop hiding out here," Tony said. "Not just from Sarah but from yourself. It's time to face the music."

"That ought to be fun." Reno snorted.

"What I don't understand is how you thought this kind of marriage could work in the first place. It's the most ridiculous setup I've ever seen, and I told you so. It caused all kinds of complications and look what happened."

How could he explain it when he still didn't understand it himself? Somehow, he'd been stupid enough to think he and Sarah could just transfer their working relationship from the office to the house. He certainly hadn't planned on falling in love with her.

At night, he lay in the bed in Tony's guest room, sleep eluding him, thinking of Sarah and how she had changed his life. Unbidden, images came to his mind of her and Molly. Looking at them, at the obvious bond between them, anyone would have believed Molly was Sarah's biological child.

He saw himself standing on the outside, locked out by his own anger and withdrawal, and his heart ached worse than his body did. His entire world had turned gray, and he had no one to blame but himself for washing away all the color she had brought into his life.

He had no idea if she even wanted anything to do with him after this, and if the answer was no, he needed to figure out how to deal with that, too. But he was through standing still. All that had done was help him nearly ruin the best thing that came into his life.

"I guess I have to stop running away from the fact I love my wife—god, have I ever even called her that? And I've screwed up to the max. I don't deserve a second chance, but I'm praying that she'll give me one."

Tony just looked at him, waiting.

"I know I have to tell her the truth about Maggie and Molly. She might run in the opposite direction, but I'm hoping she doesn't."

"Sarah loves you," his brother said. "Any fool can see it, and you're not just any fool. I hope you're a smart one."

"Me, too. I'm going to call her when we're through here and ask her to come back to the house so we can talk."

His phone rang, and he looked at the display. Nick.

"Sarah's back at the house. I'm not sure you can call it home, but whatever. She and Molly are both there, and apparently she has her shit together better than you."

"Isn't that the truth," Reno muttered. "Okay, no more running away." He hung up and looked at Tony. "Thanks for letting me camp out here, but it's time for me to see if I can get my family back."

Family. He liked the sound of that word. He just hoped he still had one. As he packed his suitcase another thought struck him. Maybe it was time for a grand gesture. One that would show Sarah how much he really loved her. And make her at least willing to listen to him.

But his good mood was shattered when his cell rang again.

"Aguilar's been spotted in Texas." Balenger's voice was sharp in his ear.

"What?" Panic stabbed him. "I thought you told me he was back in Mexico."

Months had gone by since the man's escape and they'd stupidly allowed themselves to be lulled by the thought that maybe the vendetta was off.

"He was, but he must have snuck out of his own estancia. One of our agents spotted him in El Paso. You know he's headed this way."

Sarah! Molly!

Fuck!

"Call me when you have something else," he told the man and disconnected the call.

He immediately punched the number for the house, but when the answering machine picked up, he cursed. Then he dialed Sarah's cell phone, but her phone went to voice mail.

Jesus God. Where the hell were they?

"Tony!" he shouted.

"I'm right here. What's up?"

"Aguilar," he told him as he ran for his car, Tony right on his heels.

Please god let her be okay. I promise to make everything right if you can just keep her safe.

But as he drove like a maniac through the streets, he was sick with fear and dread.

Chapter Eleven

Consumed by fear, Reno called Balenger and the local cops as he raced for the house. Why the fuck did his brother have to live clear across town? He had Tony continue dialing both the house and Sarah's cell but without any luck. By the time he pulled up in his driveway two patrol cars were there, and Balenger was just pulling up. An ambulance was just coming down his street from the other direction. The garage door was open, and two of the cops were bending over something on the floor.

Oh, Jesus! No. No, no, no.

He shoved the car into Park so hard it rocked. Throwing open the door, he raced up the driveway and roughly shoved aside the kneeling men. He almost passed out at the sight of Sarah crumpled on the floor, blood staining her side and pooling on the floor.

"Sarah!" His chest tightened with anguish. He lifted one of her hands, frightened at how icy cold it was.

"Reno?" Balenger touched his shoulder. "Reno, the ambulance is here. Let the EMTs get to her.

He moved around so he was kneeling by her head, leaving room for the medics to work. He barely heard what they were saying as they took her vitals. So much blood. Shit. Even the pressure bandage they applied didn't seem to be doing any good.

Then something struck him and he looked up at Balenger. "Molly?"

"Gone. He left a note." He snapped his fingers, and another man in a suit handed him a plastic envelope with a sheet of paper inside. Reno read it, trying not to throw up.

Come and get what's yours, if you can, gringo. This time I'll be sure to kill you.

"He's taken her back to Mexico," he guessed.

Balenger nodded. "We're pretty sure of that. And you know he's got a slow death planned for you."

"He can kill me as long as Molly's safe and Sarah doesn't die."

The medics lifted Sarah onto a stretcher and began to back out of the garage.

"I'm going with her," he told them.

"You can't ride in the amb—" one of them started to say.

Balenger flashed his badge. "Make an exception."

Reno remembered little of the mad dash through the streets, sirens screaming. He held Sarah's cold hand in his, thinking if he could warm it up, she'd be okay. Praying she'd live. Praying that Molly would be unharmed. Aguilar wouldn't hurt a baby, would he?

"I love you, Sarah. I love Molly. If I can just have you both back safe, I'll tell you every day for the rest of our lives."

Then they were at the emergency entrance, and Sarah was being handed over to the doctors and nurses who had rushed out with a gurney. Tony, who must have driven his car to the hospital, tugged him away.

"I can't leave her," Reno said.

"Let the doctors have her," his brother said in a soft

voice. "Here." He held out a handkerchief.

Reno took it, realizing his cheeks were wet with tears he hadn't even realized he'd cried. He was standing there mopping his cheeks when a man in scrubs walked up to them.

"Which of you is Mr. Sullivan?"

"I am," Reno told him.

"I'm Dr. Redfield. I'm the surgeon who'll be operating on your wife. We're going to take good care of her."

"Don't let her die," was all he could manage.

Redfield gave him a reassuring smile. "That's the plan. I suggest you go up to the second floor where the surgery waiting room is. That's where I'll look for you."

"Can I see her again before she—before you—"

"Go ahead up there now while she's being prepped. I'll make sure they get you before they wheel her into the surgery suite."

"Come on." Tony tugged gently on his arm. "Let's go."

He let himself be led into the elevator and up to the surgery waiting room on the second floor. They were barely inside the room when Nick entered.

"Lindsey wanted to come," he told Reno, "but I didn't think this was the best place for a pregnant woman."

Reno just nodded, his throat so tight with unshed tears he could barely talk.

"Here." Tony handed him a paper cup filled with coffee. "Drink some of this."

He took a sip, scarcely noticing that it scalded his tongue or tasted like battery acid.

"How did this happen?" he asked Nick. "I should have assigned someone as a permanent bodyguard."

"We hadn't heard a thing about Aguilar in months. And Sarah never would have stood for someone glued to her twenty-four/seven. It's obvious Aguilar and his men observed her and you. He knew there'd be a security system in the house so he had to wait for just the right opportunity. Sometimes things happen no matter what you do. But Sarah will pull through and we'll get Molly back safe and sound."

"If Sarah pulls through, I'm going to tell her everything," he told the two men.

"*When* she pulls through," Tony corrected.

Reno nodded. "And throw myself at her feet and beg forgiveness." He swallowed. "If she just pulls through." He tried to draw in a full breath. "And Molly. Jesus. Will I lose her before I even have her, tell her I love her?" He looked at Nick. "We have to get a team—"

"Already in the works. Sit down. I'll bring you up to date. Balenger's been a big help. He hates it that the FBI can't go into Mexico for her."

"I want to go with the team to Mexico," Reno insisted.

Nick shook his head. "You aren't fit for this kind of rescue operation. You'll do something stupid and endanger all of us, including Molly. Have enough brains to realize that."

"But—"

"No buts. And Sarah will need you here. She'll need you with her when she finds out about Molly and waits for news. You know I'm right."

The worst part was, he agreed with Nick. And he

certainly wasn't thinking clearly enough to lead a team into danger. Anyway, he didn't think he could tear himself away from Sarah.

"Mr. Sullivan?"

Reno looked up, saw a man in scrubs at the door to the room, and leaped to his feet.

"That's me."

"If you come with me, you can see Mrs. Sullivan for a minute before we take her into surgery."

Reno nearly ran into the hallway where Sarah lay, as white as the sheets, on a gurney. He almost passed out when he saw her. He wrapped both of his hands around one of her small ones, the one without the IV needle in it, and squeezed gently.

"Sarah, if you can hear me, I love you. I love you more than I've ever loved another soul, and when we get past this, I'm going to spend every day showing you. You and Molly, because we're going to get her back. That's a promise."

He placed a gentle kiss on her lips, lips nearly as cold as her hand.

"Mr. Sullivan?" The nurse touched his shoulder. "We need to take her now."

Reluctantly, he released his hold on her and backed away. As they wheeled her through the double doors, he felt tears coursing down his cheeks again. He had really fucked up big time, but he was going to make it right.

"I want to go on the mission," he insisted to Nick.

"That's a big fat *no*."

"But Aguilar took Molly as bait for me. I'm the one he wants."

"And he'll get you and kill you. In fact, the shape

you're in, you'd get us all killed." Nick's cell phone buzzed, and he looked down to see a text scrolling on the screen. "And that's my cue to get my ass in gear. Everything's ready. Balenger got us maps of Aguilar's compound, and everyone's ready. We are wheel's up in thirty so I need to boogie."

"Go."

"Remember. We have to wait until dark to do this. But the helo will drop us far enough away that we can hike toward the compound and keep an eye on things. We don't want to risk anything happening to Molly."

"I know. I know."

Nick squeezed Reno's shoulder. "Everything will be fine. Sarah will come through this, and I'll get Molly back." He looked at Tony. "He's all yours. Take good care of him."

The two men shook hands, and then Nick was gone.

Reno thought the next few hours were the longest he had ever spent. Every minute seemed like an hour, every hour like a day. He checked his cell phone every five minutes, even though he knew it would be a while before he got confirmation from Nick.

When he couldn't stand it anymore, he did something he hadn't done in as long as he could remember. He went to the hospital chapel and prayed.

****

Nick had assembled a team of five men, all former Special Forces and all skilled in hostage rescue. This was nearly the same team that had done the extraction from Aguilar's compound the last time so they were familiar with the area and the layout. They were dressed in camouflage, their faces blackened and web harnesses crisscrossing their body to hold all their equipment. And each man carried an assault rifle.

"Okay, let's review it all one more time," he said over the noise of the rotors as they headed for Mexican airspace. He opened his laptop, called up the map of the compound, and held it so everyone could see the screen.

"We're going to assume they have Molly in the same room they held the hostage the last time. Aguilar's daughter visits sometime, and that room has a crib in it."

"I can't believe that animal has children." Evan Noble grunted. "Spawn of the devil."

"Actually," Nick told him, "you hit the nail on the head. She's become a vital member of his operation. If we take him out, there's not a doubt in my mind she'll step in and rebuild the organization."

"Maybe we should take her out, too," one of the men commented.

"If that was our mission, we would," Nick agreed. "But our sole purpose is to rescue Molly Sullivan. Destroying the compound will be a part of that. So let's get back to business."

He went over everything with them until he was confident each man had his assignment memorized. He really wasn't worried. In Special Forces, they'd executed missions like this a number of times. They were silent for the rest of the trip, each man busy with his own thoughts, running details through his mind.

The helicopter dropped them five miles from the compound, far enough away not to raise suspicions and in a heavily forested area to give them concealment.

"I'll call for extraction as soon as we have Molly,"

Nick told the pilot. "By that time you can extract closer to the compound." He pointed to a spot on the map on the tablet the pilot was holding. "Here. Got it?"

The pilot nodded. "Got it."

They synced their watches, and Nick waved the helo away.

They remained silent as they walked through the jungle, their footfalls nearly soundless. There was nothing to talk about yet, and they knew from before where Aguilar had cameras placed. When they got close to the compound, they set up far enough back that their images weren't picked up.

Nick took the thermal imaging reader from a pocket on his harness, opened it, and turned it on. Immediately, tiny red dots appeared both inside and outside the estancia. If Aguilar was true to form, the baby would be upstairs in the room that overlooked the courtyard, and he would have someone staying with the little girl. Nick looked for a room with two dots in it and sure enough... There it was, right where he expected it to be.

Of course, it could be two other people, but he went with his gut. If he was wrong, they'd just check every room, shooting whoever they had to as they went. His preference, of course, was to grab Molly and get the fuck out.

He showed the screen to everyone so they could fix it in their minds. Then they all hunkered down, took out their binoculars to watch what was going on, and prepared to wait.

Not much happened during the daylight hours. Nick noted with some interest that there were only two guards at a time in the courtyard and one on the back side of the house. They'd taken note of that the last time, and apparently, Aguilar hadn't learned anything from the last invasion. Arrogance had its drawbacks.

At last, the sun went down and gradually darkness descended. By nine o'clock, Nick was convinced they had as much cover as they would need and he signaled quietly to each man. Ned Dropo, former sniper, stayed on the hill. As the others began to move out, Ned sighted along his scope and quickly and efficiently took out the front guards. Then he duck-walked toward the back and took out the man there.

Slowly, the others spread out, Dropo keeping his rifle trained on the estancia, ready to pick off anyone who ventured outside. They circled the surrounding wall, bending low, and set charges along the way until they reached a point where they could haul themselves over. Someone shouted in the courtyard, and Nick heard the voice raised. Obviously, someone had discovered the two bodies. The man began to shout but was cut off in midsentence.

Good. Dropo was doing his part.

As soon as they were in the courtyard, Nick and two of the men scrambled up the outside stairway, placing charges along the wall and leaving Dropo and two other men to cover the courtyard. At the top of the staircase was a set of French doors. Locked. Nick smashed the glass with the butt of his rifle, reached inside to flip the lock and pulled the door open.

Thank god I chose the right room!

In front of him stood a plump woman with her gray hair in a bun, wearing a black dress and holding Molly protectively against her chest.

"*Por favor, senorita.*" Nick reached for the baby. "I

need to take the child." He reached out for her. "Molly, come to Uncle Nick."

She must have recognized his voice because she reached out to him. "Unka Nick. Want Unka Nick."

The woman stared at him, frightened, holding Molly even tighter.

Nick brought up his rifle. "Hand over the baby. I don't want to hurt you."

Jim Clayton said something in Spanish to the woman. She looked from one man to the other, then reluctantly handed Molly to Nick.

"Thanks," he told Jim. They heard loud voices raised in the house, more gunshots, and the voices coming closer. "Let's get the fuck out of here."

He secured Molly against his chest with straps from his harness, placing a reassuring kiss on her forehead. Then he and Jim ran down the outside stairway. He was almost out of the courtyard when he heard a voice next to him.

"Give that child back to me," Aguilar said in is guttural voice, "or I kill both of you."

Nick wasn't sure how he would have handled it, but the choice was taken out of his hands. He heard a soft *pop!* When he turned, he saw a round hole in the center of Aguilar's forehead. In the next instant, the man fell to the ground.

Thank you, Dropo!

"Let's get the hell out of here," Jim Clayton urged, running toward the gate in the wall.

As he ran, Nick punched a button on the radio he wore on his wrist.

"Ready for extraction," he told the pilot.

By the time they reached the crest of the hill, the

helo was already setting down, rotors still spinning. Two pairs of hands helped Nick and Molly into the helo first, then the others scrambled in afterward. Molly, who had either been frightened silent or felt secure with "Unka Nick" had started crying with all the commotion.

"Shh, little one," he crooned. "I'm taking you home to Mommy and Daddy."

Despite all the activity and the noise, she hiccupped in mid cry and looked at him. "Mama?"

"Yes, sweetheart, Mama. And Daddy."

It amazed him when she plopped her thumb in her mouth and leaned her head against his chest.

As they lifted off, Jim Clayton took a small remote from his harness and depressed the button.

Boom!

The explosion from the charges they'd planted rocked the night air and lit up the sky. In seconds, most of Luis Aguilar's estancia was a pile of rubble. Dropo lifted a shoulder, positioned a missile launcher from the cabin of the helo on it, and as they pulled away fired the projectile. The last thing they saw was the conflagration consuming Aguilar's coca fields.

"Good riddance, asshole," he whispered, holding Molly tightly against his chest.

Then he took out his satellite phone and punched in a number. This was one call he was happy to make.

Chapter Twelve

Reno didn't know how long he sat in the chapel, praying to a God he'd long ago forgotten about and begging forgiveness, begging for Sarah's life, begging for Molly's safe return. Promising anything and everything, and meaning it. It was time to purge himself of the poison he'd been carrying around and hope he could build a life with the wife and child he now realized he loved more than anything.

He jerked when a hand touched his shoulder, and he looked up to see Tony standing there. His heart nearly stopped beating.

"Is Sarah— Did she— Is she—" He couldn't get the words out.

"She's okay. The nurse came in to tell you the surgery is over, and the doctor wants to talk to you."

Reno nearly knocked his brother over as he rose from his seat and raced for the door. He reached the waiting room just as Dr. Richards was exiting the surgery suite.

He smiled when he saw Reno. "I gather you were in the chapel. Always a good place to be when someone we love is in surgery."

"Is she— How is—" Again he couldn't get the words out.

"She came through the surgery just fine. Let's step out of the hallway here."

Reno did his best to curb his impatience as they

moved into an alcove away from hall traffic.

"Tell me everything," he demanded.

"The bullet entered just below the rib cage. It's a miracle it didn't damage any vital organs, although it did a lot of soft tissue damage. We were able to repair everything surgically and replace all the blood she lost, which was considerable."

"But she'll be all right," Reno persisted.

"Yes. She'll be fine." Dr. Richards smiled. "She has a long recovery ahead of her, but she's healthy and in good shape. That will help."

"When can I see her? Now?"

"Reno," Tony began.

"No, that's okay," Richards said. "I understand where he's coming from. She'll be in recovery for at least another hour. Then we'll transfer her to a room—"

"Private room," Reno interrupted

"Of course. The nurse will come and get you when she's ready."

"Why can't I see her now? Please. It's really important." If he didn't get to touch her pretty soon, he might pass out.

Dr. Richards studied him for a moment. "Are you the Reno Sullivan who owns Guardian Security?"

"I am. Why?"

"I believe your agency caught the people stealing drugs from the hospital and installed a new security system."

Reno nodded. "That's right."

"Okay. Give us ten minutes to get her settled, and I'll have someone come and get you."

Reno nearly fainted with relief. "Thank you, Doctor. Thank you so much."

"Come on." Tony nudged his elbow. "Let's get you some coffee while we're waiting."

"First tell me if you've heard from Nick yet."

"Only to let me know they'd arrived at the insertion point and were waiting until dark."

Reno looked out the window. "It's already dark, so why haven't we heard?" He didn't want to examine all the ugly possibilities. "I want to know the minute you hear from him."

"Of course."

"God. I hope that bastard hasn't hurt Molly." He would destroy the man with his bare hands if he had.

Tony tried to get him to sit down, but he couldn't stop pacing, burning off his impatience. It seemed forever before the nurse came to fetch him, although when he looked at his watch, he saw that barely fifteen minutes had passed.

"You must be someone pretty special," the nurse told him, leading him through a set of double doors. "I didn't think even God could get back here. Well, maybe God." She chuckled. "Okay, here you are."

She led him into a curtained cubicle, where Sarah lay on a hospital bed looking as white as the sheet. An IV bag was hooked on a stand next to her and several machines beeped and blinked around her.

"This is all just to monitor her vitals," the nurse explained. "She took quite a hit, but Dr. Richards is a miracle worked."

She pulled a chair in from against the outer wall and slid it next to the bed.

Reno dropped into it and took Sarah's free hand in both of his. And once again, tears dripped down his cheeks, but he didn't care. She was alive, and he'd spend the rest of his life telling her how much he loved her.

In another hour, they came to move Sarah to her private room, and Reno moved his vigil to another chair.

"Why hasn't she woken up?" he asked the nurse who came in to check her vitals.

"She was under pretty deep anesthesia, and they gave her a heavy dose of pain meds. She's still getting them. Give her a little time."

What if she never woke up?

In his mind, his treatment of Sarah and the shooting were all tied up in one tangled ball. If he lost her, he didn't know how he'd live with it.

He was sitting next to the bed, again holding her hand, barely aware of how dark it was outside, when Tony came into the room.

"You need to come out into the hallway with me for a minute."

Reno frowned. "Why? I can't leave Sarah."

"You can leave her for this." He showed Reno his cell phone. "They'd rather we didn't use it in the room. Come on."

"Molly?"

Tony grinned. "Stop talking and come out here with me."

As soon as they were outside the room, Tony pressed the button to kill Mute and handed the phone to Reno.

"Nick?"

"In the flesh." His partner laughed. "Someone here wants to say hello to you."

Reno heard him talking, then, "Dada? Dada, Dada,

Dada?"

Reno felt so weak in the knees, he was afraid he'd collapse. "Hey, Molly girl. Yes, it's Daddy. I can't wait to give you a big hug."

Then he heard a shuffling sound as Nick obviously retrieved the phone.

"She's fine," he assured Reno. "Not hurt at all. And kind of excited about her helicopter ride. You've got a long way to go to compete with this, buddy."

Reno's throat tightened. "I don't know how to thank you. I can't—"

"It's all good, Reno. We blew the shit out of Aguilar's compound and his coca fields."

"Bring her to the hospital as soon as you get back. I want to see her for myself."

"Will they allow it?" Nick asked.

"I'll make damn sure they do."

"Okay. Lindsey insists on giving her a bath and changing her clothes, and then we'll be along. It might be close to midnight. You sure you wouldn't rather we took her to the ranch so she could get a good night's sleep?"

"The hospital," he insisted.

"Okay. She's your kid."

"Yes, she is." And as he said it, a tremendous feeling of peace came over him.

He strong-armed the staff into bringing a crib into Sarah's room. He planned for Molly to get her sleep right there.

He had just sat down again when Sarah groaned and shifted slightly under her covers.

"Hurts," she moaned.

"I know it does, sweetheart. Let me get the nurse."

After taking Sarah's vitals again and checking her bandages, the nurse injected more medication into the IV drip.

"She can take a few ice chips," she told Reno. "Her throat's probably sore from the intubation." Then she looked at the crib. "Really?"

"Our daughter was kidnapped. I may never let her out of our sight again."

"Kidnapped. Damn! Then you call us if you need anything for her."

It was close to midnight when Lindsey and Nick arrived with Molly in Nick's arms. The little girl's eyelids drooped, and she was sucking hard on her thumb, nestled against Nick's shoulder.

Reno took her and, for the first time in almost a year, held his little girl. He was so overwhelmed with emotion, for a moment, he couldn't breathe. And when he kissed her cheek, he felt tears filling his eyes again.

As he was about to lay her in the crib and settle her for the night, he heard a soft moan. Turning, he saw Sarah open her eyes.

"Reno?" Her words were slurred from the medication.

"Right here, sweetheart." He moved close to the bed. "And look who I've got here."

Molly, who had been leaning against his shoulder sucking her thumb, perked up when she heard Sarah.

"Mama!" She leaned away from Reno, reaching toward Sarah.

"Mama doesn't feel so good, sugar. She can't hold you right now."

"Mama," Molly insisted.

Sarah reached the hand without the IV out to him.

"Let me just touch her. Please?"

Reno bent down so Sarah could close her fingers around Molly's little hand.

"Mama," the little girl said again. "My mama."

"Yes, sugar." Reno had to swallow against the lump in his throat. "It's your mama. And if you go to sleep, when you wake up, she'll be right here beside you."

The whole process was so foreign to him it took a few minutes to settle the little girl in the crib. Finally, she was down for the night, her little bottom up in the air, her thumb in her mouth.

Reno turned back to his wife—his wife!—and took her free hand in his.

"I love you, Sarah." Tears pricked his eyelids, and he had to stop and swallow against the lump in his throat. "I love you with all my heart. I'll never, ever let you down again. Just promise me you won't ever leave me."

"Molly?" she slurred.

"Molly, too. God, yes. I can't believe how much I missed with both of you because I was such an idiot. But that's done now." He took a breath. "I promise to love both of you forever."

He lifted her hand and kissed her fingers, noticing the tears sliding down her cheeks. He plucked a tissue from the box on the bedside table and carefully wiped her eyes and her cheeks.

"Love…you, too."

Her face was creased with pain, and he could see what a struggle it was for her to speak.

"As long as you love me, we can do anything. I promise you."

The nurse bustled in to give Sarah her pain meds, but Reno never moved, standing beside the bed, holding the hand of the woman he loved more than life itself. And right next to him the little girl he'd nearly lost through his own stupidity. He had a long way to go to deserve the two women in his life, but he was damn sure going to give it his best shot.

At last he pulled a chair between the bed and the crib and fell asleep, one hand on the crib rail, the other holding Sarah's hand.

****

Sarah was in the hospital for another two weeks. Lindsey and Nicki shared babysitting duties during the day, but Reno insisted they bring the little girl to the hospital to sleep near her mother at night. For himself, he told Nick he'd be at the office whenever they saw him, and he didn't know just yet when that would be. Over those two weeks, the three of them bonded in a way that hadn't existed before. By the time Sarah was discharged, the family unit was coming along nicely.

Agent Balenger stopped by, bringing flowers for Sarah and thanking Reno and Nick for doing what they did.

"And what would that be?" Nick asked, all innocence, knowing Balenger couldn't acknowledge any of it.

"Nothing I can discuss," Balenger joked.

Finally, Reno was able to bring Sarah home. He'd had the cleaning crew come in and clean everything from top to bottom. He'd even thrown out all the sheets and had Lindsey buy new ones.

"Kind of an out with the old?" she'd teased.

He nodded. "And anything else you think needs

replacing."

"Why don't we leave that to Sarah when she's feeling better?"

"Of course." He smacked his head. "Good idea."

****

Sarah had been home for three weeks, healing nicely and enjoying the miracle of being a real family with Reno and Molly. She was able to do more things each day, although Reno watched her as if she might break. Nicki came afternoons to help her, and Reno became more and more involved in Molly's care. Sarah's heart turned over to see the two of them together.

If there was one fly in the ointment, it showed up when Kip Balenger stopped by and dropped a little bombshell.

"You know Marina Aguilar isn't going to let this go. Word is she's out for blood to avenge the death of her father."

"Marina's a loose cannon," Reno reminded him. "She could just as easily shoot herself by mistake."

"Don't kid yourself. She's out for your blood. We'll keep or eyes and ears open and do our best to keep you in the loop. But trust me. This isn't over yet."

Sarah could tell that something else was brewing in Reno's mind, too. Something that for, whatever reason, made her edgy. They had yet to get to the reason for his outbreak Thanksgiving night, everything that followed and everything that had led up to it. She was on pins and needles about it and swallowed a sigh of relief when he finally broached the subject.

He caught her after she put Molly to bed one night. "Come sit with me in the den and have a glass of wine."

"Okay. What's up? You've been edgy all day."

He heaved a sigh. "I think it's about time I stopped running from my past."

A knot began to form in her stomach. "I was hoping we'd get to that sooner rather than later. But things have been so good these past few weeks, I didn't want to rock the boat."

"It's time." He handed her a filled wine glass and raised his own. "A toast. To the most magnificent woman in the world. And a prayer that you'll have some understanding of what I'm going to tell you."

"Why don't you sit down?"

"I think I'll stand for the moment. I can talk to you better this way. I want to get this all out right now before I lose my nerve." He looked hard at her face, as if searching for some indication of her mood. "Sarah, I'm so sorry about Thanksgiving. There's no justification for any of the things I said or did. You deserve much better than that."

"Yes, I do." She caught her lower lip between her teeth but still sat there calmly.

Reno raked his fingers though his hair. "I've been so terrified of losing you. The things I said that night? I wanted to take them back the minute they were out of my mouth, make them go away, but you were already up the stairs. I felt worse when I finally admitted to myself how I feel about you, but I didn't know how to fix things."

"So you decided to get drunk instead." She said the words flatly, watching him.

"No. I was just trying to blunt the pain and find some answers. By the time I realized they weren't in the bottle, I was already wasted."

"Why didn't you let me know how you felt?" she asked. "What did you think would happen? That I'd run away?" She fiddled with her wine glass. "Surely you had to sense I had feelings for you, too."

"Truthfully? I was afraid."

She stared at him. "Afraid of what?"

"Of my own life, I think." He took a healthy sip of wine. "And in the end, afraid of what you'd say if I came to you sober and gave you the whole story."

"What story?" she cried. "What is it that's so hard for you to get out? The real issue here, whether you want to see it or not, isn't what happened the other night. The root of the problem is Molly. Everything leads back to her. These past weeks you've been wonderful with her and we've been bonding as a family. You told me in the hospital you love me. Love her. Is that a lie? If you can't tell me the truth of what's behind everything, it's all going to fall apart."

"You're right." He drew another deep breath, as if sucking courage from the air. How could he tell her he was so afraid of what she'd think of him? They had just found their footing as husband and wife, as a family. If he lost it all, he didn't know how he'd handle it.

"Trust our love," she told him. "Trust what we are finally building here. I don't care how awful you think it is, we'll get past it. You know why? Because I know the man you really are, the one you don't even recognize. The man who owns my heart. So let's hear it. No more evading the issue."

Help me, God. Don't let me make a mistake here.

"I need to tell you things you should have known from the beginning. I was just so sure if I did, you'd turn me down. Then what would I do?" He sucked in a breath. "This is an ugly story that doesn't make me look so good, but you deserve to know it all. Then I guess the rest is up to you."

He shoved his hands in his pockets, and with his head bowed, told her a tale that, by turns, shocked and saddened her. In short sentences, he told her about the death of his parents when he was still in college, his fight to hang on to Tony who was four years younger. The decision he and Nick made to open their own company.

"Nick and I spent fourteen years building Guardian Security into what it is now. I made it my entire life." He shook his head. "Nick put a failed marriage behind him and moved forward. Now Nick has Lindsey and a child, with another on the way. I was connected only to my work, avoiding all but the most casual relationships."

"I knew you were a workaholic when you hired me," she told him. "It only took me two weeks to figure that out."

"Then, two years ago, I took my first vacation ever. If you recall, Nick threatened to lock me out of the office unless I did."

"I do."

"Maybe the tropics weren't such a good idea," he went on. "Beautiful scenery, warm nights, sensual music, and drinks that can knock you on your ass. And there was Maggie—voluptuous, exotic, and predatory. She'd apparently targeted me that first night. I didn't know which went to my head more, her expressed desire for me or the potent drink I kept slugging down."

"Women like Maggie troll for men like you," Sarah pointed out. "The fact you succumbed to her takes nothing away from who you are."

He gave a short little laugh. "Yeah. Go figure a sharp guy like me would get taken, right?"

"You're a smart man with a national reputation. You learned everything you could. You just forgot to study women."

"I had another problem," he went on. "The reason I seldom drink. I have an inability to properly metabolize alcohol. That's why the most I ever have is a glass or two of wine."

He stopped, as if gathering his thoughts.

"But there you were," Sarah said in a soft voice, "thousands of miles from home where no one could see if you made a fool of yourself."

"And a week of the basest kind of lust where I never remembered one sober minute. But I do remember my haste to get away from her when I finally stopped drinking."

"But the baby…" God, what a thing to smack him in the face.

"No one was more shocked than I when she called me with the news. Even drunk, I'd been careful to use condoms. She reminded me they sometimes don't work. Apparently, this was one of those times." He rubbed his forehead, as if trying to erase memories. "I offered her a lot of options, but the only thing she wanted was marriage. Made me realize how much I wanted a child, even if I had to take her with it."

"But you were so distant from Molly," she pointed out, still not understanding. "It wasn't until she was kidnapped—"

"I know." He held his hand up. "Let me go on here. I was able to keep Maggie off the booze while she was pregnant. I was frightened to death of fetal alcohol syndrome. But the baby wasn't a week old before she was binging again."

"And what about Molly?" She had to know how he'd felt when the baby was born. He'd said he wanted her and loved her, so what had happened? How much worse had the nightmare gotten? "What about when she was born?"

"That little baby captured my heart right away. She was healthy and happy and so damn sweet. A miracle." He rubbed his forehead. "The moment I held her in my arms, I knew she'd made it all worthwhile. She gave my life new purpose. Then Maggie destroyed it all."

Sarah wanted to get up, to go to him, and put her arms around him, but she forced herself to sit still, even as her heart was breaking for him. She knew what came next was bad, and she steeled herself to hear it.

"We had a knock down drag out one night about her drinking. She was already half in the bag when I got home and found the babysitter caring for Molly. I told her this was her last chance to sober up or I was filing for divorce. And I'd make sure she didn't get a nickel from me. She knew I could do it, too."

Sarah bit her tongue to keep from saying anything and clasped her hands tightly in her lap.

"She said she'd get her revenge, because I'd be raising another man's child."

Even as he said the words, shock ran through Sarah like an electric charge. Molly wasn't his? What a cruel joke to play on him.

"She said she actually got pregnant when she went back to New York, but the guy didn't have a dime to his name. She wanted the rich prize with the big bucks." He snarled the words. "And she said it just like that." He stopped pacing and looked down at his feet, as if ashamed of his next words. "Since then, I've hardly been able to look at Molly without being reminded of how I'd gotten myself in this position and how I'd been trapped and betrayed." He lifted his head and looked at her, pain vivid in his eyes. "I know, I know. It isn't her fault. But still, when I looked at her, all I saw was Maggie's bitter face."

Sarah sat rooted to her seat, stunned. She didn't know what she'd expected to hear, but it wasn't this awful tale of greed, deception, and betrayal. How could a woman be so uncaring with the lives of a wonderful man and a beautiful child?

"I acted like a fool," he rasped. "Something I try not to do very often, you know. Just—" He shrugged. "It happened. I was drunk, and thought I was the one taking advantage of her." He began pacing again. "I don't think Maggie and I even liked each other. What we had was lust of the basest kind. She knew how to punch my buttons and get whatever she wanted. I let her do it. You can't be any more disgusted with me than I am with myself. I deserved what I got."

So here it was at last.

She'd known it had to be something this bad to make him behave the way he had. She'd worked with this man for five years and been married to him for eight months. She knew him underneath it all—a good, decent person whose only failing was to be human. So much was clear to her now.

"I know you must hate me for the way I've treated the child." He shook his head. "It was very painful admitting to myself that a big part of this was my

195

pride." He took the poker and stirred the logs in the fireplace, obviously giving himself something to do. "Please try to understand. I only married Maggie because she said she was pregnant with my child. And I wanted that child. When Maggie told me the baby wasn't even mine, I was destroyed. I'd gone through the marriage from hell for nothing."

Sarah thought of Molly, the unknowing center of the turmoil, a constant reminder of everything. Her throat tightened with emotion.

"Sarah?"

She heard the edge of fear in his voice as he waited for her to break her silence. "That's why you'd never let me into your bedroom, isn't it? Because Maggie slept in there with you."

He nodded. "I didn't want you touched by her filth."

"And why there are no pictures anywhere in the house."

"Yes."

"I thought it was because you loved her so much you couldn't bear to be reminded of her," she whispered. "I thought you wanted a contract marriage because you were never going to get over the death of your wife."

"God, no." A harsh laugh escaped his lips. "That's so far from the truth it's not even on the same planet." He rubbed his forehead again. "When I asked you to marry me, I didn't realize what a selfish thing I was doing. I was concerned with my needs, not yours. I don't know how you've put up with everything. You've been far more than I could have expected."

"What did you expect?" she asked, her voice soft.

"Not nearly what I got." His eyes searched her face again. "And I certainly didn't expect to fall in love with you. Maybe Nick and Tony are right, and I've been in love with you since the day I hired you. My feelings for you kept growing stronger. It got to the point where I could hardly be near you without getting hard."

"But then you ran away," she said.

"Because I knew what a jackass I've been. Everything got so mixed up. I reacted without thinking. So, jerk that I am, I went off and got drunk. And the rest, as they say, is history."

"How do you feel now?" Her voice was so soft he almost didn't hear her.

"Everything that's happened in the past few weeks was a real wakeup call for me. I realized what I had and was on the verge of losing." He looked at her with everything he felt in his eyes. "Sarah, I want this to be a real marriage, if you'll just give me the chance. I want a life with you more than I've ever wanted anything. I love you so much I can't see straight. I've been terrified that I'd chased you away." His voice was agonized. "We've had a fresh start here. Can we put all of this behind us and move forward?"

"And Molly? None of this is her fault. What about her?"

"Yes, what about her." A look of intense sadness crossed his face. "You're right. She's the innocent in all this. The way I've treated her, I think, is the greatest crime of all. I never realized it more than when Aguilar kidnapped her."

"You've loved being Daddy these past weeks."

He grinned. "I sure have." The grin disappeared. "And being your husband. Can I be a real husband to you, too, Sarah?"

"I think we've certainly made a good start in that direction. But let me ask you a question. Didn't you have a DNA test? That would have been proof."

A muscle jumped in his cheek. "Of course. Nick insisted. The results weren't good. But I'll try to get past that. Sarah can you forgive me for the rotten way I've behaved and build a family with me. Take what we've started and nurture it?"

The next move was up to her. There were still problems, all right, but she saw with sudden clarity how empty her life would be if she turned him away. Once she admitted this to herself, the rest was easy.

Rising from the couch, she put down her wine glass and walked to where he stood.

"Sarah?" He raised his eyes to hers, and the fear of what she might say was written in them. When she lifted her arms, he pulled her into an embrace. "I love you," he murmured. "So much. Please believe me."

"I do. After everything that's happened, I know you wouldn't say it if you didn't mean it."

"You have no idea how much I want to make love to you, but I'm afraid of hurting you."

"Well," she drawled, "at the last visit the doctor pretty much gave me a clean bill of health. He did say no skiing or snowboarding or running marathons, however," she joked. "So what do you say we give it a try?"

"I say yes."

He swept her up in his arms and carried her upstairs. They had been sharing her room, sleeping together yet keeping physical contact to a limited embrace. He'd told her he didn't think he'd ever be able to get away from the bad memories of his own room. She had been content with him holding her through the night, but now she was ready for so much more.

He stood her beside the bed and spent a long moment looking into her eyes. "God. I can't believe how close I came to losing you."

His kiss began so gently but soon turned demanding, filled with desperation. His lips were soft yet bruising. He thrust his tongue into her mouth, plundering it, devouring it, tasting every inch.

Sarah slid her tongue against his, returning movement for movement. His taste was heady, intoxicating, flavored with the bite of the wine. The kiss went on and on until she couldn't breathe.

When they finally broke apart, he lifted his head and looked at her, studying her eyes. She could tell he saw something that made him relax just the slightest bit. He took off his jacket and tossed it on the couch, rolling back the sleeves of his shirt.

"Tonight, I'm totally sober, and I plan to remember every minute of what happens."

He took his time undressing her, removing each piece slowly and peppering her skin with kisses. Closing his mouth over a nipple, he sucked it, then scraped his teeth over it before turning his attention to the other one.

He paused when he came to the scar, still an angry red slashing across her midriff.

"Don't be upset," she told him. "It's my battle scar. And I see what happened as the catalyst for everything good that's happening now."

When she was completely nude, trembling slightly under his intense gaze, he kissed the rest of her—hips, thighs, her mound. He jerked back the covers on the bed as if his control had frayed and placed her carefully on the sheet. His gaze never left her as he took off his own clothes.

Sarah was transfixed by his nudity. He reminded her of some primitive god, ready for the mating ritual. His cock stood out from his body, the root settled in a thick nest of dark hair, his sac lying heavy against his thighs.

Just like in my dream.

She wet her lips, captivated by the sight of him in the flesh, and pressed her hands against his warm skin. He was so hard and muscular, his chest matted with a thick carpet of dark curls begging for her fingers to touch them. A soft line of down trailed along his abdomen and down into his groin. When she touched his thick shaft, it was more enormous in real life than in her dream, so large it mesmerized her.

"Reno." Sudden shyness and uncertainty intruded on the wave of desire sweeping through her.

"I know." He leaned down and brushed his lips across her forehead. "It's all right, Sarah."

Then he was beside her on the bed, kissing her again. He bent his head to hers again, slanting his mouth to capture her lips. When he slipped his tongue into her mouth, she welcomed the taste of him, reveling in the texture of his tongue and its demanding thrusts. He tasted wonderfully of mint toothpaste and the smoky Merlot, reminding her of that first kiss they'd shared.

With a touch that felt almost reverent, he skimmed her with his fingertips, running his hands over her breasts, her waist, her flat stomach, and the curve of her buttocks. He caressed her breasts, teasing her nipples, trailing his fingers down her body to reach the lips of her pussy.

Every place he touched ignited another lick of flame.

"No other woman has ever affected me this way." His voice was hoarse and not quite steady. "You reach into my very soul. I want you, every bit of you, every way I can have you, and I never want to stop."

Sarah circled his erection with her fingers, but he grabbed her hand.

"Not yet. This is for you, darlin'. Just for you."

He let his hand drift lower until he reached the soft feel of her curls. Placing his palm over her mound, he slid his finger between the folds of her pussy, seeking her opening. With a feathery touch, he stroked up and down her slit in a gliding motion, touching only the outer lips.

With a soft moan, she opened her legs to him. He slid one finger into her hot sheath, then another, seeking her center.

"You're already wet for me," he said, desire thick in his voice.

"I know."

Her pulse raced, every nerve firing. Her body, frozen in cold storage for so long, thawed and warmed in the heat of their passion. The touch of his body next to hers was as electric as a live wire. She could feel the definition of his hard muscles, the sweet roughness of the hair on his chest, the silkiness of his hair when he bent his head to her.

Slowly, almost lazily, Reno stroked in and out of her cunt, watching her through slitted eyes. Her eyes became heavy with passion, her breathing ragged. He moved his thumb up to find that sensitive nub and circled it teasingly. She caught her breath and began to move her hips, urging him to enter her deeper, but he held back.

"Tonight when you come," he said in a low voice, "I want it to be the most shattering climax you've ever had. Don't deny me that."

He curled his fingers, finding the hot spot, and she thrust hard against his hand. When the first little flutters began, he withdrew altogether.

"Oh, god, Reno, don't stop now. Please." Her blood felt like liquid fire, and her skin felt too tight. "Make me come."

"I will, sweetheart, but not yet. Definitely not yet."

He slid down her body until he was lying between her legs. Grasping her thighs, he placed them over his shoulders. When she was wide open and vulnerable, he thrust his tongue inside her. She went wild, bucking against his mouth. He teased her with his tongue, with his teeth, with his hands, all the time holding her in such a way as to give him full access to her pussy.

Sarah couldn't stop moving. Her labia and her inner sheath felt hot and swollen, with so many nerve endings sparking, she didn't know why she wasn't burning alive. He was controlling her now, building her tension. Every time she reached the edge, he brought her down a little, keeping her in a constant state of arousal, drawing it out as much as he could.

She felt sensations gripping her body, quivering as he skillfully used his mouth, his tongue, and his long, gentle fingers. This was beyond anything she had ever felt before, the tension so prolonged she didn't think she could stand it. She was wild with hunger for him, wanting to feel the fullness of him inside her. He made love to every inch of her, and she responded with wantonness, a glorious sense of abandonment she'd never thought herself capable of.

"Please, please, please," she begged. It wasn't his fingers she wanted to feel or his mouth. It wasn't enough. She wanted—no, needed—to feel him inside her, filling her.

"I don't want to hurt you," he said again.

"Then be gentle," she teased, "but don't make me wait."

"Okay, darlin'. One minute here. Let me just get a condom."

But when he started to rise from the bed, she held him back. "No. Don't use anything. The chance of me getting pregnant are slim to none, but if we can make it happen, I want it." She wanted to give him this so much.

Reno stared at Sarah for a long moment, his eyes filled with a swirl of emotions. Then he nodded.

Slowly, slowly, he eased into her, pulling her toward him so her hips slanted, giving him greater access, allowing her to take him deeper. There. Now. Oh, God, he was all the way in, and the feeling was beyond anything she'd experienced.

The friction of his cock against her inner walls set off more spasms. With every movement she knew he was claiming her, making her his. She was on fire, pulses throbbing, blood rushing hotly through her veins. Sex had never been like this before. Ever. Not even with Mike. The need in her rose up and up, spiraling like an unwinding coil.

She was there...almost there...almost... Now!

He thrust hard once, twice, three times and, with a hoarse cry, carried them both over the edge. Their bodies shook with the crushing intensity of the orgasm. Spasms gripped them until she was sure they would break into a million pieces.

By the time the orgasm subsided, leaving only tiny aftershocks, they were both limp and boneless, completely spent, utterly sated. This…*this*…was the cataclysmic joining she'd dreamed about. *This* was completion beyond anything she could have imagined. *This* was the wild ride down the mountain she'd dreamed about, only it was better than any of her dreams.

She closed her eyes, letting the myriad of sensations wash over her.

And prayed it could always be like this.

Chapter Thirteen

Every muscle in Reno's body felt as if it had been stretched to its extreme then released. All the strength had been drained from him. It was almost too much for him to realize.

In all the years of his sexual experience, he had never experienced this. His body had just exploded with his release, shaking him with its intensity. The wet fist of Sarah's delicious cunt had gripped him and hadn't released him until the last vibration died away. None of Reno's vast sexual experience had prepared him for the way this reached his very soul.

In that moment, he realized there was no uncertainty on his part, no question about his emotions. He truly loved this woman. He just prayed he could always be what she needed.

When he could move, he tried to shift his weight to give her breathing room, but she kept her arms wrapped around him, holding him.

"I must be too heavy for you." His breathing was choppy and uneven, and his heart beat loudly against his ribs.

"No. Stay. Don't move."

He rained soft kisses on her cheeks, her eyelids, her forehead, the tip of her nose. "Was it all right for you?" he asked, his lips against her ear. "I'm a little out of practice."

"I don't think I could stand it any better." She bit her lip. "I worried that I wouldn't satisfy you, that I wouldn't be…experienced…enough for you. Wouldn't know enough."

"You can believe this or not," he said, "but nothing I've ever done before was even close to the feeling I had when we came together." He brushed the damp tendrils of curls away from her face. "Sex doesn't have to be sophisticated to be wonderful, darlin'. I'll teach you anything you want, but believe me, I don't think we can improve on this."

"Yes, I want you to," she whispered. "I want to know everything you like, all the things that make you feel good. I want to be able to give you as much pleasure as you gave me." She lowered her gaze, a delicate blush creeping up her cheeks. "I have to confess something."

He frowned. "What? I thought we were through with confessions for the night."

She refused to look up at him. "I-I've been having dreams. About you."

"Dreams?" He tried to keep his voice even wondering if she, too…

"Yes. Erotic dreams." She turned her head away. "About you and me."

Reno took a deep breath, reaching for control. Was this possible? Had they both been having the same dreams, night after night? God, how many times had he fucked her in his mind? Tasted of her essence, taken her into his mouth?

"I shouldn't have told you," she said when he didn't speak.

"No. I mean, yes, you should." He rolled to the

side, taking her with him. He brushed her hair back from her face. "You definitely should have told me, because the same thing has been happening to me. I've been having my own dreams."

Her eyes flew open, and she looked straight at him, an erotic thrill racing through him. "It has? You did? About us?"

"Yes." He smiled. "Almost every night since we made this stupid bargain."

"Why didn't you ever say anything?" she asked.

He brushed his lips across hers, their mouths touching as he spoke. "Why didn't you?"

But he knew the answers to both questions, and the knowledge brought him a fresh wave of self-loathing. Deliberately, he banished those thoughts. Tonight was a new beginning, and he wasn't going to drag the past into it.

"Tell me what you dreamed about," he urged. "About us. Don't be embarrassed," he said when a dark blush colored her skin again. "I want you to be able to say anything to me."

"I don't know if I can." She caught her bottom lip in her teeth.

"Did I do this?" One hand kneaded her breast gently, thumb rasping over the nipple.

"Yes," she whispered.

"And this?" He took the nipple into his mouth, raking his teeth over it and pressing it hard against the roof of his mouth. Her body tensed beneath him, and she arched up into his mouth.

"Yes," she murmured again, her voice thickening.

"And this?" He moved down her body to run his tongue over the soft skin just above her mound.

"Yes, yes, yes." She moaned and twisted beneath him.

He paused, studying her. "Please tell me I didn't hurt you. That I'm *not* hurting you."

"I'm fine." She smiled. "More than fine."

He eased two fingers inside her, curling them to hit that sweet spot. She bucked as he moved them in and out, adding a third and stretching her to the fullest. He felt the tiny quivers begin in her pussy and increased the tempo of his strokes. When her orgasm broke through her, he held her in place, feeling the tremors as her inner walls spasmed around his fingers.

When the last aftershock died away, he shifted so he was looking directly into her eyes. "Good?"

"Better than I imagined."

He nipped at her earlobe. "Me, too. But oh, god, Sarah, I have to be inside you again. Right now."

Positioning himself, he entered her again with one slow stroke, pausing only to give her time to adjust. This time there was no foreplay, no drawing things out, but it was just as cataclysmic. At last, they collapsed, spent, hearts thudding, breath rasping, a fine sheen of perspiration coating their bodies. The heady aroma of musk mingled with Sarah's perfume and his aftershave, filling the room with the carnal scent of sex.

"Are you all right?" He stroked the scar with a gentle touch. "I'm so afraid of pushing you too hard."

"I'm fine. I promise to let you know if I'm not."

"We may not live to see Christmas at this rate," Reno joked, then he tightened his arms around her. "It's a wonder we haven't killed each other tonight with all that pent-up sexual energy."

She turned a deep pink, and Reno laughed again.

"I don't think I've ever seen anyone blush all over before." He caught her hand. "You're beautiful naked, Sarah. Don't cover yourself, okay? I want to look at you and be able to touch you whenever I want to."

She nibbled on her bottom lip again then nodded. Her eyes dropped to his cock, still large and heavy even at rest.

As if he could read her mind, he said, "Yes, you took it all. Every bit."

She blushed again.

"I should get the wine to celebrate, but I think that's beyond my energy level right now."

"We don't need wine. This was better than a drink."

"I wanted to drink to the future," he told her. "To us."

He buried his face in her neck. "God, Sarah. When you were shot and Molly was taken, I died a thousand times. The thought of life without the two of you was so bleak I couldn't even contemplate it."

"Then isn't it nice we've been given this second chance, and you don't have to."

"Yes, it is." He tucked her up against him and pulled the covers up.

"Don't you think it's strange," she asked, "that we've both had such…erotic dreams about each other?"

"I think someone was trying to send us a message. And I think that's why everything tonight has been so explosive. It's been building all this time."

"I just hope we don't kill ourselves," she teased.

****

When morning arrived, they were still wrapped around each other, naked bodies pressed together. And despite Reno's morning woody, it was more emotion than passion.

"I think I could use a long, leisurely bath," Sarah told Reno.

"Why don't you take one? Then I'll take you and Molly out to breakfast. It's Sunday, and we have the whole weekend to do as we please."

"Mmm. That sounds good." She pressed herself against him.

He stroked her back and arm with a gentle glide of his fingers. "Do you think we made a baby last night?"

She tensed, and he looked down at her. "Sarah? Is that a problem? I thought—"

She searched for the right words. "There's something I probably should have told you before, but the terms of our *bargain* made it irrelevant." She bit her lip. "I was sure it wouldn't matter so I just kept it to myself."

"What is it, Sarah?" Suddenly, he was the voice of concern, shifting so he could reach out his hand and touch her. "What didn't you think you needed to tell me? Are you sick? Is it something we can take care of?"

She shook her head, then dropped her gaze. "Not sick. No." Her sigh was heavy enough to split the thick silence. "After my miscarriage, when Mike was killed, the doctors told me I'd probably never conceive another child." She raised her eyes to look at him again. "Molly may be the only one we'll ever share. That's why this is so important to me. Why I wanted us so desperately to be a family."

He pulled her into his arms, holding her against his body. "I am so sorry. No wonder you thought I was such a heartless bastard where Molly was concerned."

"When Aguilar took her that day—" She shook her head. "I don't even want to think about it."

"Then don't. It's over and we move forward."

"If by some miracle we make a baby, I don't want Molly to be relegated to second place."

"That's not going to happen."

"You say that now, and I know how you've been with her since the hospital, but…" She bit her lip. "What if you have flashbacks about Maggie and that awful scene?"

"I promise I won't close up, okay? I'll tell you, and we'll deal with it."

"I can't ask for more than that."

"I held that child every day for two weeks when she was born," he said, his eyes staring at a point beyond her. "I rocked her in my arms and felt her tiny heart beating against mine. She was my child, my flesh. Then, in seconds, I found out what a cruel joke it all was." His face twisted in pain. "Now I hate myself for all I missed out on. And all that Molly missed."

"This is a new beginning for all of us. Including Molly."

He hugged her, then grinned. "You may have to give me regular treatments to keep me in line, though."

At that moment, they heard Molly calling out her usual babbling from the nursery.

Sarah gave a mock groan. "I guess Mommy and Daddy time is over. She needs to be changed and fed."

"I'll do it. I'm getting real good at this. You take your bath."

She wasn't about to turn down that offer.

The soothing bath did much for her sore and aching

body. She leaned back and let the scented foaming water drift over her as images of the night just past kept floating at the edge of her consciousness. Her body began to tingle just from the memories, and she lay there for a long while with a smile on her face.

Dried and sprayed with her favorite perfume, she dressed in a new sweater and a pair of tight, chocolate, suede jeans she'd bought in a moment of frivolous impulse. They clung to her hips and accentuated her legs. The outfit was so different from her usual dull, functional wardrobe. She put on what she thought of as her wedding earrings and brushed her hair out until it fell in thick, shimmering waves.

In the mirror, she saw an unfamiliar image, a woman full of life and exhilaration. Her eyes sparkled, and she glowed with passion and joy.

"You're so beautiful. You take my breath away."

She looked up. Reno stood in the doorway, clad in chinos and a bright blue sweater that stretched over his powerful muscles and accentuated his dark hair and features. She saw such emotion in his eyes that her heart turned over. She went to him and wrapped her arms around him. "You make me beautiful."

"You should dress this way all the time," he told her. "Except other women would most likely object. They'd pale into insignificance."

She laughed, not used to that kind of compliment. "I'm going to call Lindsey and see if it's okay to drop by. They might have plans."

But Lindsey was thrilled they were coming out and insisted they stay for dinner. "Come on out. We're excited to see you guys."

Chapter Fourteen

The day was one of Texas' glorious winter gifts, the sun blazing yellow, the sky a heavenly blue. To Sarah and Reno everything seemed newly washed, the way their lives had suddenly become. The air had a fresh scent to it, and even the birds seemed to be singing just for them.

When they pulled up at the ranch, Sarah got out of the car and Reno came around to her side, pulling her body to his. He leaned down and kissed her with such thoroughness her knees were weak. He had held back for so long. Now the dam had broken, and he couldn't keep his hands away from her.

"Careful," she told him, "or we night find ourselves naked in the dirt right here."

He chuckled. "At least, it will give those idiots peering out the window something to look at."

Sarah looked over his shoulder to see Lindsey racing toward them from the house, followed more slowly by Nick and Tony.

"I'll get Molly," Reno told her.

"Sarah, it's so good to see you out and looking so great." Tony winked at her. "My brother's lucky he got to you first, or I'd give him a run for his money."

"Well, she's taken," Reno told him, even as he smiled.

Lindsey hugged Sarah. "You look absolutely

amazing. As if you're a whole new person."

"I feel like it," Sarah said, laughing.

"And you're recovered from your surgery?"

Sarah nodded. "The doctor said I heal fast. I'm glad, because I want us to put that whole nightmare behind us."

Lindsey looked over her shoulder to where Reno was holding and cuddling Molly.

"But something good came out of it," she reminded Sarah.

"A lot of good." She lowered her voice. "He told me about Maggie last night."

Lindsey's eyes widened. "Good for him." She hugged Sarah. "I see all good things ahead for the two of you."

"Me, too."

"For the first time in what seems like forever, he's relaxed and at ease. He's actually smiling."

Reno shook hands with both men. Nobody said anything, but the emotion that passed among them all was almost tangible.

"I think Molly's about ready for her nap. Is the other crib still set up?"

"It is. Let's get her upstairs. Jason's already napping. We'll have a few hours to act like adults."

The afternoon was tranquil. That was the only word for it. They watched football games, Sarah and Reno next to each other on the couch so close not even a sheet of paper would fit between them. He held her hand most of the time, the rough texture of the warm skin feeling good against her palm. Even when they ate, he found excuses to touch her in some small way.

When it was time to leave, Sarah got Molly ready.

She smiled as Reno, without prodding, put the baby seat in the car and took Molly's things from Mary. She loved seeing the two of them together. If they never had a biological child of their own Molly would be plenty for them.

The little girl dozed on the ride home and barely woke when Sarah took her in the house. When Sarah came into her room after settling Molly in her crib, Reno was stretched out on her bed, stark naked, hands behind his head and a lazy grin on his face.

"We should think about redecorating the room," Sarah told him, dragging her eyes away from his swollen, waiting cock. "Something that would personalize it and make it truly ours. New colors, new furniture." She tilted her head. "Does that appeal to you?"

The look in his eyes told her he was only interested in one thing. "Sounds interesting. We'll talk about it in the morning. Tonight, you'll have to be satisfied with just me." He reached out a hand to her. "Come to me, Sarah."

She drew her sweater over her head, tossing it to the side, then shimmied out of her jeans. After the previous night, she found herself surprisingly unselfconscious undressing in front of him.

"You take my breath away," he told her as she joined him on the bed.

"Same goes."

They made love as if they'd been doing this forever, knowing the secrets places on their bodies and how to move just so.

"I hope we get ourselves under some kind of control soon," he muttered when they lay back, spent.

"Otherwise we're going to die from happiness."

Sarah laughed, a warm, bubbling sound. "They say that's the best way to go."

He rolled onto his side and tucked her up against him, pulling the covers over them both. "I love the feel of you in my arms," he told her. "Sleep, baby. We'll have good dreams."

****

When Sarah brought Molly downstairs the next morning to feed her, she found Reno already in the kitchen. She was grateful to see he'd brewed a pot of coffee and poured a cup for each of them. He leaned against the counter, drinking his while he watched her feed Molly.

He wasn't dressed in a suit today, even though it was Monday. He'd pulled on gray slacks and a red V-neck sweater. Casual clothes. While she finished with Molly, he called Angela, his new secretary, to tell her he'd be out for the day. Sarah wondered what that was all about.

"You don't have to stay home today," she told him. "We'll be okay."

"Much as I hate to admit it," he said grinning, "I think they'll get along at Guardian without me. I just hope they don't find out."

Sarah settled Molly in her playpen with her favorite toys and turned on the mobile attached to one side. That would keep her occupied while she fixed breakfast for herself and Reno. She could feel his eyes on her as she moved around the kitchen.

They were some time getting through breakfast, because it turned into a sensual exercise. Sarah made scrambled eggs and sausage, and Reno insisted on feeding her the sausage by hand. As he placed each spicy piece on her tongue, she sucked at his fingertips, touching the edges with her tongue. That made him lean over and trace her lips, licking the taste of the sausage from them. He fed her the eggs one forkful at a time, first himself, then her, his tongue tracing her lips after each taste. When he thrust his tongue into her mouth, she sucked on that, too, loving the mingled taste of coffee and Reno.

Cleaning up became even more of a challenge. She stood at the counter in her nightgown while Reno cleared the table. With each delivery she felt his hot erection probing at her buttocks. She had barely gotten the last dish in the dishwasher before he swept her up in his arms and carried her upstairs.

Pulling the covers back with one hand, he deposited her on the bed, pulled her gown over her head, stepped out of his sweat pants, then mounted her. She was wet, as she always seemed to be when he touched her. In two days, she had gone from ice maiden to wanton, carnal need consuming her so strongly she couldn't shut it off.

His mouth took hers in a hungry, greedy kiss, his tongue dueling with hers, her own twisting against his. He licked the roof of her mouth and the inside of her cheeks, each stroke of his tongue sending sensations straight to the heart of her pussy. She threaded her fingers through the heavy silk of Reno's hair, pulling his head even closer to her.

His hands slid down her body to find her nipples, pinching and rolling them until they stood up in hard, stiff peaks. Her heart raced and her pulse throbbed as her body responded to his touch. He shifted his body back and forth so his cock rubbed against her clitoris, driving her need higher than she'd thought possible.

She slid her hands around to find his flat nipples, pinching them as he had hers and scraping her fingernails over them. Reno lifted his head, the rhythm of his breathing changing and becoming uneven.

"I want you now," he rasped.

She opened her legs as he moved into position. They were both so ready, when he slid his cock inside her, she took the entire length of him in one stroke. They lay still for a moment, savoring the feel of her slick inner muscles grasping at his shaft. Then the room was silent except for the sound of skin against skin, heavy panting, and their mingled shouts of joy as their climax crashed through them.

Reno collapsed against her, catching his weight on his forearms as they struggled to drag air into their oxygen-depleted lungs and calm their galloping hearts.

"That was…incredible," Sarah said in a weak voice when she could speak again.

Reno kissed her softly. "Every time with you is incredible."

"Did we save enough energy to transfer all your clothes to my room?" she asked. "That's on our agenda for this morning. Remember?"

"I don't think I could move my body, much less my clothes." Reno chuckled, but he slid off the bed and pulled his pants back on. "All right, woman. I'm up and on my feet. Let's get busy."

When they were finished moving his clothes and personal belongings from one room to the other, Sarah surveyed the results with great satisfaction. To her, the sight of their things mingled together was an affirmation of the pledge they had made to each other and the night before.

"Pretty pleased with yourself, aren't you?" Reno wrapped his arms around her from behind and tucked her head under his chin.

"You bet. Now I feel as if we're married."

"Oh, we're married all right," he told her in his deep voice. "Trust me. There's no doubt about that."

"Don't forget, I want us to think about making some major changes in here."

"We will. We'll do something. But I have other things on my mind at the moment." He stood for a long moment, looking at the closet again, scanning the clothes. He had the same speculative look in his eyes Sarah had noticed in the kitchen.

Sarah hugged herself nervously, wondering if something about the closet bothered him. He turned her around to face him, a somewhat unsatisfied look on his face. Was something making him uncomfortable?

"Is my face smudged?" she asked at last. "Why are you staring at me that way?"

"Because it gives me enormous pleasure."

She could see desire smoldering in his eyes. And something else, something she couldn't quite identify.

"What's going on behind that smile?" she asked. "Are you hatching something?"

"You bet." He grinned at her. "Do you think your folks would take Molly until after supper?"

"I'm sure they would if they don't have plans. They love having her with them. Why?"

He rested his hands lightly on her shoulders. "I want to take my beautiful bride shopping, if that's all right."

"Shopping? For what?" She was totally bewildered.

"A new wardrobe."

"But Reno, I have—"

"Not what I want you to have. You need more things like the outfit you wore yesterday. It gives you, oh, I don't know, electricity?" He placed his hands on either side of her face and studied her. "Please let me indulge you. I had such a scare when you were shot, I don't think I'll ever stop wanting to do things like this for you." He winked. "And wear that outfit from yesterday."

Reno had other things in mind, too, but he'd need to make a few calls to accomplish them. He'd do it while they shopped, when Sarah was tucked out of sight in a dressing room. He had always looked at money as just a means to an end. He'd never had it when he was younger so he'd worked hard to get it. Now that he had more than he knew what to do with, he enjoyed being able to use it in a manner that gave him real satisfaction.

Sarah's parents were delighted to babysit as she'd expected and even offered to keep Molly overnight. Soon, Sarah and Reno were headed downtown to the Rivercenter Mall.

"I feel as if I've stepped into a reality television show," she told him as he moved her along from store to store.

"Believe me, it's real enough." He grinned.

One thing was certain. The man had unerring taste. He sorted through displays, shooing her into dressing rooms, salesgirls following her with arms loaded. There was no question he was in charge today, but he was relaxed and comfortable, a man showing off his wife. He was having fun and so was she.

Sarah chuckled in one store at the sight of him lounging in a chair with an ankle resting on the opposite knee, looking magnificent.

"All the women are drooling over you," she whispered when she came out to model an outfit for him.

"If you ask me, I think it's the men who can't take their eyes off *you*." He touched her hand possessively. "I must be sure to let them know you're taken."

They smiled at each other, a smile full of intimate secrets that shut out everyone else.

While Sarah tried on clothes, Reno put the rest of his plan into action. He made calls on his cell phone, speaking in a low voice and watching for Sarah to appear. Things were coming together exactly the way he wanted.

By the time they stopped for coffee late in the afternoon, she was glad to have a minute to catch her breath.

"You must be out of your mind," she protested again. "I don't need all these clothes."

"Yes, you do. You need more color, more...everything. Besides, I love buying things for you, so don't argue with me. I'm a man who knows his own mind. Or so they tell me." He chuckled.

"I feel like a kept woman." She smiled.

"You are," he said. "And I'm the one who's keeping you. For a very long time."

"Where did you learn so much about women's clothes, anyway?"

"Watching my brother. And don't ask me for

details." He grinned. "My lips are sealed."

Reno had planned for dinner on the Riverwalk, but by the time they finished at the mall, he agreed with Sarah that home looked a lot better. "We can pick up pizza or something on the way," he said. "That okay with you?"

"You bet. I'll be glad to get home."

It took both of them to carry the bags to the bedroom. Sarah hung up the things that needed hanging and left the rest for the next day.

"Right now, all I want is a shower," she said.

She was already standing under the streaming hot water, letting it work on her still sore muscles when she felt him beside her, a hand sliding the soap along her spine.

"I believe this is my bathroom now, too," Reno said in a low voice. "And my shower."

Her fatigue dissipated as he slowly lathered her body. He made her lean forward, bracing her arms against the wall, while he covered her back from her shoulders to her ankles, up the insides of her thighs and into the cleft of her buttocks, his fingers lingering there and moving in a gentle motion. Then he turned her around and did the same with her front, circling the nipples and sliding lathered fingers into her sheath, paying careful attention to the sensitive flesh inside. As she began to shake with desire, he stopped and handed her the soap.

"Not yet," he said. "My turn."

He stood while Sarah moved the soap over his rock-hard body, covering every inch, rubbing his flat nipples until they were stiff, spreading the lather over his erection, running her finger over the tip, watching his face darken with desire. He turned off the shower, dried them both off, and carried her to the bed. She had thought herself too tired to want this tonight, especially after making love that morning, but his touch inflamed her and gripped her with a violent need.

He made slow, careful love to her, drawing out each orgasm until she was sure she would lose her mind, bringing her to climax again and again before entering her.

"Tonight I want nothing from you except to enjoy what I do to you," he murmured in a husky voice. "You make me feel like a man possessed, Sarah. I can't get enough of you."

He was fierce and wild, at the same time gentle, claiming her with his love.

At last, he let her rest, tucking her in against him, her head on his shoulder. The last thing she remembered was saying, "We forgot to eat the pizza," and hearing his laugh rumbling deep in his chest. Then she slept.

Chapter Fifteen

"I've been thinking," Reno said the next morning. "I want us to have some time alone away from this house. We never had a honeymoon. I guess it wouldn't have been too appropriate before, but things have changed."

"Yes." She grinned. "They certainly have."

"I'm not talking about some big trip here," he went on. "I just want to hide us away somewhere for a while." He smiled at her. "A client of ours has a weekend cabin up in the hills about an hour from here. Right now, he's taking his family to Bermuda for two weeks so he was glad to give me the keys."

"How long will we be there?"

"Just two or three days. I wish it could be more, but Nick said the Colorado contract's been signed so I need to get back to the office."

"But who will watch Molly?" She tried to think what arrangements she could make. "An agency is out, Nicki has school, and I think more than one night would be too much for my folks. She's getting to be a real handful."

"Already taken care of." He sounded pleased with himself. "She's going out to the ranch. With Mary and Emilio there, Lindsey can manage nicely."

Sarah's jaw dropped. "You already arranged this?"

His lips turned up with a self-satisfied smile.

"Didn't think I could do it, did you?"

"I guess I think you can do anything," she said, still flabbergasted. "Oh, Reno, what a nice thing for you to do."

"Think we can find something to occupy us?" he teased and laughed as heat crept up her cheeks. "You can bring some of your new finery, although I might not give you a chance to wear much of it." He looked at her with uncharacteristic nervousness. "So, is this okay?"

"It's wonderful." She jumped up and threw her arms around him, kissing him. "When do we leave?"

"Today, as soon as we pick the baby up from your folks. We should pack now so we can leave right from there."

Their arrival in Cibolo created a flurry of activity. Emilio, stolid and implacable as ever, carried in all of Molly's paraphernalia, and Mary took the little girl off to find Jason. Nick gave Reno the key to the cabin and the directions he'd picked up the night before.

Then, at last, they were off.

****

If Sarah had wished for heaven on earth, it would have looked like the cabin in the Hill Country. Although *cabin* couldn't begin to describe their vacation hideaway. Rising majestically on the crest of a hill, its limestone exterior looked as if it had been quarried out of the very ground on which it sat. Guarded by ancient oaks and sycamores, with crepe myrtles blooming in riotous profusion, it had the appearance of a painting on the cover of a western novel.

Deer roamed over the hundred acres that

surrounded the house, along with wild turkey, rabbits, and hundreds of birds flying in every direction. The air was redolent with the aroma of mountain cedar and Texas sage. A soft breeze rustled the finery of the oak trees and swayed the giant oleander bushes.

Sarah gasped in wonder at her first sight of it, stunned by the magnificence the entire scene displayed. She wanted to capture it in a painting and hold onto it forever.

"Like it?" Reno grinned at her, helping her out of the car.

"You're kidding, right? What's not to like? My god, it's unbelievable." She drew in a breath, her nostrils filled with the clean scent of outdoors.

A massive limestone fireplace that soared to the ceiling dominated the center of the house. She could almost see the flames crackling in it.

"Great for blazing fires at night," Reno said, coming up behind her and gathering her in his arms. "We seem to do very well in front of fireplaces, don't we?"

Sarah blushed at the obvious reference to the night of their reconciliation.

"I like a bride who can still blush," he teased. "I can't wait to see you in the firelight again."

Sarah felt her heartbeat accelerate at the anticipation of the evening to come and the rest of the nights in this hideaway at the end of the world. She felt almost giddy with expectation and turned and hugged Reno tightly, pressing her face to his chest.

"Thank you for this," she said. "Thank you so very much." She moved away from him, walking to the front to look at the view again. "This whole place is so beautiful. It's like God's country."

Reno stood beside her, one arm draped over her shoulders. "I know. I get the same feeling when I'm at the ranch with Nick and Lindsey. It's like being in another world. No wonder Nick sold his house in the city when they got married and chose to live in Cibolo. I don't blame him. It's paradise."

They made no plans but just let each day happen, choosing activities as the moment struck them. Sometimes, they hiked the property, which covered a hundred acres. Other times, they roamed the countryside, stopping at out of the way places for lunch or dinner. In the evenings, they hunkered down in cozy comfort with one of the movies from the owner's collection, munching on hot, buttery popcorn and cuddling on the couch as if they were teenagers.

And of course, they made love whenever the mood struck them. They were ravenous for each other, feasting in greedy hunger, driven by their newly acknowledged love. She was always ready for him, hot and wet and waiting. He took her everywhere—in bed, on the couch, on the floor, standing up in the shower. He used every bit of expertise he had to give her total satisfaction, driving them both to exquisite peaks of desire.

Three days seemed to fly past them as if they were only seconds. On their last night, after sharing a bottle of wine, brie and crackers, they stretched out in front of the fireplace one final time.

"I want this to work out for us, Sarah." Reno's voice was serious. "I promised you I'd try with the little girl and I will, but what if I can't make it work?"

"Reno, I know in my heart if you try that you can

finally open your heart to her. You'll never lose me. The rest we'll just figure out as we go along." She lifted her face to him. "I'm in for the long haul, cowboy."

Would they ever get to the point where he'd tell her how he felt? Would he ever say I love you? She just had to hope.

"Thank god." He smiled at her lazily.

"I hate to think of leaving tomorrow," she told him. "This has been incredible."

"You like it here?" he asked.

"Oh, yes. This whole area is magic."

He leaned down and kissed her. "I agree. Let's enjoy every minute we have left here."

Tomorrow, he'd have another surprise for her, and he hoped she'd be as excited as he was.

Chapter Sixteen

Sarah looked through the car window with mixed regret and excitement as they pulled away from the cabin. She felt sure that these few days had really cemented the marriage and turned a bizarre bargain into a real relationship. Too bad, they couldn't have stayed longer, maybe have brought Molly out to be with them. She had a distinct feelings that, in someplace other than that house filled with bitter memories, Reno would be able to find his way back to the little girl.

Closing her eyes and giving herself over to the motion of the car, she jolted upright when she realized they had stopped. She had no idea where they were except they were parked off the road between huge oaks. Nothing looked familiar.

She looked at Reno, confused. "Where are we?"

"About two miles from Lindsey and Nick." He grinned at her. "I told Nick what I wanted and had him scout it out." Reno went around and opened the car door for her, then urged her forward until she realized they were standing at the top of a hill. "Ten acres, with a creek running through it and plenty of space for a home, a yard, maybe even a couple of horses. You've got a horse farm to the right and a small cattle ranch to the left." He turned to her, anxiety written on his face. "What do you think?"

She was stunned. "I love it. Didn't you think I would? But—"

"I don't want to remodel the house, Sarah. I want to be out of it. Start fresh, with no memories of any kind."

"Any kind?" she teased.

"Well," he drawled, "maybe a few. Listen, I had Nick tell the real estate agent someone might be interested. Would you be happy with this?"

Sarah threw her arms around him. "More than I can tell you."

A house of her own, built just for them. She couldn't have asked for more.

By the time they reached the ranch, Sarah could hardly contain her excitement. And when she went into the room where Molly sat in a playpen and the child reached out her arms for her, her heart was so full she had to turn away to hide her tears.

"Was she good?" she asked Mary.

"As gold," Mary answered. "I told Lindsey she should order a baby girl just like this one."

"She's been great," Lindsey said, "but she's been looking for you every day."

Sarah hugged Molly to her and rained kisses on her cheeks. The little girl smelled deliciously of cookies and chocolate and baby powder, a scent that made her heart turn over. Molly patted her with her chubby little hands, then shifted in Sarah's arms as she spotted Reno walking in behind her. Bouncing up and down, the little girl lifted her arms out to him, cooing.

When Reno smiled and lifted her in his arms, Sarah's smile stretched her cheeks. Two months had passed, and she was still getting used to the new relationship between father and daughter. Sometimes she held her breath, wondering if it would suddenly fall apart.

On the way out to the car, Lindsey pulled Sarah aside. "By the looks of things, I'd say the delayed honeymoon exceeded expectations."

"Better than you can imagine. We still have some hurdles to get past, but we'll get there. Everything between us is so wonderful, Lindsey."

"I'm so glad for you both. He's such a special person."

"Yes, he is. I'm very lucky."

"No," Lindsey said softly, "Reno's the lucky one."

"So did you give her the nickel tour?" Nick asked.

Reno nodded. "Call your agent and set up a meeting. It's a go."

Lindsey clapped her hands. "How wonderful. We'll be so close together."

"Remember," Reno warned, "we have one house to sell and another to build before this all happens."

"But it will." Lindsey kissed his cheek. "That's for luck."

They drove home in a quiet silence, happy just to be with each other. There was no need for conversation. The time in the cabin had said it all.

While Reno carried all the suitcases into the house, she took Molly up to her room. Mary had fed the little girl lunch, and her eyes were drooping now. When Sarah put her in her crib, she popped her thumb in her mouth, closed her eyes, and was asleep at once.

Sarah went into the bedroom to unpack. She had no idea where Reno was. In the doorway of the room, she stopped, frozen. He was lying on the bed, eyes closed, and one arm thrown across his forehead.

"Are you okay?"

He opened his eyes. "I kick myself daily for all the times I missed with Molly because I was such a bitter bastard. What would have happened if she hadn't been kidnapped? She's so adorable and a child anyone would be proud of and excited to claim as their own. Holding her in my arms is unbelievable joy. But sometimes…sometimes I remember Maggie's words and I—"

Sarah placed her fingers over her lips, then she lay down next to him, nestling her head on his shoulder, touching his face. "When that happens, tell me. I'll help you all I can. And one of these days it will cease to even cross your mind."

"Promise?"

"I do. I am always here for you. You have to know that."

Reno held her to him as if he'd never let her go. She wanted to weep herself, for all the pain one person had caused. Instead, she molded herself to him as tightly as she could and let her hand rest on his muscular chest, trying to infuse his body with her warmth. After a long time, they dozed, clinging to each other.

Later, Reno went out to pick up Chinese takeout. But both were tired and they were glad to get into bed early. She crawled into bed, excited about the land they were buying. She had barely closed her eyes before she heard Reno come into the room and strip off his clothes. The mattress dipped as he lowered his body next to hers. His warm hand cupped her cheek, turning her face toward him.

"Everything's going to be fine," he promised. "Just hang onto me and don't let go."

As if she would!

****

Obviously tired from her three days of excitement, Molly slept later than usual the next morning and so did Sarah. When she came downstairs with the freshly diapered child, Reno was already at the kitchen table, drinking coffee, and talking on the phone. When Sarah looked at him, he held up one finger signaling to wait, he was almost through.

"All right," he said into the receiver. "Tell them that's the best offer they're going to get. I'll be at my office in an hour. Call me back as soon as you get an answer." Disconnecting the call, he leaned back in his chair with a self-satisfied look on his face.

Sarah raised an eyebrow as she settled Molly in her highchair. "You sure look like someone who won the lottery. What's going on?"

"I called the real estate agent on that property and made an offer. He's going to call me back at the office, but I think they'll take it. It's close enough to their asking price that I think they won't bargain."

"What happens then?"

"As soon as we close on it, we need to hire an architect, meet with him and get some plans drawn up."

"Wow!" Sarah tucked her hair behind her ears and sat down to feed Molly. "Moving at the speed of light, are we?"

He reached across the table to touch her arm. "I can't get out of this house fast enough if you want to know the truth."

Sarah was silent for a moment, working to get

more food in Molly's mouth than on her chin. An idea suddenly took root in her brain. When Reno returned to the table, his coffee mug refilled and carrying one for her, she turned to look at him. "I have an idea in that direction."

"Yeah?" Reno sipped the hot liquid in his mug. "Okay, let me have it."

"We could move into my house. No one's ever lived there but me," she hurried to assure him. "You've had the landscape and cleaning services there once a week so it's in good shape. I know it's a lot smaller than this place, but it would do for the short term. We can sell it when the new house is ready."

When he didn't answer, she glanced at him nervously. He was staring at her.

"Bad idea?" she asked.

"No, it's a great idea. Why didn't we think of this before?"

"Because before," she said very carefully, "it didn't matter where we lived. Now it does."

"You'd sell your house?"

She shrugged. "It's only a building. No memories. Someone new will make their own. We'd have to put all this furniture in storage."

"Get rid of it," Reno bit off. "Sell it with the house. Burn it. I don't care. How soon can we move?"

Sarah laughed. "As quickly as I can air out the place and call the movers. We need to take Molly's stuff, our clothes, the things from your den…"

"Buy something new. Order it today and have them deliver it and set it up."

He came to stand behind her and placed a kiss on the top of her head. "Do it. Call today. As soon as I get to the office, I'll call a real estate agent we've done a lot of work with and get this place listed." He drained the rest of the coffee and put his mug in the sink. "I'd better get going. This is shaping up to be a busy day ahead."

****

Everything kicked into fast forward. In less than a week, they finalized a listing agreement, hired an architect, and moved forward with their plans. Sarah's parents were delighted when she told them, although not too excited about having them living farther away.

"It won't be that far, Mom," Sarah assured her. "I still have to be close enough so Reno won't have a long drive to the office. And we drove it yesterday. It's only twenty-five minutes between our new place and yours."

"Well, all things considered," Ellen said, "I do think getting out of that house will be good for both of you. Forgive me for saying this, sweetheart, but being the second wife sometimes has its drawbacks. It never helps to cook in another woman's kitchen."

Sarah had never told the Madisons the Maggie story nor did she intend to. It was Reno's secret to share, not hers. But Ellen, with her uncanny intuition, had sensed an air of imbalance in the house that she couldn't quite define. Sarah could tell she was pleased that they were going to make a fresh start in a new place.

The following night Reno was home earlier than usual, looking very satisfied with himself. He dropped a large envelope on the counter.

"An early Christmas present, darlin'. They accepted our offer. We now own a big piece of land in the middle of somewhere."

"Oh, Reno. Really and truly?" She leaped up and threw her arms around him. "But that's wonderful."

"All you have to do is sign these papers tonight, and I'll have someone drive them to the agent's office tomorrow. The seller has already signed."

"I've been busy, too." She grinned. "The nursery furniture will be delivered and set up tomorrow and the movers will be here Wednesday. They'll pack up everything I tell them to, including our clothes, and we'll just leave the rest." She frowned at him. "Are you sure that's what you really want to do?"

"You don't know how much." His face was suddenly grim. "I just want to walk out the door and never look back." He glanced at Molly in her highchair.

"I'll get her upstairs and bathed in just a minute," she said hastily. "You came home a little early, is all, so I'm running just a bit behind."

"No worries." He patted her ass. "Now, why don't you go do whatever it is you need to do, and I'll get rid of this jacket and tie. I brought home some champagne so we could celebrate before dinner."

****

The next morning, she drove Lindsey out to see their property.

"This is gorgeous." Lindsey's eyes sparkled. She turned to hug Sarah, somewhat of a problem with her now bulging stomach and Molly in Sarah's arms, but they managed. "I'm so very happy for you. Both of you. Reno deserves every bit of happiness you bring him."

"We still have some bumps in the road," Sarah said, "but we're getting there, one step at a time."

As if Fate wanted to rain on their parade, Reno

came home that night tense as a rubber band.

"What's the matter?" she asked. "Oh, god, not trouble with the land."

He shook his head. "Balenger called me today. It seems Marina Aguilar, Luis's daughter, is on the warpath and she's headed this way for revenge."

For a moment, Sarah was afraid she'd pass out. "Will we never be done with them?"

"He's got eyes on her and her entourage. They aren't making any secret of this, apparently. When are the movers coming?"

"Tomorrow."

"Good. They won't find us here." He brushed a kiss over her lips. "I'm not going to work until this is over. And Gary Stern will be hanging out with us. I'm not taking any chances."

"God." She raked her hands through her hair. "How long is this going to go on?"

"I'd say only a few more days. Balenger is putting some of his men on it, too."

When Sarah crawled into bed that night, the excitement of the move had dimmed somewhat with this new threat. She said a silent prayer they'd all come through it safely.

The following morning, the movers showed up on schedule, and by five that afternoon, juggling a cranky Molly whose naps had been hit or miss, Sarah walked back into her house where the furniture fought for space with piles of cartons. Several of them were stacked in her garage and wouldn't be opened until the new house was ready, and her house was half the size of Reno's, which doubled the problem. Plus the fact that her rooms were a miniature of the ones Reno was used to and likely to give him a case of claustrophobia.

Well, no matter. We'll be a little crammed, but we can make it work. We just need to get the plans finished, settle on a builder, and get him in high gear.

Reno, true to his word, stayed home. Gary Stern was already there waiting for them. With the two of them, moving stuff around turned out a lot easier. If only she wasn't tied up in such a tense ball.

She unpacked some of their clothes and Molly's things, fed and bathed the little girl, and put her down for the night. At last, she collapsed on the couch, catching her breath. At six, Reno ran out for pizza and sodas.

"My hero," she told him. "Just what the doctor ordered."

"You're an amazing woman," he said, looking around. "I can't believe how much you've gotten done." He leaned down and kissed her. "If you're not too tired, maybe later, I can show you just how much I admire you." He winked and leered at her.

"Don't forget we have a guest," she reminded him.

"I'll tell him to sleep on the car."

"Reno!" She gave him a playful slap. "Be nice to him."

After supper, Gary settled himself uncomplaining on her couch, and she and Reno retreated to the bedroom.

"You know," he told her as they got into bed, "except for the cabin, tonight is the first time we've slept together that I didn't feel a phantom hovering over my shoulder. This house is clean, Sarah. The only spirit in it is yours. And now ours."

"I feel as if we've closed one door and walked

through another."

"That's the plan, my love. That is, indeed, the plan." He hugged her close to him, molding her against him, and they fell easily asleep.

Chapter Seventeen

They were all up early the next morning. It wasn't just the need to tend to Molly. They were all on edge. Sarah had even taken to strapping her gun to her waist, putting it down only when she was holding Molly.

"You look like Annie Oakley," Reno teased.

Gary just raised an eyebrow and gave her a tiny smile.

"I have a lot to get done," she told Reno, "and I want to make something special for our first dinner here. So go to work and keep your magic fingers busy until tonight."

Reno's cell rang, making her jump. He answered, and when he hung up, he had a tight look on his face.

"What?" she asked.

"Balenger. Marina Aguilar is in San Antonio. She was spotted checking out the old house. The FBI had agents there, but she never got out of the car. When she spotted them, she took off and our guys lost her. I'm sure, with her network, they've managed to find where you are now. They've got eyes out there everywhere, but these people disappear like smoke. He's pretty sure she'll be showing up here any time. He's on his way right now with some of his men." He looked at her. "And you, Miss Deadeye, keep yourself scarce."

She laid a hand on her gun. "I'll just keep this close in case."

"She's not afraid to show her hand," Balenger told them when he arrived. "Her father waited for the right moment. She'll come in with guns blazing, then hightail it to their local contacts to hide."

****

They were all tense, waiting for the shoe to drop. Reno, wearing a holster with his own personal gun and wondering when the hell Balenger was going to get there, insisted Sarah set up Molly's playpen in her room and stay in there with her. He waited a few minutes, watching her reading to the little girl, before he turned to close the door. In the next moment, he heard the sound of breaking glass at the front of the house.

"Take Molly and go in the closet," he ordered. "Just in case."

Sarah clutched Molly to her, whispering to the little girl who didn't seem too happy to be taken into a dark place. Reno closed both the closet and bedroom door and hustled out to the front of the house in time to see Marina Aguilar standing at his broken living room window. Two of her men flanked her.

"You killed my family," she screamed, lifting a gun and pointing it at him. "Now I will kill yours."

Reno ducked behind the couch as the first shots split the air. He didn't want to get into a shooting war with these people, as outnumbered as he was. The best he could hope for was to get in a couple of strategic shots. He wished he had Nick or one of his top agents with him. Or that Balenger, damn him, would get here.

Another volley of shots flew through the window and embedded in the wall behind him.

"You can't hide for long," she shouted again. "My men will drag your wife out of wherever she is hiding and fuck her until she is dead. Right before your eyes. Then we will kill you, slowly and painfully."

No, no, no, no.

All the spit in his mouth dried up, and panic raced through his system.

Hold it together. You've been in spots like this before. Just think. You can outflank them.

A car screech to a stop outside.

"Give it up, Marina." Balanger's voice rang out. "We've got you outflanked and outnumbered."

"Over my dead body," she shouted.

"As you wish," Balanger called.

A loud volley of shots followed, some of them again hitting the living room wall.

Then silence.

"We're good, Sullivan," Balanger called. "Come on out."

When Reno rose, he glanced around the room, cringing at the number of bullet holes in the wall. When he stepped outside, the two men with Marina lay on the ground, handcuffed. In front of the house, Marina lay on the grass, arms flung outward, the front of her blouse soaked in blood.

"She's dead," Balanger told him. "With vermin like her, the only good Aguilar is a dead one."

"I can't say I'm sorry." Reno blew out a breath. "I was afraid you wouldn't get here in time."

"Traffic was so fucked up I nearly called for a helicopter. But I'm glad we made it when we did. Where did you hide Sarah and Molly?"

"Oh, Jesus. In the closet."

He loped into the house, into the bedroom, and opened the closet door. Sarah was still huddled in there, clutching Molly.

She looked up at him, wide-eyed. "Is it over?"

"It is." He reached out to help her up, then wrapped his arms around both of them. His heart still raced at the thought of what could have happened.

"So fast?"

"I told you. Marina Aguilar runs on emotion, not brains. She thought she could just come in here with guns blazing and take us out."

He took Molly from her and hugged the little girl to his chest, kissing her curls. Then he reached for Sarah again, pulling her tight against him.

"Come on. Balenger wants to see us. Then we're getting out of here."

When Sarah saw that the picture windows in the living room and dining room had been shot out with glass scattered over everything, she nearly cried. Reno wasn't looking forward to her seeing the walls of the house.

"At least we're all alive," she told him in a shaky voice.

Kip Balenger walked inside, two men behind him.

"Mrs. Sullivan, sorry your house is such a mess. I wish we'd had time to move you all out of here but…"

"But we were bait," she guessed.

He didn't answer, which was an answer in itself.

"Where are they now?"

"Marina's dead. No loss there. My men are transporting the others to the federal detention center downtown. At least the nightmare is finally over."

"Thank the lord for that."

They shook hands all around before Balanger left with the rest of his men. Reno called someone to come and board up the windows. Tomorrow, he'd get a full crew in here to begin repairs. Then they packed up what they'd need for a few days and he would take them all to one of the corporate apartments Guardian kept.

"Tomorrow, I'll get the crew in to put this place back in shape. Then maybe we can finally have some peace and quiet in our lives."

After that, the days moved along quietly, all of them adapting to the house much better than she'd expected. Reno suffered from claustrophobia for the first week or two, but before long, he adjusted to the more confined situation. She gave him the tiny den to use, realizing he still needed a room to hide himself in now and then. That seemed to increase his comfort zone.

Molly was consumed with delight. She had new corners to poke into and new areas to explore. The problem was her inquisitive nature propelled her into all sorts of trouble. Sarah had Reno remove the inside door from the enclosed back porch and turned it into a playroom. It gave the little girl a place to expend her energy, and Sarah some peace of mind.

They managed, after a fashion, but she'd be glad when the new house was finally built.

Reno's house had only been listed for a week when the real estate agent called to tell them they had a buyer. The people had made an offer, asking if the furniture went with it. Sarah called Reno at the office, barely able to contain her excitement.

"The agent has a buyer." She was almost dancing with glee. "The people from the Sunday showing. Almost the full price, too. And guess what? They also want all the furniture and stuff."

"You're kidding." Reno laughed. "I think you're right. This was meant to be."

She cleared her throat. "It will be nice for you to spend Christmas someplace else."

"You are so right," he said after a moment of silence. "And it will be our first together."

Our first Christmas. I have to make it special for him.

The day they closed on the sale of the house, they left Molly with her parents and went to dinner to celebrate. Reno took her to the Italian restaurant they'd eaten at before, and they took a long time over dinner.

"This is the beginning of everything new." Sarah touched his hand gently, praying silently that she was right. "A new door is opening for us."

"You're good for me." He rubbed his fingers across the back of her hand. "If I hadn't been such a fool, we could have had this a long time ago."

"Forget about that. We have it now. That's all that matters."

Smiling at each other, they toasted their new life.

****

The meetings with the architect went better than either of them had expected. Deciding not to build his own house and borrow trouble, Reno chose a homebuilder he had high regard for. They met with him to finalize arrangements, and everything was a go for the first of the year.

Determined to fall in with the holiday spirit, especially now that they were in new surroundings, Reno took two days off and went shopping with Sarah for a tree and ornaments.

"Not much," she reminded him. "Next year, we'll

decorate in the new house. But I can't let the season go by unnoticed. And it will be good for Molly."

They hauled the tree to her house, and Reno helped her decorate.

"I haven't had a tree since my folks died." His eyes were suddenly sad.

"We'll more than make up for it." Sarah hugged him. "From now on, every Christmas will be special."

Christmas was a joyous celebration. They opened presents in the morning, watching Molly's unrestrained pleasure in everything. Then they all, including her parents and Tony, trooped out to Cibolo for a holiday feast at the Vanetta ranch.

They celebrated New Year's very quietly, not wanting to share this first one with anyone. At midnight, they toasted each other with champagne.

"To our wonderful life," Reno said.

"The best," Sarah agreed.

They looked at each other with feelings of deep satisfaction and pleasure, aware of how blessed they were with a love that grew more each day.

"The land is cleared," she told Reno one night after a trip out to the property, unable to contain her excitement. Her eyes danced, and she couldn't stop smiling. "Oh, it looks so wonderful. And they have the house staked out to give us the best view. Right on the crest of the hill."

"Did the builder say when they'd be pouring the concrete?"

"Tomorrow." Sarah felt like a kid at Christmas. "It's going to be just fantastic."

Two or three times each week, she bundled Molly into the car and drove out to the site, checking progress and meeting with the builder. And of course, there was a never-ending array of things to select—paint, flooring, fixtures, counters, appliances. The list went on and on. Reno was busier at the office than ever. Guardian had three new projects going. Still, he managed to steal time here and there when Sarah needed him. Some nights, they were so tired they just crawled into bed, looked at each other and fell asleep.

Sitting at the kitchen table one morning, sipping the last of her coffee, she was reviewing everything in her mind. The house was quiet. Reno had gone to the office for a rare Saturday meeting, and Molly was with Nicki. The teenager had picked her up earlier to take her to a birthday party for one of the myriad Vanetta nieces and nephews. Sarah had looked forward to this time to do some uninterrupted work, but her mind kept wandering.

Since the week in the cabin, their marriage had been incredible—warm, passionate, loving. Reno was more open with her in every way than he'd ever been to anyone in his life. He had torn down walls he'd spent years erecting, reaching out to make her a part of himself. It was everything she could want. Almost.

Now and then she allowed herself a moment of sadness for the fact she'd never conceive a child herself. Then she reminded herself how lucky she was to have Molly.

Sighing, she drained her coffee cup and placed it in the dishwasher.

Be grateful for what you have.

****

Time seemed to be passing so swiftly now with the activities that consumed each day. Before they knew it, their first anniversary was approaching, and Reno wanted them to do something special.

"Not go away," he said quickly. "I know the timing isn't right for that. But think about some place you've always wanted to go for dinner. Or something we can do that's always been on your wish list."

"You spoil me." She kissed him. "I'll give it some thought, okay? And try to come up with some suggestions."

At that moment, though, she was so tired nothing appealed to her. And deadlines were looming. The house was nearly complete. All it needed were the last finishing touches. Then they would call the movers and put her house up for sale. They'd decided to take their time shopping for furniture, using hers in the interim. She knew Reno was anxious to actually be settled at last, and she was doing her best to get ready.

Sarah was so relieved he was willing to wait on the furniture she could have wept. The thought of more shopping, more choosing, exhausted her. A fatigue enveloped her that she just couldn't seem to shake. She'd felt it for days. Then one morning, she woke up and couldn't drag herself out of bed.

"I think I have the flu." She had just thrown up for the third time. "It's been going around. Remember when Nicki had it? What with all the moving around and everything, I just realized I forgot to get my flu shot. I don't think I'll be up to much celebrating on our anniversary. I'm so sorry."

Reno, concern lining his face, brought her some tea and made her lie down with a cold cloth on her forehead. "The important thing is for you to get well. You've worn yourself out with moving and working on the new house. I should have seen what was happening and put the brakes on."

"It wasn't a big deal," she protested. "If I had just gotten that stupid flu shot, I'd be all right."

Molly was bouncing up and down in her crib, babbling her familiar sounds.

"I have to get up." Sarah tried to sit up without much success. "Molly needs to be dressed and fed."

Reno forced her back down to the pillow. "I'll manage. You're in no condition to do anything."

"But you don't—"

"I can do it." He smiled at her thinly. "I run a company with massive projects. I should be able to take care of one small child."

"Come get me if you need help," she called in a weak voice.

He headed down the hall, his body unnaturally stiff. She worried about how he'd deal with being forced into the situation, but she was too sick to care. She put her head on the pillow and fell asleep at once.

When she woke, she was nauseous again and stumbled to the bathroom. Reno must have heard her because he was upstairs and beside her in what seemed like seconds. He helped her back to bed, wiped her face, and gave her some water to drink.

"Can you hold anything in your stomach?" His face was taut with worry.

"Some tea, maybe. I'll come downstairs if you'll help me."

"Not on your life. I can fix a cup of tea, and I'll bring some crackers—one thing my mother was always good at was treating the sick. Crackers and tea, her cure for everything. Then I'm going to take you in the shower with me, and when we get out, I'll change the sheets. You have to feel sticky."

"Where's Molly?" she asked, her forehead creased with anxiety.

"In bed asleep."

"Did you find everything for her okay? What did you do about breakfast and lunch? And how did you handle her all morning?"

"Everything was fine. She's very good, which helps a lot. I may not have fed her what you would have, but we made out all right."

She tried to smile at his mild attempt at humor. "Nicki can come in after school and help."

"Let's wait and see how you feel tomorrow. If you're still sick, I just might call her."

The shower felt good. She was grateful to have the sour feeling of nausea washed away. Reno was very gentle with her, holding her while he bathed her, sitting her on the vanity so he could dry her and put on a fresh gown. He placed her in the slipper chair while he did a hasty job of bed making then carried her over and laid her down with the pillows fluffed under her head.

"I know I'll be better tomorrow." She tried to subdue the nausea that never seemed to leave her. "And you have to go to work. I know how busy it is when you take on new projects."

"I do believe they're learning how to get along without me." He grinned. "What a blow to my ego. Nick doesn't miss a beat, just picks up whatever slack he needs to. I told them to expect me when I show up. Quit worrying about everything, and let me take care of things. That's an order."

She sank back on the pillows, thankful to leave

everything in his hands. She drank another cup of tea and promptly fell asleep again.

But the next morning, she wasn't any better. The nausea hit her as soon as she opened her eyes. Reno held her head, wiping her face and holding a glass of water so she could rinse her mouth. She kept down tea and crackers then slept. She couldn't seem to keep her eyes open, which was a blessing because when she was asleep at least she didn't throw up.

In moments of wakefulness, she wondered how Reno was surviving with Molly. He was out of bed instantly each morning when he heard her voice, his face set in granite but determination in every line of his body. He had taken her advice and called Nicki, who blessedly came in each day after school.

Sarah strained to hear the noises of the house, expecting disaster, but all she heard was Molly's familiar giggle and Reno's deep voice. She wanted to get up and help, but she barely had the strength to make it to the bathroom and back. Nicki was now coming in right after school and staying until Molly was in bed for the night.

"Are you doing okay with her in the morning?" Sarah asked one evening, full of anxiety. She had been sick for four days now and didn't seem to be getting any better. She knew Reno was increasingly worried about her.

"We haven't had any disasters yet," he told her. "Everything is fine."

She knew what a supreme effort it was for him and ached for the internal struggle she was sure he was having. What a situation.

By the fifth day, she was beginning to feel a little

better. She wasn't racked with nausea all the time, and she could keep down some broth as well as tea and crackers. She was lying on the pillows in the late afternoon, wondering if she should try and get up, when she heard a crash and a scream from downstairs. Her blood chilled and panic clutched at her. The scream was Molly's.

She forced herself up from the bed, found her robe, and made her way downstairs, clinging to the banister and hoping she didn't pass out. Molly was still screaming and over that sound she heard Nicki's scared voice, and Reno's, tense but in command.

She leaned into the doorframe in the kitchen, supporting herself and shaking at what she saw. The highchair was lying on the floor, glass and blood were everywhere, and Reno was holding Molly. Blood was spurting from her arm at an alarming rate. Nicki had grabbed dishtowels and was trying to apply pressure.

"That's arterial blood," Sarah whispered, her voice shaky with fear. "She needs a tourniquet."

Dizzy and weak yet somehow finding the strength to move, she grabbed another towel and twirled it to form a wide strip. With Reno helping, she placed it around Molly's arm, tying it over the other towels to form a pressure pad.

"Hold her arm up," she ordered. She tried not to look at the long, deep cut on the little arm. "Did you call 9-1-1?"

"I'm taking her right to the emergency room," Reno said, his jaw clenched. "The hospital isn't very far."

"I'm coming with you," Sarah told him.

"Sarah, you're sick and you can hardly stand up.

Besides, you can't run around in a nightgown. Please get back in bed."

"Nicki." She turned to the terrified teenager, forcing a strength she didn't feel. "Grab my raincoat, would you? It's spring, for heaven's sake. It's already balmy here. And my shoes, too. Hurry. I'm going. I want to be with her. Nicki. Go now." Somehow, she found the strength to hold it together, but barely.

"I'm so sorry, Mrs. Sullivan," Nicki said, twisting her hands. "It's all my fault."

"No, it's not," Reno insisted. "I was here, too. But right now, we need to get to the emergency room. Help me get them both in the car. You'd better come, too."

Reno drove like a madman, honking his horn at every vehicle in his way. Nicki was wedged in the front seat between them, helping Sarah with Molly, keeping the bleeding arm raised. They both tried not to notice how pale the little girl was. Sarah's own discomfort was forgotten for the moment as she focused on the emergency at hand.

"I was irresponsible," Reno said, anguished. "I should have paid better attention. We had her in her highchair, but I didn't check to make sure she was securely strapped in. I know she tries to stand up in it all the time. I've seen her do it."

"Did she just fall?"

"I had a glass of soda on the counter," Nicki said miserably. "Molly reached for it. Lost her balance, and she and the highchair both fell, pulling the glass with them. When she landed, a jagged edge cut her arm." She was caressing the little girl's face, wiping her tears, trying to soothe her. "I'm a terrible baby-sitter. I wouldn't blame you if you fired me."

"Nicki, accidents happen with children." Sarah tried to sound reassuring, but she was fighting back a new wave of nausea and dizziness. "You do the best you can and pray about everything else."

Reno pulled up to the emergency entrance, slammed the car in Park, and ran around to take the baby from them. He was already racing into the reception area when Sarah struggled out of the car.

I will not faint. I will not be sick.

Sarah clenched her jaw and exerted as much control as she could muster. Reno could worry about her later. The baby came first.

Nicki helped her inside, and she collapsed into the chair nearest the door.

The emergency room was in chaos, people hurrying everywhere, voices raised. Although the seating area was full of people waiting their turn, rules and regulations didn't exist for Reno Sullivan. People seldom argued with him about anything. With his usual expectation of compliance, he carried Molly up to the desk, corralled a nurse who yelled at once for a doctor, and they all disappeared into a curtained area.

Sarah sat huddled into the chair, letting the noise swirl around her, holding her coat to her for warmth. Nicki stood next to her, wringing her hands, unsure what to do next. Sarah could see the teenager was running on nerves at this point. She wondered if anyone would come and tell her anything.

The combined odors of illness and medicine were threatening her fragile hold on her heaving stomach. She kept her eyes closed, calling on what little strength she had to survive this without passing out or throwing up on the hospital floor. Reno was right, she shouldn't have come, but she couldn't have let him take Molly without her.

All she could think was *what a mess.*

Sarah was leaning back with her eyes closed, willing the nausea to go away, when a gentle hand touched her arm and a soft voice said, "Mrs. Sullivan?"

She pried open her eyes.

A nurse was beside her with a wheelchair. "Mr. Sullivan is worried to death about you. He says you have a bad case of the flu. It's sure been going around. He wants a doctor to take a look at you. Come on, let me help you into the wheelchair." She smiled reassuringly. "If you pass out on the floor here, it doesn't make us look too good."

"Molly?"

"Your little girl's being taken care of. The doctor's with her and so is your husband."

"The bleeding?" Sarah was almost afraid to ask.

"They've got it under control. I'm just going to get you into an area here, then tell them where you are. Someone will come and let you know what's happening real quick."

"Is it all right if I go call my mother?" Nicki asked, after helping the nurse with Sarah. She was fighting back the tears that threatened to spill out of her eyes.

Sarah nodded as she was wheeled away. In a minute, she was lying down in a treatment area, being covered with a blanket, the privacy curtain pulled around her. She felt the nausea rise again and with great effort fought it back. She was trying to get herself under control when someone pulled the curtain aside, and Reno was there with the doctor.

"Where's Molly?" she asked, her voice thin and

thready.

"She'll be fine," the doctor said. His nametag read R. Moreland, M.D. "The nurse is with her at the moment. We've stopped the bleeding and put an inflatable tourniquet on her. I gave her some light medication for the pain so she's more comfortable. While she's calm, I thought we'd come here and bring you up to date. Nasty, nasty cut, but we're taking care of it."

Reno stood next to Sarah and gripped her hand. She could feel the nervous tension vibrating through his body.

"We have a plastic surgeon coming to stitch her up," Dr. Moreland continued, "so she won't have much of a scar. We will want to give her a general anesthetic, though. Otherwise, the suturing can be quite traumatic for her, since the cut's so deep. Your husband wanted me to check with you before he signed the papers."

Sarah could only nod.

The doctor handed Reno a clipboard with forms attached, and Reno scrawled his name.

"We also will need to give her some blood. She's lost quite a lot, and we don't want to run into other problems during the surgery. We prefer to check the parents first before using our own supplies. We always prefer family, if possible." He looked at Sarah critically. "Not you, my dear." It was apparent he was unaware of the situation. "I think right now you need all you've got."

"Molly isn't my biological child anyway," Sarah told him, "although our blood type might be compatible. I've never checked."

Reno's face tightened in embarrassment that he

didn't know this simple fact. "I'm sure it's in her medical records at the pediatrician's, but I never paid attention enough to ask."

"No matter. Your wife's in no shape right now to be a donor under any circumstances. But the lab tech is right here, so Mr. Sullivan, I guess you're it."

Reno opened his mouth to say something, closed it, and swallowed hard. "Actually, I'm not her biological parent either."

"Then this is an adoption?" the doctor asked. "Well, let's test you anyway. If you have the right blood type, you can still be a donor."

He nodded, his face rigid, and Sarah squeezed his hand weakly, trying to give him assurance. He looked so uptight she was afraid he'd break apart any minute.

A technician entered with all his paraphernalia. He was quick and efficient and, in just seconds, handed a vial of Reno's blood to a waiting lab messenger.

"I'm going to see if the surgeon's come down yet." Dr. Moreland looked at Reno. "The nurse has been with your daughter since we sedated her, but you might want to come with me, Mr. Sullivan, in case she's at all aware. Just to reassure her until we take her to surgery."

Reno was torn, wanting to be two places at once.

"I'll be all right," Sarah told him. "Please go be with Molly."

The lab tech had moved to the bed to stand next to Sarah.

"We're going to take a little blood from you, too, Mrs. Sullivan. I need to run some tests before we try to prescribe anything for you. And the nurse will come and take your vitals. We'll be as quick as we can. I know you're in rough shape. Can you handle it until then?"

Sarah moved her head in a weak nod. "It will be all right. Just go. Molly needs all of you more than I do right now."

Reno kissed her forehead, then turned and followed the doctor.

After everyone had left the area, she dozed, rousing only when the nurse came to check her blood pressure and other vital signs. She was vaguely aware of the activity around her beyond the curtains, but as long as she lay perfectly still, she was all right. She wondered when someone would come to tell her more about Molly. An icy knot of fear curled in her stomach as dozens of unpleasant possibilities flashed through her brain.

When she opened her eyes again, Reno was beside her bed, holding her cold hand in one of his large warm ones, reassuring her with his presence. But who was comforting him? The harsh lines of strain cut deeply into his face, and tension vibrated through his body.

"They're just waiting for the lab results," he told her. "Meanwhile, the medication's put her to sleep."

Before Sarah could comment, they heard footsteps enter the room.

"Oh, good, you're both here." Dr. Morehead moved the curtain aside and entered the treatment area. "Mr. Sullivan, I'm somewhat puzzled here. You say Molly is adopted?"

"Not…exactly." Reno's face flushed a dark red. He didn't want to tell this doctor about Maggie and her lies. "Why do you ask?"

"First of all, your blood type is a match. You're both A Positive, and while that's not a particularly rare blood type, it is a little uncommon. Secondly, with a child this young, we try to match the blood as much as possible so we do something called the HLA test. We routinely use it for tissue compatibility, as well. It determines certain proteins found in the outer coating of nearly every cell in the body. Everyone has a small, relatively unique set inherited from their parents."

"So what are you saying?"

"I'm saying that while it doesn't prove paternity, it can disprove it. If father and child do not have one antigen pair identical to each other, it rules out paternity." Dr. Moreland paused for the space of a heartbeat. "This test shows you and Molly have matching pairs, which means you definitely could be Molly's father. I don't mean to pry into your business, but..."

Reno's face was frozen in shock. He had to force himself to speak. "But I had a DNA test done that proved the opposite."

"Where did you have this done if I might ask?"

Reno named the lab, and Dr. Moreland shook his head. "I'm sorry to say, that lab is under major scrutiny right now. They hired unqualified lab technicians, and many of their test results were incorrect."

Sarah thought Reno was going to have a heart attack. The blood drained from his face, and he staggered, falling into the chair next to the bed.

"We can do another test if it would reassure you," the doctor went on, "but right now we need you to give blood so we can get your daughter into surgery."

Dazed, Reno let himself be led away.

Sarah lay back, eyes closed, her lips curved in a smile. She should have looked past the blonde curls to see the thick dark lashes so like Reno's and the eyes with a hint of gold fleck. When she could stay awake for more than ten seconds she'd take a closer look.

She roused a little when the nurse came to check on her again and let her know the doctor would be back very soon. They would give her something for the nausea as soon as her test results were back, if she could just hold on.

Chapter Eighteen

The next time, she awoke she felt a warm hand touching her. Opening her eyes, she saw Reno sitting upright in a chair beside her, his eyes glazed, his breathing slightly erratic. Shock. But a good shock, after all.

"You are not allowed to say I told you so," he said when he noticed she was awake.

"I told you so." She tried for a faint grin. "You can't hit me when I'm sick."

He bowed his head, rubbing his temples with the tips of his fingers. "I can't believe this. All these months, I've been so miserable to her, shutting her out, withholding love. What a bastard I am. I don't deserve her. Or you. Either of you."

"Stop that." Sarah summoned what strength she had. "You had no way of knowing the test was flawed. You could only go on the information that was given to you."

"You don't know how terrified I've been, watching them take care of her." He wiped his hand over his face as if brushing cobwebs away. "I looked at her lying there, so panicked at the sight of her still, little form, and realized, in the end, it didn't matter what any of these tests show. You've been right all along. Biology has little to do with it."

Sarah blinked her eyes against the tears crowding

her lids. "You've always loved her. I sensed it, but you were just in too much pain to show it."

"Selfish pain, Sarah." He gently squeezed her hand, holding it as afraid to break the contact. "I took out my own damaged ego on a child who was the innocent bystander in this little melodrama. She's my daughter—our daughter—and just the way it happened with you, it took a near disaster to show me what a damn fool I've been." He leaned back in the chair, eyes closed, lines of anguish scoring his face. "God, what if something goes wrong, and I never get to tell her how much I love her?"

"She'll be fine," Sarah reassured him. "You heard the doctor. You got her here in plenty of time. She's got a full medical team taking care of her. Please stop beating yourself up. Children survive worse things."

"I love her, Sarah." His eyes were bright with unshed tears, and the hand holding hers shook. "I love both of you. I'm going to spend the rest of my life showing you just how much."

She'd waited so long to hear those words she almost couldn't take them in.

"Loving us is all we ever asked of you, you know." Her voice was soft, and she squeezed the hand holding hers with what strength she had.

He reached into his pocket and drew out a small box.

"I, uh, ran out for a bit while you were still knocked out. I wanted to give you something that would make up for being such a dickhead all these months."

"You didn't need to get me anything," she protested.

"Yes, I did. For the mother of my child."

His child. Pleasure flooded through her and warmed her at his words. She watched, holding her breath as he opened the box.

He leaned over to give her a kiss filled with both desire and promise. Then he handed the box to her. "This is my heart," he said solemnly. "I give it to you willingly with all my love."

Sarah gasped when she opened the jeweler's box. Inside were tiny gold earrings in the shape of hearts, outlined in pearls and diamonds. Tears welled in her eyes as she lifted them out.

"I will always keep your heart safe," she said, her voice husky. She closed her fingers around the box and pressed it to her chest.

"I love you," he said again. "I plan to say it so much you'll get sick of hearing it."

"Never." She shook her head.

"What agony that woman put us all through."

Even in her weakened condition, Sarah found the strength to silently curse Maggie. She heard the traces of residual anger in his voice. She'd work on getting him past that.

"She wanted to strike back at you, hurt you the only way she knew how. She saw how much you loved Molly and knew that was where she could strike at you to cause the most pain."

"How can I ever make it up to Molly?" He visibly fought the tears now, his throat muscle working reflexively.

"Children know things, Reno. They sense things. It will be fine. I promise you."

Sarah wanted to say something else, but she

couldn't make herself think straight any more. The nausea was coming in waves, swamping her and receding. She wished someone would come back with her test results so they could give her something to keep it at bay.

Reno, fidgeting in the chair, glanced through the curtain toward the door. "Can I leave you for a minute, sweetheart? Are you okay here? I'm sorry. I just have to know how she's doing."

"She's doing fine." Dr. Moreland came through the curtain before Reno could move. "She's out of surgery and doing very nicely." He made some notes on one of the charts he held. "She had no adverse reaction to the anesthetic, but she's got quite a lot of stitches in that arm. I'd prefer to keep her for a couple of nights, just to monitor her and give her some IV antibiotics."

"Of course," Reno said, standing up. "Whatever's best. Can we see her?"

"As soon as they get her set up. Right now, she's in pediatric recovery, and I need to discuss with you where we're going to put her."

"I don't understand." Reno was instantly alert, ready to take command. "Is there some problem?"

"No. There are just a few other things we need to address." He made one last note on the second chart, then flipped it closed.

"What things? And what about my wife? What have you found out about her? Can't you do something for her?" His voice rose as the worry he'd been battling surged to the forefront. "She's had this virus or whatever you want to call it for five days now and doesn't seem to be getting much better."

The doctor nodded and opened the chart again.

"Mrs. Sullivan, have you ever been told you have a major hormonal imbalance?"

"Yes, I know about that. I had a miscarriage several years ago, and my hormones haven't been right since then. I used to take a low dose of birth control to try and straighten it out, but the pills made me sick. Why?"

"I'm sure that's the reason you're having such severe nausea. You don't have the flu, my dear. You're pregnant."

Sarah and Reno stared at him as if he'd grown an extra head.

"Pregnant?" Sarah managed to croak. She had a sudden urge to laugh hysterically.

"Yes, your lab tests confirm it. About two months, I'd say. I always run the test before we medicate, just in case. Don't want any problems, you know. But the hormone imbalance has exacerbated what we usually call morning sickness and also made you drowsier than normal. So." He closed the chart and smiled at them. "I'm assuming this is good news."

Sarah was the first to find her voice. "Yes, doctor, thank you." She clung to Reno's hand with a fierce grip. "It's very good news."

"You'll need to see your own obstetrician as soon as possible. With your condition and history, you should be monitored carefully. Meanwhile, I'm going to keep you for a couple of nights, too. You're severely dehydrated from all the vomiting, and your blood pressure's a little low. We discussed it and thought you might want your daughter set up in the room with you."

Reno swallowed several times before he finally managed to speak, although his voice was barely recognizable. "Yes, we'd appreciate that very much. Thank you."

"All right, then. The nurse will give you something for that nausea now, Mrs. Sullivan, and set up an IV. Then they'll come and get you as soon as the room is ready." He shook hands with Reno and left the room.

Reno lowered himself back into the chair beside the bed, still clutching Sarah's hand, still unbelieving. The tears he'd been trying to hold back were now rolling down his face, and his throat was so tight he couldn't say anything. The look on his face made Sarah's heart ache.

"A baby." He was having trouble taking everything in. First the news about Molly. Now this. "I don't deserve all this good fortune." His voice was thick with emotion.

"I think everything was meant to happen the way it did." Sarah managed to summon a smile. "We are truly blessed."

He raised his head, and they looked at each other, stunned by it all.

They were still trying to absorb it all when the nurse came in carrying a tray with several items on it.

"These shots should make you feel better real quick. And I'm going to start an IV drip, so we can get some fluids into your body. That will help a lot, too."

Reno moved out of the way until the nurse was finished, then he was back at Sarah's side in an instant. He laid his hand over her lower abdomen.

"That night right before our anniversary." His voice was quiet, loving. "I knew there was something different when we made love. I swear that's when it happened."

"I think so, too. My periods have never been regular since the miscarriage so I didn't suspect anything unusual. I just thought this was the flu," Sarah told him. "Everything happens for a purpose, you know. We can put the past behind us now, once and for all. Life is good." She grinned weakly. "And I'm even starting to feel a little better."

"I love you so much, Sarah."

He leaned over to kiss her, wanting to hold her but afraid of dislodging something.

"Mr. Sullivan?" The nurse was at the curtain again. "Your daughter's doing fine. It will be just a few minutes now, and we'll get both her and your wife upstairs. There's a young lady out here in great distress, though, who wants to see you. Is it all right to bring her back here?"

"It must be Nicki," Reno said. "Yes, please. Go and get her."

It was a tear-stained and shaken Nicki, who appeared, with her mother behind her.

"I told her everything would be all right, but she's been a wreck," Mrs. Vanetta said.

Reno went to her and took her hands in his. "Nicki, if it's anyone's fault, it's mine. I was right there and wasn't paying attention."

Sarah wished she could hug the unhappy, scared teenager. "Molly's fine," she told her. "Accidents happen. Please don't keep blaming yourself. You take such good care of her. We trust you, honestly. And she's doing fine. They've already finished stitching her up. They'll keep her a couple of nights as a precaution, but I promise you she's okay."

Nicki burst into tears again. Reno looked at Sarah

helplessly, then put his arm around Nicki and moved her over closer to his wife.

"You'd better pull yourself together because we're really going to need you now," Sarah smiled, reaching for Nicki's hand. "We're going to have a baby."

Nicki looked up through her tears. "Honest? A baby?"

"Yes and we need your help before it comes and afterward. You'd better get in shape for this."

"She was so worried you wouldn't want her to sit anymore," Mrs. Vanetta said. "I told her it's all right. She should know about accidents. She and her brothers and sisters kept the emergency room in business when they were younger."

When the orderly came to get Sarah, Reno sent Nicki and her mother home. He walked along beside his wife, still clutching her hand, as they rolled her toward the elevator.

In minutes, Sarah was settled in the hospital room, her IV checked and her vitals taken once more. When the nurse had finished with her, they rolled in a hospital crib with Molly in it. She looked so white and still that both Sarah and Reno panicked.

"She's fine," the nurse assured them. "She woke up from the anesthetic with no problem. She's sleeping normally now. We'll be checking on both of you throughout the night. Doctor wants regular reports. I'll be back after a while."

Reno stood at the crib, motionless, his eyes fixed on Molly. She looked so small, so fragile. Her dark curls were tousled around her pale face. Her left arm was bandaged from wrist to shoulder and an IV needle was taped to her right hand.

Why hadn't he looked at her more closely before? All he'd seen were Maggie's blonde curls and her rounded cheeks. But Molly had his thick eyelashes and his dark, gold-flecked eyes. He'd been so blinded by anger and rage he'd seen nothing except his love for this child ripped from his heart by hateful words.

His eyes moved to Sarah, drowsy from the medication, her eyes closing as she drifted off. What an incredible woman she was. He'd hired her as if employing a servant, and she'd stepped in where others would have fled. She was a loving mother to the daughter he'd refused to acknowledge, and she'd given her heart to him willingly, despite how little of himself he'd given back to her. When he'd turned to her for love, she had accepted him without reservation.

He thought agonizingly of all the time that had been wasted, time when he and Sarah could have had a real relationship. Time he could have spent as Molly's father. He was more fortunate than any man had a right to be. He would spend the rest of his life making it up to both of them and to the new little life that he and Sarah had created.

He watched them until he was sure they were both sleeping, then tiptoed from the room to find a place to use his cell phone. He needed to call Nick and Lindsey as well as Sarah's parents. He was sure the Madisons, in particular, had called the house and been worried when no one answered.

Ellen Madison burst into happy tears at the news, then handed the phone to her husband who had a hard time controlling his own emotions. Nick and Lindsey could barely contain their excitement. Reno told everyone, when they asked, that they could check on his family in the morning. His family! What a nice ring that had to it.

Both Sarah and Molly were still sleeping when he returned to the room. Torn between finding a place next to his daughter or his wife, he finally solved his problem by moving the crib even closer to Sarah's bed. Situating himself in the chair, he reached out one hand to touch Molly and placed the other on Sarah's arm. He sat for a long time, his heart so full he thought it would burst.

At last, the specter of Maggie had been chased away.

****

When Sarah opened her eyes, light was pouring in through the window, the sun casting shadows against the wall. She turned her head and smiled at what she saw. Reno was slumped in the chair between the bed and the crib, rumpled and unshaven. One hand rested on her arm and one of his large fingers was clasped tightly in Molly's tiny ones. The little girl was still sleeping, but Sarah could see her breathing was even and regular and her color much better.

She shifted a little, and Reno came awake at once.

"Are you all right?" He lifted his hand from her arm and rubbed his eyes. "How do you feel?"

"Better, I think. How's Molly?"

"Pretty good. She woke once during the night. I think her arm was bothering her, so they gave her some baby aspirin. That's why she's still sleeping now."

"Not anymore. Take a look."

Molly had her eyes wide open and was trying to sit up. Reno bent over the crib and lifted her gently.

"They showed me how to hold her," he explained.

"The bandage on her arm is so big because they want to protect all the stitches. But they took out the IV early this morning, so she can move around better now. They took yours out, too. They said you were pretty well re-hydrated, and you could now take medication by mouth. They want another twenty-four hours, though, to see if you can keep food down."

Reno settled Molly on his lap, taking care with her arm and showered her face with soft kisses. He couldn't take his eyes away from her. He touched her hair, her cheeks, her tiny mouth, kissing her over and over again.

Molly, reveling in the attention, giggled and reached up to pat him with her good hand.

Sarah felt tears gathering in her eyes and blinked them away.

"I called Lindsey and Nick and your folks," Reno informed Sarah. "And Tony. I figured Nicki's mother would have passed the word on the Vanetta grapevine. And I didn't want your folks to worry when we weren't home, knowing you'd been sick."

"Did you tell them we're fine now?"

"Yes. They said they'd probably come by later today. I expect to see my partner and his wife this morning, though, and maybe even Tony."

A nurse's aide bustled in, carrying a tray that she put on the bed table. "Breakfast for the ladies," she called out. "Mrs. Sullivan, your orders say you should try some weak tea and dry toast. How's the nausea this morning?"

"Much better," Sarah told her. "And I don't feel quite so dizzy." She didn't. The room had settled around her, everything staying in one place even when she moved.

"Good." This from the nurse entering the room. "Here's your morning meds and baby aspirin for your daughter. She'll need this for a few days until the worst of the soreness is gone. Doctor will send you home with some medication for the nausea, Mrs. Sullivan, but he wants you to see your obstetrician as soon as possible."

"We'll take care of it right away," Reno stated, his voice firm.

"I'll let you get started on your breakfast." The nurse smiled at Molly. "I'd say you need a highchair to feed this little angel. I'll send one in right away."

Reno shook his head. "I'll hold her on my lap and feed her."

****

The doctor had put a rush on the preliminary DNA test the night before, and the day seemed to drag by while they waited for the results.

"I'm convinced it's positive," Reno said at one point. "Not a doubt at this point."

"Even if it's not," Sarah pointed out, "it won't make a difference."

"It will be positive." Reno's voice was firm and confident. "I just know it."

He helped Sarah eat and fed Molly. Then, while Sarah dozed, he held the child on his lap, crooning to her, until she, too, fell asleep. He knew he should put her back in the crib, but he couldn't get enough of holding her.

The nurse arrived with the evening medication, and the doctor walked in right on her heels.

"First things first," he said. "I have the results back on the preliminary DNA test." He grinned. "Good thing you said cost didn't matter because I think they charged through the nose to rush it. However, there's no doubt you're Molly's father, Mr. Sullivan. I hope that pleases you."

Reno could only nod, so gripped by emotion he couldn't speak.

"Well, everyone seems fine here. I'll just check my patients over, but I think both can go home tomorrow."

Finished with his exam of mother and child, he made notes on the chart, then told them he was writing discharge orders for the next day. He wanted the two of them there one more night, but they could all go home in the morning.

Reno collapsed back in the chair, still amazed by the turn their life had taken.

Sarah, feeling immeasurably better, grinned at him. "Life sure is good, isn't it, Daddy?"

"Better than I deserve." He leaned over and kissed his wife firmly on the lips, then picked up Molly and sat back in the chair. Nestling the little girl against his chest, he reached for Sarah's hand and twined his fingers through hers.

And that's how they were, Reno feeding Molly and Sarah sipping at her tea when Nick and Lindsey appeared in the doorway. Sarah looked up and waved them in.

Lindsey came over to the side of the bed and hugged her. "Reno called last night."

"I figured he would. We're fine. Honestly."

"He told us the good news, too. Oh, Sarah, we're so very happy for you. For both of you. It's a shame it took this kind of an emergency to turn things around, but I knew everything would work out sooner or later."

"The best news is we had another DNA test done,

and it proves without a doubt that Reno is Molly's father." Sarah beamed.

"Oh, my god," Lindsey gasped. "That is just too much." She kissed her friends soundly while Nick shook Reno's free hand. Emotion was very thick in the room.

Sarah turned her head and looked at Reno, cuddling his daughter. Then she looked at Nick, with his arm around Lindsey, glowing with her pregnancy. Two of the best friends in the world.

Her marriage to Reno might have begun as a bargain, but it had certainly turned out to be a good one for both of them. Sarah touched her abdomen where the baby was growing, the child she and Reno had conceived with their love.

A new home, a new child, and a new life.

Chapter Nineteen

The scene could have come straight from a painting. The blue Texas sky, dotted with puffs of cloud, was a backdrop for a golden sun. A soft breeze fluttered the leaves on the oaks and sycamore and drew ripples in the little stream. Next to the barn, in a paddock fenced with white split rails, four horses nickered gently as they nuzzled one another. The aroma of hay and horseflesh drifted on the air.

The house of gleaming limestone and weathered wood sat on the crest of the hill. Huge windows, that filled the house with light, reflected the sun.

On the wraparound porch, two cats snoozed on the wide railing, tails curled comfortably around them. In one chair was a large, muscular man in jeans that molded to his strong thighs. A denim shirt accentuated the breadth of his shoulders, and on his feet were scuffed boots. A graceful-looking woman sat next to him. Her golden sweater picked up the tawny highlights of her thick coffee-colored hair and soft suede jeans clung tantalizingly to her hips.

The man held a little girl about two years old, her head with its tousled curls nestled happily against his chest. The woman, her hair loose about her face and cascading over her shoulders, held a tiny baby against her body. Her cheek rested against the soft, downy head, her lips pressing against the skin.

They rocked in rhythm, unwilling to disturb their sleeping children. Their faces held a look of total peace and serenity. And a love that was so strong it shut out everyone and everything else. People who saw them envied the strength of what they had.

They sat and rocked as the sun began to dip from the sky and the light of day faded. Their children slumbered peacefully in their arms. They had weathered a difficult journey, but now they had reached nirvana. Life was good.

About the Author

Known as the oldest living author of erotic romance, Desiree Holt has produced more than two hundred titles in nearly every subgenre of romance fiction. Her stories are enriched by her personal experiences, her characters by the people she meets.

After fifteen years in the great state of Texas, she relocated back to Florida to be closer to members of her family and a large collection of friends. Her favorite pastimes are watching football, reading, and researching her stories. She lives with her three cats, who love to sit with her when she writes.

~*~

Desiree loves to hear from readers.
www.facebook.com/desireeholtauthor
www.facebook.com/desiree01holt
Twitter @desireeholt
Pinterest: desiree02holt
www.desireeholt.com
www.desiremeonly.com

~*~

To chat with Desiree Holt and other Wild Rose Press authors of erotic romance, join us at www.groups.yahoo.com/group/thewilderroses.

Also Available
Silencing Memories
Guardian Security Book Two
By Desiree Holt

http://a.co/cR79510

Just when architect Alexis Craig thinks she's gotten her life back on track, the terrible nightmares return, and out of nowhere, a stalker sends a note to her office. Photos follow, then emails, and she can't dismiss the threat any longer. Hiring security seems the logical answer, but there's nothing logical about her body's reaction to the sinfully sexy expert bent on keeping her safe.

Guardian Security partner Nick Vanetta believes there's more behind the situation than a simple fixation, and he wonders if the answer is buried somewhere in her past. As they dig deeper into her family history, the sizzling attraction between them burns hotter and the job becomes much more than playing bodyguard to this headstrong woman. To protect the woman he loves, he must find the stalker...before it's too late.

Also Read
Sin City Alibi
By Sophia Ryan

http://a.co/0x3Gbku

Sometimes what happens in Vegas follows you home.

Jumping libido-first into a cliché Vegas fling is the last thing on Dani Parker's mind when she flies to Sin City for some R&R after her lover/boss, Elliott, dumps her. But an innocent night of flirty fun with a sexy hunk she knows only as Matt whirlwinds into a sinfully hot weekend. Back home, she discovers her boss has been murdered, her Vegas fling is heading the investigation into financial irregularities for the company she works for, and she's smack-dab in the middle of both.

Matt Collins has filled his life with work and no-strings sex since the day his heart went on lock-down. No woman ever cracked that lock. Until Dani. Now all he wants is her in his bed and in his life, but the odds for success are stacked against him. She can't accept his conditions for love, there's evidence suggesting she and her former lover embezzled from the company, and the cops arrest her for Elliott's murder. His gut tells him she's innocent and he wasn't just an alibi, but his heart remembers the brutal past that still haunts him.

When everything Matt and Dani hold dear is on the line, they'll learn that sometimes risking everything leads to the most satisfying payouts.

Thank you for purchasing this
publication of The Wild Rose Press, Inc.
If you enjoyed the story, we would appreciate
your letting others know by leaving a review.
For other wonderful stories, please visit our
on-line bookstore at www.thewilderroses.com.

For questions or more
information contact us at
info@thewildrosepress.com.

The Wild Rose Press, Inc.
www.thewilderroses.com

Stay current with The Wild Rose Press, Inc.
Like us on Facebook
https://www.facebook.com/TheWildRosePress
And Follow us on Twitter
https://twitter.com/WildRosePress